Ministers for Breakfast

Beth Staas

Book cover and interior designed by Ellie Searl, Publishista®

ISBN: 9798218172121
LCCN: 2023904943

Qualified Press
Westmont, IL

CHAPTER 1: JOY

"NO MATTER WHAT, you have to follow the paycheck." That's how Gary announced his new job gotten through grit, luck and a Positive Mental Attitude.

Our boys were in high school, not a good time for them to move, what with football and soccer. Then there was the house that we'd just re-decorated. But Gary would be vice president of sales and in charge of franchise at *Marty's Quick Stop,* so he grabbed it fast. In a New York minute we were out of Pittsburgh and moved to a podunk town named Worthington. We'd be big fish in a small pond, which suited Gary just fine. Moving always came with new opportunities, this one with country club membership. We would be expected to join the most prestigious church in town. Nothing like a Sunday morning to establish contacts.

It took some getting used to, especially going to church, us being the kind who sleep-in on weekends. But you can adjust to anything if the price is right. After all, my name is Joy. And being religious was not required to join. Amity Community Church asked only that you be contributors of record and attend often enough to be recognized by the ushers. I myself had never gotten past Daily Vacation Bible School with carry-home leaflets of Joseph and his brothers which my mother would say *how nice* then toss into the trash. But I'd always wanted some kind of religious training for Jason and Matt so they'd be part of the conversation.

At first it was easy and fun. I'd trained for this all my life, learning to scope out who was important, latch onto the power force at a party and flirt without a commitment. These are things you learn by watching, not something that's taught in school.

After getting settled, which meant locating doctors, dentists, sports clubs, barbers, tanning salons, beauty shops, cleaning ladies and yard help, all with the help of Gary's secretary, we were ready to make our debut into Worthington's so-called society.

We began with the country club, a membership that would help with contacts. While the boys were taking golf lessons, Gary and I would sit at the pool chitchatting with whoever happened to be around. It's something we do pretty well even though we're on the downside of thirty, being tanned and buffed and always in style but not so much that it scares people. And that's how I met Carol Stone.

Now Carol is about twenty pounds overweight but it's not so gross that she can't wear a bathing suit if it's one piece, preferably with a skirt. She has a pretty face and nice hair that's professionally streaked and white teeth that contrast against her tan. I first saw her at the shallow end of the pool with two cute kids, a boy and a girl. Gary and I were at an umbrella table at the opposite end with two couples we had just met, being clever and funny and laughing a lot. Carol kept looking at us with that wistful smile that said she wished she was part of our group instead of being on duty. So I pretended a trip to the bathroom, and as I walked by, admired her kids, which is always a good opening, then introduced myself. Within five minutes I learned that her husband was also in sales and she was in her high school marching band like me, although she played the drum while I was the majorette. She was about my age but we were a little ahead since she and her husband Tony had taken time to go to college.

On the way back, I stopped and invited Carol to join our group, having seen Gary's eyes signaling it was okay. She only made polite sounds about having to go, so after saying again how cute the kids were, I went back to our table, watching out of the corner of my eye as she packed up to leave.

Gary and I stayed for another hour or so, then we walked over to the golf shop to pick up the boys, going home to shower and change, then back to the club for dinner. It was their Saturday night buffet, which is a great way to meet people while waiting in line. Right on target we ran into one of Gary's customers and his wife so we made up a table for six, with the boys joining in the conversation from time to time, learning how to behave in public. We talked about golf and I added a few comments although I have no desire to go out in the baking sun to play such a stupid game, preferring to get a massage at the gym.

On Sunday we got ready for church, being stylish and hip without overdressing. Like Gary says, there's no second chance to make a first impression. We decided to attend the eleven o'clock service since only the old and retired go early and they're pretty useless as business contacts anyway. It was a comfortable drive, having gone by the church a couple of times, making sure we didn't look like we were lost.

Amity was housed in an ultra-modern concrete building, the whole front wall being a series of stained-glass windows. The roof peaked to a tower like two hands in prayer with a gleaming crucifix at the tip of the fingers. It stood in the middle of a beautifully landscaped park framed by flowering shrubs and a lawn that was lush and green. Someone famous designed it, the name which escapes me.

When we arrived, cool but out of breath, we joined the swarm of people in the foyer waiting to be handed programs before finding seats in the sanctuary that looked more like a conservatory. Imagine my surprise when we practically crashed into Carol Stone. I recognized her right away, which was an accomplishment since makeup and street clothes always make a difference. I introduced her to Gary and presented the boys, skimming over Gary's lame joke of wanting to name them Pete and Repeat.

"You chose an important Sunday to attend," she smiled. "We're candidating a new minister and will vote after the service. But you're welcome to stay." Sizing up the boys, she continued, "Our Youth Group meets every Sunday night. Maybe you'd like to come and join them. They're a nice bunch of kids."

I guess I looked surprised, because she laughed, saying that she was Religious Education Director, something not mentioned when we met at the pool. Then the organ started, so we got in line to find seats, which of course had to be up front since we were late. But that was okay. We'd come to be noticed.

The oak pews were cushioned in red velvet with just the right amount of padding. As we waited for the service to begin, Gary filled out the guest card tucked next to the hymnals and the boys and I read through the program. Pretty soon the music softened and conversation hushed like at a play or a concert before the curtain goes up. Then the music swelled and a choir wearing long white robes trimmed in red came down the aisle singing in a foreign language, which I guessed was German, and everyone stood up. A door opened next to the altar almost automatically and the Right Reverend Neville Leighton, whose name was on the program, emerged. He mounted the dais which was banked with potted flowers and the lights slowly turned up, the whole scenario looking like a movie or play with the hero making a grand entrance. Neville Leighton certainly looked the part.

I'm not easily impressed, but I had to admit that this place was first class and so was the minister. He was not especially tall, but today men don't have to be, as long as they are well put together and trim, and Neville's body was the kind people call controlled and taut. You could tell he spent time working out and taking care of his skin all smooth and tan. His hair, slightly gray around the temples, made me guess him to be about fifty. The haircut probably cost two hundred dollars, and worth every penny. He was wearing a tan suit of light wool and Cordoba brown loafers, an important touch since a total match would have been obvious, like in a Sears catalog. He looked out at the congregation, and I swear, our eyes locked. It was only a split second and not the first time that ever happened to me, but it was rewarding and I decided that church attendance wasn't going to be so bad after all.

As he spoke, I studied his hands, a class ring on his right, a white gold band on the left. His voice, a rich baritone, rose and fell in rhythm to his gestures, like everything, understated. He would've made a good salesman.

The sermon had something to do with Daniel in the lion's den and how that applied to trust in today's society. God spoke to Daniel. Daniel trusted God. Today we need to trust one another. Contemporize. Relativize. Like I said, a good salesman. No one coughed or sneezed until he was finished. Then the choir sang a number and marched out while we stood up again, and afterward people moseyed out, pretty much like at a concert or a play.

We took our time, smiling and nodding to people who introduced themselves, shaking hands with a few, including the minister, remembering as many names as possible. Then in the foyer, there was Carol Stone again, her head bobbing around like she was looking for someone. Knowing how important it is to find a familiar face whenever you're entering new territory, I walked up right in front of her, making sure she saw me. "Lose the kids?" I asked, showing I remembered the two little ones at the pool.

"Oh no," she smiled. "They're downstairs with the sitter. Actually, I was looking for you. Would you like to join us for brunch at the club? Normally we have a coffee hour after church, but it was cancelled because of the vote."

I ducked my head and looked at Gary, letting him take the lead.

"That would be great," he replied in his hearty salesman's voice. "Maybe the boys can keep an eye on your kids."

I could feel Jason stiffen.

"Thanks, but I'm dropping them off at my mother's. So let's just meet at the club at about one."

People now clustered toward the front of the sanctuary where a long table was set up for the officers and bigwigs presiding. It would be an up or down vote on the candidate for minister. It didn't impact us then. But what happened next would affect the future of this church, and everyone involved with it, including us.

CHAPTER 2: CAROL

THE ONLY SOUNDS came from birds chirping outside the window. Maybe I could sleep another hour before the kids woke up. Suddenly I heard footsteps moving about in the next room. I reached over to nudge Tony but he wasn't there. Alarmed, I stumbled toward the bedroom door flinging it open just in time to see Tony at the kitchen counter, bending over my purse. His thick dark hair was tousled and his clothes rumpled as though he'd gotten dressed in a hurry. "What are you doing?" I hissed.

He looked up as he shoved something into his pocket. "Go back to bed. It's still early."

"What are you doing?" I repeated, my voice going up a notch.

"I've got two sales calls this morning and I'm almost out of gas."

"What did you take out of my purse?"

"Shush. You'll wake the kids."

"As if you'd care."

"Honey, I just needed your credit card. Mine's maxed out. I'll bring it back on Tuesday. You still have some cash to carry you over."

I grabbed my wallet. "You left singles and a ten, plus some change. That's supposed to take care of us? Maybe *I'm* out of gas. Maybe I need to buy groceries. And what if there's an emergency?"

"Nothing's going to happen. And if it does, you can call your mother."

"No Tony. Give it back!" I tried to reach into his pocket, but he grabbed my wrist, twisting it behind my back. Then he put his other arm around my waist and while I struggled, kissed me hard. "That doesn't work any more, Tony."

"Gotta go. Back on Tuesday. Sorry about missing church."

And that's how my day started. It didn't get any better. Someone had used the religious education office to make posters and my files were scattered helter-skelter. So I missed most of the worship service. Then the babysitter was swamped, so it was Carol to the rescue. A replacement appeared later so I was able to go in when the vote was taken, but I missed the discussion.

Now I prepared to take the kids to Mom's and my car wouldn't start. I knew it needed a tune up. On the other hand, it could just be flooded. But the fuel gauge pointed to empty, and I mentally cursed Tony for not filling it up after his Saturday errands. Never mind about planning ahead. That's what wives were for - gassing up the car, going to the cleaners, making ends meet. I turned around, checking the kids' seat belts, then gave it another try. After grinding four more times, it coughed and caught, sending out a plume of blue smoke.

"Miss Watson says ice cream is one of the seven food groups," Scott declared as I backed out of the parking spot. "She says it's okay to have as much as we want."

"I don't care what they say in your science class. We're going to Grandma's house, not to the grocery store. And we're late."

Jennifer began to cry. "Ice cream, ice cream…"

I gritted my teeth. It was only a mile. With luck I'd make it.

Scott began bouncing up and down. "Ice cream, you scream, we all scream…"

"Is that the way a seven-year old behaves?"

"That's what Daddy says."

I rounded the corner and pulled up in front of the house where I'd grown up. "Honey, Grandma will give you some."

With that, Scott jumped out, loudly announcing our arrival. Lifting Jennifer up, I followed inside.

"I always have ice cream in the freezer." Mom's voice echoed from inside the refrigerator door.

"Scott was afraid there'd be none left."

"For my babies? Never." She took two bowls down from the shelf. "Tony out of town?"

I nodded. "Sundays are the best times for selling. Farmers in town, stores open…"

"How'd the morning go? Did Neville pass?"

I nodded. "Let's just pray he's what we need."

"Stability is what we need."

"If it's the right kind." I looked at the clock. "I have to go. We can talk later."

She turned and took a twenty-dollar bill out of a canister on the shelf and tucked it into my breast pocket. "The banks are closed on Sunday."

I felt my face warm with embarrassment. "Thanks Mom. Next week's payday."

"No hurry. I have a steady job."

"So do I, Mom. And Tony's working. It's just that straight commission takes some getting used to."

Her scowl showed she wasn't convinced.

Tony and I had met in high school, the same place where Mom taught Home Economics. I was in the marching band. Tony was on the football team. I never figured why he asked me out. When he kissed me goodnight that first time, his touch, rough and hard, sent electric currents racing up and down. At seventeen he was distinctly male, all gonads and testosterone. I couldn't resist. I suppose being raised without a dad had something to do with it. My first boyfriend turned out to be my one and only. I followed him to college. Pretty soon I was buying him drinks, lending him money, and screaming about his other women. Then I became pregnant and Mom bought him off, trading his tuition loan for a wedding ring.

The baby was never born. A miscarriage is no one's fault. It just happens. But Tony acted like he'd been scammed. So I hit the skids in silence, depressed and almost suicidal for five years. When I finally came back to the real world, I found my husband out of a job and myself pregnant. Three years and two jobs later, I was pregnant again. Blessedly, both children were healthy and there was no further depression. I never told anyone, not even the doctor.

I gave Mom a peck on the cheek. "I'll be back as soon as I can."

Driving two blocks to the gas station, I spent five of my precious dollars, then rushed to the club where Tony's company had paid for membership, expecting it to generate business. If meetings didn't produce a sale, at least we'd have had a free lunch or dinner and a take home doggie bag. Sometimes that, plus Tony's per Diem, was all that kept the wolf from the door.

After Jennifer was born, I realized I'd have to go back to work, bracing myself to teach in the inner city, the only openings available. Then Melissa, Amity's Director of Religious Education, moved to New York and the job fell in my lap. It was only part time but I could bring Jennifer with me, or work from home. So for now it was okay.

I parked next to the Presser's Lexus just as they were getting out. I'd known Bill and Kim Presser forever, first as a toddler in the church basement standing in awe of the big kids, then as a junior bridesmaid at their wedding, a notable honor, given Kim's family prominence. As the current president of Amity's board, Bill was technically my boss, at least until a new minister was hired. So I put on a hearty smile, a Member of the Team. "Let's hear it for Amity. We did it!" I hugged Kim as she got out of their car and shook Bill's hand, a big man where hugging was impossible. "I'm glad it's over, aren't you?"

"He was the best of the lot," Bill replied.

I laughed. "Sounds like buying a horse."

Bill clicked his remote to lock the car and we walked toward the club's dining room. "Not much different. People, property, products, they all come and go. Neville happened to be available. We were ready to hire."

"And what about the human factor? What about finding the right mix, the right personality, making the right choice."

"Praying the right prayer? Come now Carol, you know better."

"Don't discount it," Kim declared. "Neville has a doctorate in education that can generate new programs, draw in more kids, bring in their parents, and so on. Back when Dr. Walsh was minister, the building was filled with happy sounds from morning to night. Pray that it happens again."

"Better pray that the deficit turns around. If not, the minister issue is moot."

"Speaking of which, I just met a new couple. He's with *Marty's Quick Stop*. You should know them, being on their board.

"Met him a few days ago," Bill said, wheezing slightly as he climbed up the steps to the dining room, moving toward the end of the room where people were seated at long tables. Then finding a chair, he caught the server's eye and got a glass of champagne, downing it before Kim was barely settled.

I sat across from them for a few minutes, making small talk, then excused myself to go to the lady's room. Sunday is my busy day.

In the bathroom I washed the smell of gasoline from my hands and dabbed color on my cheeks and lips. The face was fine. The rest of me wasn't. Bill had been told to lose weight for the sake of his health. I needed to lose weight for the sake of my appearance, my morale and maybe my marriage.

Back into the dining room, I scanned for Amity members and friends. Church school had started and I was still one teacher short. This might be my lucky day. After all, how much does it take to teach a four-year old to sing *Jesus Loves Me?*

Kim was at the table, her manicured fingers forming a tick-tack-toe on the tablecloth. I sat down in Bill's empty chair. "How's everything going?"

She took a deep breath, letting it out slowly. "Okay, I supposed."

"You and Bill fighting?"

"Civilized people don't fight."

"You need to get out more. Meet people. Rub elbows with others. Glory in diversity. Make use of your education. After all, how many people graduate summa cum laude from Vassar?" My voice invited her to smile.

"If you want me to teach that pre-K class, you can forget it."

I shifted in my seat. "Actually, it would be good for you."

"Carol, you know I don't like kids."

"You're rattling around in that big house. The boys are on their own. Bill is gone all day. You need to do something with your time."

"I'm thinking about it."

"Life's too short to sacrifice for one man. Burn your bra and live a little."

She laughed dryly. "And allow Sunday school to rescue me? No thanks."

"Then what are you going to do?"

"Carol, Carol, you push too hard. Should anything change in my life, I promise you'll be the first to know."

I sat back and grinned. "Really? The very first? You mean before anyone else? For sure?"

She burst out laughing, a hearty sound echoing from deep inside the belly. She patted my hand, her face now clear of anger. "For sure. If anything remarkable happens in my life, you'll be the first to know."

Kim was not easy to reach, this rich girl who was a throwback to Freudian angst. But just then more people were coming in and I caught sight of Joy and her husband. In the flurry of introductions, the moment was lost and I got up, returning to the project at hand.

Chapter 3: Joy

EVERYONE WAS GATHERED at the club by the time we arrived. Carol waved us over, introducing us to Bill Presser, Amity's outgoing chairman of the board who couldn't have looked more perfect for the part. Gary had already been introduced to him. Heavyset and balding with jeweled cufflinks and a pinky ring, he towered over us, flashing a perfect smile that made me feel like I was back in the principal's office. I took his hand and looked way up, returning his smile, barely flinching because he had what's called a firm handshake.

"It so happens I'm on *Marty's* board," he boomed. "Let me give you my card."

And Gary, like a real pro, didn't bat an eye.

"Let's not talk business," interrupted the woman at his elbow. "Today is Sunday. Sufficient unto the day…"

"Kim thinks it's her job to keep me focused," Bill said wryly.

"And don't you forget it."

Some people smile when they fight, but these two were dead serious.

"The line is getting shorter." This came from a dark-skinned lady with a red dot in the middle of her forehead dressed in a green silk sari, meaning she was probably Hindu.

I hate being in the middle of spats, so I hurried to join Gary and Carol in the buffet line making polite comments about the salad and desserts, smiling at the chef waiting to slice orders of beef or ham.

Carol must be smart, because she caught on right away. "Pay no attention to the Pressers," she whispered. "Bill's a nice guy after he's fed."

Back at the table, the wine steward came to pour champagne into hollow-stemmed glasses. I found the wine fruity and dry, and held out my glass for more, then began to nibble at my salad. Conversation centered on the church's business, and I sat back and listened. Like with Kim, it was my job.

Amity Congregational Church'd had a much-loved minister for some fifteen years, a Doctor Jefferson Walsh. Back then it was a city church, centrally located in town. But membership began to drop when the economy expanded and people began moving to the suburbs. Still, Amity was the most prestigious church in town, where everyone who was anyone wanted to belong. Of course, Worthington wasn't much, so everyone who was anyone wasn't much either.

Then a new Interstate was built a quarter of a mile from the church. Suddenly the land was valuable. So the Board of Directors sold the land at a big profit, moved out of the inner city, and furnished it with the best. Once more, people came in droves. Who wouldn't? It was like an afternoon at Boca Raton, all for a dollar or two in the collection plate.

Then Dr. Walsh dropped dead of a heart attack and the next minister, a Reverend Billy Oliver, was a disaster. Maybe he didn't understand that asking and wanting were different. For example, if parishioners asked for Bible study, it meant they wanted cocktails at the nicest house on the membership list, not Wednesday night in the church basement memorizing the Begats. And when Social Action asked to take on the homeless, they wanted to see it on the six o'clock news, not smell the great unwashed in the church parlor. Even I knew that much and I've never belonged to a church.

Then the Metropolitan Church started a parish and rented Amity's facilities for its Saturday night service. Now everyone knows Metropolitan is a Gay church and members are plenty rich because most gays work in technology making lots of money. If some just happened to join Amity along the way, it could add to the treasury big time, even though some thought it wasn't worth the price.

But what really sunk Billy's boat was renting space to Alcoholics Anonymous without first checking with the church board. To do that all by himself was seen as a power grab and the board got ready to slap him down.

After a lot of digging, the board learned that Billy was from some other denomination and lacked full fellowship. In other words, he was on probation. So Amity didn't renew his contract. It was that simple. The central office took pity and gave him an administrative post where he could cool his heels and decide if he was really cut out for the job even though he'd been a minister for twenty years before.

Meanwhile, Amity's pulpit was filled with white-haired grandfathers or young Turks saying *Ya' Know* at the end of every sentence. It was a year before they began to candidate again and another year to make a choice. By then, membership had slipped. The Reverend Doctor Leighton would have his work cut out for him.

But at this very moment, Neville Leighton was probably on a plane returning to his family, hoping the congregation would issue him a call. I sympathized, having watched Gary more times than I'd like to remember, waiting for a confirmation.

By now I'd had two glasses of champagne and was mellow, feeling no responsibility for conversation, although I usually take that part seriously.

There were more than a dozen at our table. Gary had planted himself close to Bill Presser at the opposite end, and they were laughing and nodding at one another like long lost buddies. Kim was at her husband's side picking at her food or staring into space, being one of those people who doesn't quite know how to join in. College doesn't teach you everything.

Across from them was a tall thin man, very blond with thick shell-framed glasses. There was no champagne glass in front of him, which made him all the more interesting. Next to him was the Hindu lady who kept going up for another helping of food that barely amounted to a teaspoonful to begin with, all meatless of course. I suppose that's what keeps Indians so thin. Though not beautiful, she was striking, her moves dramatic. What she saw in Mr. Paleface was a mystery. Maybe he was smart or rich - or both.

Then there were the scattering of country club types you have trouble remembering because they all look like Barbie and Ken. No one was talking to me directly, so after sitting with a smile pasted to my face until it hurt, I decided to take a walk. When I came back, Carol Stone gave me a welcoming nod like she wanted me to sit next to her, which was okay since she could get me started with the others.

"Lose the kids?" Her voice had a husky quality that I'd not noticed before.

I smiled. "We've never been regular churchgoers. But they'll come around eventually." I widened my eyes, moving my head up and down to show I was sincere.

She laughed a deep throaty chuckle. "All in good time."

"Dr. Leighton is an interesting speaker. And everyone is so friendly." I said. "We'll be back."

Now she became animated. "The Women's Group is planning a tea for Neville's wife. We'll need help with things like arranging flowers and doing place names. It's a way to get to know people. Interested?"

I tried to get Gary's attention, a little nervous at how Carol was coming on so strong. But he was busy talking to Bill. So I said yes, took out my appointment book and in the square marked October 8 wrote *Leighton, 3:30 p.m. at the church* followed by Carol's phone number, hoping I wasn't committing myself to something I'd regret.

Just then Gary turned toward me and signaled it was time. So I picked up my purse and gave everyone my best smile, walking toward the door, a little giddy from the over-heated room and the champagne.

On the way home, we compared notes the way we always do. Gary reported that Bill Presser was an attorney and president of the Chamber of Commerce in addition to being on *Marty's* board. He would sponsor Gary and invited him to the JC's breakfast meeting. I guess they get points for new members. Steve Rothberg, Mr. Paleface was Amity's Finance Chair and a CPA. His Hindu wife, Mirabelle, taught World Religion at the

Community College. He had been her escape from an arranged marriage in India. She was his meal ticket while he finished school. One hand washes the other.

Then it was my turn. I told about the Social Committee and he thought that was just fine which surprised me because the whole idea seemed fast and risky. I mean, what if I got stuck doing volunteer work in the kitchen instead of where I'm better qualified? But Gary was unfazed. If it turned out to be a mistake, I could always switch to tennis or golf.

CHAPTER 4: KIM

I WATCHED HER Leave, swaying ever so slightly, probably a little drunk. It was a polished performance, head high, hips tucked in and legs that moved like a skater, each step a slithering stroke. I knew I'd meet her eventually, perhaps at a luncheon, but I never expected to see her at church. Joy Volkman, marginally pretty in a magazine girl kind of way, making the most of what she had - wispy hair carefully colored and just the right length, body firm and tan, upper management and nouveau riche, one of those swelling the fringes of Worthington. I knew her type - smiling too much, trying too hard, commanding the sandbox at pre-school, always taking charge. She seemed to be in her early thirties and judging from her conversation, hadn't cracked a book since high school. Good looks might be visible, but intellect survives.

Bill sat elbow to elbow with Steve Rothberg talking business. Boring. Were this a serious discussion about humanities or literature, I might be interested. I'd experienced college as offbeat with a strong feminist focus, mentored by a few professors. I'd visited their quarters and remember it being pleasant. But that was a while ago. By the time I graduated, the avant-garde had faded. So I went home to marry Bill who was already immersed in his law practice. Still under thirty, he was going bald and putting on the pounds that were to become his albatross. But he was a familiar presence and it seemed the most natural thing to do. I'd had my fling. It was time to settle into a community where family meant something. Even now I'm at a loss as to a better alternative.

I shifted in my seat and sighed ostentatiously, hoping to catch Bill's attention, but garnered only a frown warning me not to interrupt. So I joined Mirabelle who was staring across the room like she was meditating. Or maybe she was only mentally screening out the riffraff. I considered asking, but that would invite another lecture on our respective cultures. So I tried small talk. "Looks like we got ourselves a new minister."

"The numbers tell the story. I understand the vote was not unanimous," she replied, turning her head slightly.

"Really? Who said that?"

"My husband, the bean counter." It was a term that offended her. I'd once used it in her presence and was rewarded with a diatribe on the misuse of language, a reference to her linguistic expertise. Mirabelle wore her academic degrees like a chip on her shoulder.

"He's not supposed to give out that information," I countered.

"Perhaps. But it will soon be part of the board minutes for everyone to see. That's stated in the bylaws."

"And I'll bet you've read every word," I said, keeping my voice light.

"Yes. If I make a commitment, I need to know what it's about." She paused, her voice suspended like in a question.

"I skimmed it. Pretty cut and dried." The cliché was intended to irritate.

"Neville had better read it as well. His future could hang on a word, a phrase, a sub-heading, in the same way as it did his predecessors."

"Oh my, we're back to that."

"Better to be forearmed."

"Neville is a trained counselor and should be able to understand behavior as well as the needs of the spirit."

"Jack of all trades, master of none."

"What's that supposed to mean?"

"We need a man of God, someone who leads us in prayer and devotion. Daniel in the Lion's Den fomenting trust in one another? Rubbish! Daniel exemplified faith in God. Anyone who reads his Bible knows that." There's no zealot like a convert.

"Good grief, Mirabelle, what's wrong with you? A little PMS?"

She stood up, hiking her sari above her thin breasts. "Why do you Americans think that hormones explain everything?" And she was gone, storming into the haven of the lady's room.

I sighed and looked at my watch. Most of the crowd had left and the buffet was being cleared for the dinner crowd. I got up to retrieve our jackets, anxious to go home.

By now Mirabelle had returned, her face once more composed. An exchange of small talk bridged the rift, and together we peeled our husbands from their seats and ushered them out the door. The men continued with their projections as we walked to the parking lot, looking to dig Amity out of a financial hole that, for all I knew, did not exist.

Bill and I drove home in silence, arriving at the house that he had inherited. It was too big, even when the boys were young. But Bill insisted we keep it.

"Time to get the trees trimmed," he said, looking at the splendid reds and yellows of early fall. "Make a note to call the landscaping service tomorrow."

"It seems a shame to cut branches before the color reaches its height."

"It'll be a saving in the long run. Fewer leaves to rake, fewer hours to pay." The garage door yawned open as he clicked the remote.

"Were I to keep a diary, it would contain nothing beyond housekeeping items in terms of price and value added," I declared.

"Why not? It made Thoreau famous. You can call it *Walden*. Titles can't be copyrighted."

Now inside, I moved to the front closet to hang up our jackets, closed the door and walked toward the living room. "I noticed you were talking to the visitors from out of town," I said. "Do you think his wife is attractive?"

"I didn't notice." He looked around the room. "Let's light the fire. It's romantic on an autumn day."

Surprised at the shift of mood, I poured two glasses of wine and sat in a chair next to the cold fireplace, waiting. My job was to take care of Bill. After that, there would still be time.

He returned and began laying the logs, scrunching sheets of newspaper under the grate, scattering kindling between the folds. From time to time he would look up and smile and I tried to smile back. Finally he sat back on his heels, surveying his handiwork with satisfaction.

"Got the matches?" I asked.

He felt around on the floor, then stood up and checked the mantel. "They're supposed to be right here. Where did you put them?"

"I didn't put them anywhere. Why am I always blamed?"

"Because you're supposed to be running this house. Go check the kitchen."

In the kitchen I found the box of matches next to the stove. Gulping down the last of my wine, I placed the empty glass on the sideboard and returned to the living room, handing the matches to Bill. "Want me to light it?"

"No, that's okay. We should be a roaring fire in a very few minutes."

I sat back on the floor leaning against the chair. The first match snapped twice but didn't light. The second went out after singing the tips of his fingers. The third lit the kindling and flamed brightly but then went out, leaving the logs untouched. "I'm getting cold. Should we turn on the furnace?"

"It'll create too big a draft. Just be patient. It's coming."

"Did you check the damper?"

"Kim, do you always have to tell me what to do? Of course I checked." He pulled the chains inside the fireplace, sending puffs of black soot onto the lambs-wool rug. "The damper's open. See?"

"So it's ready to start."

He looked down at his hands, now blackened with soot. "I'll need to wash up first."

"It would have helped to think ahead."

"You don't have to preach!" Then his voice softened. "Sometimes a man gets sick of thinking ahead. For once it would be an adventure to be spontaneous like the animals we are.

I shuddered. "Do I ever feel like an animal? No, thank God."

"No, of course not. According to you, man is spirit and mind and soul. The rest isn't worthy of a footnote." He stood up. "I'm going upstairs to take a shower. Don't hold dinner."

I didn't protest. Instead, I watched him storm up the stairs and listened for the sound of the water, then followed, going into the bedroom to change into a knit pantsuit, then back to the kitchen to find something that would be suitable for a cold supper. Male menopause. Christ, would it ever end?

I was setting out a platter of cold chicken and an array of salads, and heard his footsteps on the stairs. I braced myself for further recrimination. *I said. Don't hold dinner.* When he didn't appear, I looked out the window, just in time to see red taillights disappearing down the driveway. And that was the end of our Sunday.

CHAPTER 5: JOY

EVERY TIME WE moved, I had to learn the lay of the land. But sometimes there were shortcuts dropped in my lap. Helping with Sheila Leighton's tea got me in with people at Amity, showing me the best florists and caterers and Amity's supply cabinets that held the silver, linen and china, all well matched and expensive. It would be a place to go when I needed to borrow something.

The meeting hall was beneath the sanctuary but could hardly be called a basement, the entire building being on a grassy slope. That gave it outdoor access and floor to ceiling windows and panels to change the space into three separate rooms when needed. Off to the side was an institutional-sized kitchen with double everything - stoves, freezers, refrigerators, dishwashers and storage-cabinets. I figured it could seat a hundred people or more.

On the day of Sheila's tea, the room was set up with ten round tables centered with floral bouquets. The sun was ablaze on the russet and brightly colored leaves outside the windows, temperature holding in the 70s, a surprise for mid-October.

I'd been working with the committee-members for a month and was beginning to feel pretty comfortable. That most of the women had come from wealthy families and gone to college didn't bother me because I still looked better than all of them put together. Kim Preston was a good example, a dowdy frump waving her Vassar degree under everyone's nose. With new clothes and a makeover, she wouldn't have given Bill a second look. Let's face it, in the marriage market, a woman comes equipped with certain skills, benefits and returns, like in a business. Investment is the promise of future gain.

Still, there were women on the committee that I genuinely liked. Marva Larson was president of the Women's Club that was putting together the tea for Sheila. She and I clicked from the get-go. Model-slender with good cheekbones, Marva was real class. Divorced from a cheating husband and the sole support of ten-year old Jayne, she went to work as a secretary in an architectural firm. That's where she met Paul who tumbled for her like a block of reinforced concrete. Determined never to lose out again, she read books on how to keep a man interested. I imagine she taught Paul a thing or two because they had two babies in their first two years. Even after five years, he eyed her with enough lust to raise some Christian eyebrows. It was fun to watch them fall all over one another like newlyweds even thought they were about our age. I like people who know what they want. Gary liked them too. That Paul was the incoming Chairman of the Board probably helped, because Gary likes to be around important people.

On this day, Marva was the first to arrive, which is to be expected of the club president. We did the hug and air-kiss thing, then Liz Mason walked in along with half a dozen others and there was another round of hugs. Liz had no particular title other than being Marva's best friend, that is, until I came along. She and her husband Dave had three children, Sue aged fifteen going on twenty, plus a retarded girl and an adorable boy a lot younger. Dave was a sales honcho like Gary except he'd been stuck in the same slot for years, showing that he lacked a Positive Mental Attitude. Still, they were good enough company in a pinch.

Now more people were arriving, including Mirabelle Rothberg, the Indian princess with the red dot in the middle of her forehead that looked like a cigarette burn. She gave me a quick nod then continued walking. I'd made a point of being nice to her even though she kept freezing me out. Now I watched her sweep around the room introducing herself as Doctor Rothberg. I tried to think of a put down that she wouldn't understand like how I wished I had the nerve to wear my hair like hers, but decided she might catch on and say something nasty.

My post was at the entrance to greet the ladies who were becoming my friends after only six weeks, knowing that friendships develop when sharing thoughts and experiences. It had started with Marva right away because she was so up-front. In one afternoon, I'd learned things about her job, her kids and her husband that would surprise his mother and even his doctor. Mirabelle Rothberg was the opposite. She went around spouting spiritualistic baloney that made no sense at all. I lean toward things that are part of everyday life like movies, TV and what's going on in the world. I mean, who cares about karma or yoga when there's something genuinely American like a sale at Bloomingdale's?

Getting to know Sheila, a minister's wife might be a real challenge, like meeting The First Lady from France. But minister's wives are different and I didn't know what to expect.

By now the room was full and buzzing with conversation. Carol arrived a little late, saying that Tony absolutely had to shower before he could take care of the kids. Kim Preston was also late, having been busy getting their guestroom ready for Neville and Sheila since the parsonage was being renovated.

I tried to imagine what Sheila looked like. Given Neville's good looks, they probably made a stunning pair. She'd have sun-streaked hair and long slim legs. Coming from Santa Ana, her skin would have a beautiful tan and she'd be dressed in the newest Rodeo Drive fashions.

Then it was 1:45 and I began to see soggy canapés and the centerpieces wilting from the sun. Already there were crumbs on the starched tablecloths from people's hors d'oeuvres. Pretty soon teatime would morph into dinner and everyone would have to leave.

Suddenly there was a flurry in the hallway and a deep baritone rumbled below the women's soprano voices. It was as recognizable and distinctive as my father's. Why was Neville coming to a women's tea?

Everyone turned and looked. And there stood Sheila, wearing a print skirt of cheap cotton barely past her knees with clunky boots that had gone totally out of style. After a stunned silence, those around the punch bowl swarmed forward, murmuring their welcome while eyeballing one another like they couldn't wait to compare notes afterward. I just stared, wondering whether Amity would be going back to being a homeless shelter or a refuge for every AA on the West Side. Better Metropolitan Church with its Gay population. At least they dressed well.

"I'm so glad to be here. I was raised in the Midwest, you know, so this is like coming home." Her voice was barely a whisper.

Sue, Liz Mason's fifteen-year old, stood balancing punch and bacon rollups like an experienced party girl. Finally she stepped forward. "Let me get you something to drink." Moving to the refreshment table, she returned with a plate of canapés, which Sheila dipped into like a trucker coming off a cross-country haul.

"I leave you in their care," smiled Neville. Giving Sheila a peck on the cheek, he backed out of the room. "I'll be in the church office if you need me."

Marva stepped forward in a friendly way letting Sheila know who was in charge. "I hope you had a pleasant flight."

"It was long, but I can catch up on sleep tonight."

Now it was Kim's turn. "You've arrived just in time. The parsonage is being redecorated so you can make your preferences known before the workers finish. Meanwhile, you'll be staying with us."

"I've been told that the parsonage is large and roomy." Her voice didn't ring with enthusiasm and I couldn't blame her. Not only had the neighborhood been picked out for her but its size and style as well.

"You're welcome to change things around, of course. After all, it will be your home." Marva's voice was cheerful, but I knew what she and Paul thought about that cold and dreary house. It had been bought before the new church was built and barely maintained since then, Amity having run out of the windfall money. "There's ample storage in the basement. After the rooms are painted, a cleaning service can freshen it up for you."

Sheila smoothed her hair. "We've been driving around all morning. Maybe I should take a minute to touch up."

"Of course. Let me show you." Kim took her arm and they walked toward the lady's lounge while everyone stood evaluating Sheila from top to bottom.

I was tempted to follow, but that would have been obvious. So I went into the kitchen where the activity was a welcome distraction, admiring the trays of canapés and hors d'oeuvres, the vegetables carved into the shape of flowers, the carafes of wine. If we'd sent out for fried chicken Sheila would have been just as pleased, judging how she gobbled down Sue's offering without even looking. A woman whose husband had clearly outgrown her. No wonder he looked at me the way he did. Poor man.

Liz Mason was in the kitchen and gave me a welcoming smile. "So what do you think?"

I ducked the question. "Do they have children?"

"Yes - two. But they'll stay in California until the moving is done. You know how hard it is for kids, especially teenagers."

"Tell me about it. They'll need all the help they can get."

"I heard that." Carol's voice came through over the hubbub.

"Oh Lord. What have I gotten myself into?" I groaned, pretending I didn't enjoy the attention.

Carol's smile was coaxing. "We're scheduling a series of neighborhood meetings to discuss a new direction for Amity. Could we have one of the meetings at your house? It wouldn't be much, just a small group discussion on the future and I understand your place is rather roomy."

"Let me call you, and we can talk about it," I said hurriedly making sure I was polite.

Through the half-opened door, I could see Sheila now seated at a table. She'd powdered her nose and added a touch of lipstick, a definite improvement. Mousy women are like that. Kim had remained at her side as four other people joined them, but there were still two empty chairs and I moved to grab one in a hurry. "You're leaving behind California's sandy beaches and warm sunshine to come to Worthington?" I asked as I sat down.

"I love California, but the Midwest is home."

"Where are you from?"

"Oh, you've probably never heard of it."

"Try me."

"It's a little bitty town in southern Indiana called Wilburding."

I laughed. "You're right. Is it named for someone?"

'Not to my knowledge."

"Is it a farm town?"

"I guess so."

"Don't you know?"

"Well, there's a canning factory there..."

I looked at Marva for help.

"Worthington is growing with most of its people as transplants. So you'll be a standout - a native daughter," Marva smiled.

"My parents are Scotch-Irish." Sheila looked around the table. "...not Native."

Everyone laughed politely.

"Moving cross-country is nothing to laugh about," Marva declared, her eyes sending a warning. "So if there is anything we can do to help..."

"We won't be moving until after semester break. Of course Neville will be here sooner. But we hope to celebrate Christmas in Worthington." She looked around the table. "I teach art. It's the end of the semester for me too."

A farm girl who taught drawing might impress the hayseeds in Wilburding. But a minister should be able to stand proud with his wife at his side. Isn't that what a wife is for?

"How sweet." Kim's voice dripped with sarcasm but Sheila didn't seem to notice.

"Two galleries in California have shown my work," Sheila added softly.

"Maybe we could arrange that right here at Amity," Marva said. "Let us know when you're settled and we'll put it on the agenda."

I tried to imagine her kind of painting. Maybe they were like the pictures of children with enormous eyes, painted on black velvet and sold off the back of a truck parked at a gas station. Or, being a minister's wife, she might do copies of the Last Supper or portraits of the suffering Jesus.

I was about to ask but then I noticed a number of women getting ready to leave. It was time to return to my post at the door. At almost five o'clock, it had been a long day and I was ready for it to end. Sheila might have been a disappointment, but for me it was a howling success. I'd met a few more women whose contacts would be useful. Gary would be pleased.

CHAPTER 6: LIZ

THE AFTERNOON WAS winding down and the women were leaving. All that was needed was to give instructions to the caterers and clean-up crew. Dave was home with Kelsey and John, capably entertaining a two-year old and our Down's syndrome girl of eight. Marva had her hands full welcoming Sheila and dealing with that awful Joy Volkman, so I offered to close things down, beginning with the kitchen.

"Good party, Mom." Sue stuck her head around the corner, eyeing the food like a burglar on the prowl. "Any chance we could take some of this stuff home?"

"Afraid not. Amity will use this for tomorrow's coffee hour. I'll have the caterers wrap everything, then we can leave."

People say Sue and I look alike, having the same coloring and strong body frame. But when I was her age, skinny was in and I had curves that wouldn't quit. The story of my life - a day late and a dollar short. Now she leaned over the table and helped herself to a caviar canapé, eying me up and down. "I really like that outfit, Mom. Can I try it on? I bet it'd fit."

"I suppose. But you wouldn't have anywhere to wear it except to church and everyone has already seen it - on me."

"I'd still like to see if it fits. Remember how Dad says we have the same body? He says he can't tell the difference."

I laughed. "I assure you, he can."

She was perched on the table, her fingers curved around the edge, swinging her feet like a movie ingénue. "I like those suits with short jackets that a lot of women were wearing. Their clothes sure didn't come from Macy's. And Joy Volkman's gray pantsuit. She probably got it from someplace back east." She popped another canapé in her mouth. "Did you see Sheila when I handed her the plate?"

"It's not polite to comment on other people's manners." I looked at the clock. "Ready to go?"

"Can I drive?"

"You are how old?"

"Fifteen plus, plus, plus…" She smiled beguilingly. "You could give me an early birthday present."

"And go to jail for aiding and abetting? No way."

"Can't blame me for trying." She moved one of the trays aside, looking for another canapé with caviar. "Sure we can't take a few of these home?"

"For whom? Kelsey would spit them out and your father says caviar's too salty. Anyway, you've already had more than your share." I put my arm around her, feeling the slim roundness of her shoulder. "I'll buy a jar and take it home."

"Only if you plan on going out."

I released my hands and gave her a pat on the butt. "If you ever touch the liquor cabinet..."

"Just kidding, Mom."

"Well, make your jokes funnier."

"Can I bring the car around? That's legal. The parking lot is private property."

"Well, maybe if you're really careful. Do you remember where we parked?"

"Is the pope Catholic?" She reached into the lower cabinet, took the keys from my purse and galloped toward the door. "I'll meet you in front."

The cleanup crew was collecting chairs and folding tables, placing them behind the sliding doors. After giving final orders to the supervisor, I walked across the room to the storage cabinets. It was time to inventory some of the Christmas decorations.

Finding the boxes I was looking for, I called to a worker across the room to help carry my load.

Outside, Sue was sitting in the car, the engine running. "I could drive home," she pleaded. "Everyone says I look older than sixteen."

"That you do. But one little fender bender and we'd be in debt forever."

She tossed her head and pouted, but obediently began unbuckling the seat belt. Then things moved fast and there was no time to call out.

Sue had neglected to put the car into Park, and preparing to exit, had gotten tangled up between the seat belt and her purse. Instead of getting out, she fell forward, her body hanging half-way out the open door. Reaching for balance, she grabbed the steering wheel. At the same time, her right foot hit the accelerator, and the car shot forward. The open door hit my head, and Sue was dragged some hundred feet before the car was stopped by a high curb along the edge of the parking lot, its engine roaring.

People came running from everywhere. One woman sprinted forward and turned off the engine. Someone else reached for Sue as she dangled out of the front seat. I ran toward the car screaming her name, feeling a warm trickle running down my face.

As people gathered around, Sue was released from the tangled seatbelt, placed on the grass and covered with a jacket. Her left hand was scraped and embedded with gravel, her shoe in shreds and her ankle streaked with dirt, the calf raw and bloody. I was shaking so bad my knees began to buckle. Someone steered me into the back seat of the car where the smell of burning rubber made me want to throw up. I heard the wail of a siren sounding off in the distance. Through a haze I kept asking whether she was all right.

"The ambulance is almost here." It was Neville's voice. He handed me a small towel. "Press this against your forehead. Head wounds bleed a lot."

"What happened?" I mumbled.

The ambulance alongside the car drowned out his response as the medic leaped out and growled, "Move back, folks. Make room for the stretcher."

People peered at the figure lying on the grass. Sheila was holding Sue's head in her lap. "Is she dead?" I whispered.

The medic peered inside the car. "Are you her mother?"

"Yes," replied Neville, taking my hand. "They're both hurt."

The medic squinted at me. "That cut might need stitches." He turned to Neville. "How about helping me get this lady out of the back seat."

I made it out of the car and into the ambulance, lurching to a seat next to the stretcher where Sue lay, her body strapped down, eyes closed, a brace around her neck. A second medic was across from me, monitoring the machines attached to Sue under a gray blanket. Neville sat by my side.

I leaned forward as the ambulance began to creep past the dissipating crowd, brushing the hair off her forehead, feeling a bump beginning to form. She must have hit her head on the doorframe or the window. "Do you hurt?"

"All over."

"Your head?"

"Oh Mom, I was being careful." Her voice was filled with anguish.

"It was an accident, Sue. These things happen. You're going to be all right."

"You won't go to jail will you?"

"No. And you won't either. Just don't talk to anyone. Do you understand? It's important."

I looked at Neville, wondering how much he had heard.

"It's okay." He smiled and put his arm around me.

I don't cry easily. It might have been the shock or the adrenaline or just plain fear. But I sobbed the remainder of the trip with my head on Neville's shoulder, smearing blood all over his sweater while he patted my shoulder murmuring, "It's okay," over and over.

At the emergency room, Sue was whisked behind a curtain where she was prodded, poked and attached to an IV. Together we were rolled to x-ray, she in a cot, me in a wheelchair. By now her bloody foot was like a blue balloon. Upon our return, we were put in adjacent carrels. A resident closed the cut in my head with three stitches, then covered the wound, instructing me to sit on the edge of the cot with my feet dangling until I stopped feeling woozy.

Through it all, Neville moved back and forth, talking to the doctors, but mostly to Sue and me. The X-rays showed Sue had only a bad sprain, so the nurses began cleaning her abrasions. Only then did Neville pull out his phone and call David, first explaining that there had been an accident, then turning the phone over to me. I took a deep breath and cleared my throat.

"Jesus Christ, Liz, are you all right?" Dave's voice shook. "I've been worried sick. Do you know what time it is?"

"We're all right," I said, keeping my voice light. "I'll tell you all about it when I get home. Are the kids okay?"

"Of course. Neville said you had to leave the car at the church. Is it drivable?"

"I don't know."

"Should I come and get you?"

I looked around, suddenly confused. "I'll call a cab. Oh Dave, Neville has been just wonderful."

"I can put the kids in my car and pick you up. They're in their pajamas watching TV."

"My God, is it that late?"

"Look outside. It's dark."

"Then put them to bed. We should be home soon."

Just then Neville returned and I handed the phone back, feeling suddenly shy. "I owe you a sweater."

He smiled. "Occupational hazard. It comes with the job."

"Sheila was comforting Sue while I sat in the car falling apart."

Neville held up his hand as though brushing away some unseen speck. "You would have done the same."

The curtain swung open, revealing Sue in a wheelchair, her injured foot resting on the leg board, the other on the foot rest in a hospital stocking. Her left arm was in a sling, the hand wrapped in gauze. Streaks of dirt remained on her face with bits of grass clinging to her hair. Now that fear had subsided, I could laugh.

"So I'm not at my best," she mumbled, smoothing her blouse. "At least the bare essentials are covered. Do you suppose the insurance will pay for a new outfit?"

"That's not what's meant by profiting by your mistakes," I replied sternly. Then seeing the dejected look on her face, I slid off the cot to give her hug, rewarded with a stabbing pain in my back. I grimaced and Neville stepped forward, then stood back when he saw I was alright.

"Sheila took my car and left for the Pressers. So if you don't mind, we can share a cab."

I looked questioningly at the attendant. "They've got all the information from your insurance card, so you don't have to stay. Whenever you're ready, I'll escort you out."

The cab was waiting at the entrance. Sue and I sat in the back, her feet across my lap while Neville sat next to the driver. Our house would be the first stop.

Dave was at the window peering out anxiously and seeing the lights, came out to meet us. The cab's overhead was dim, but he still winced as he got close, seeing us as a bloody mess. Together they helped Sue out, guiding her into the house while I followed, aching with each step.

As Neville turned to leave, Dave touched his arm. "Please stay. I need to unwind and I suspect you could use some comfort, companionship and a strong drink. I'll drive you to the Pressers later. Unless you think Sheila will be worried."

"Not at all," replied Neville. "She's used to this. As a matter of fact, a drink would be most welcome."

So Dave ran back out to pay the cabby while Sue and I made it upstairs.

It must have been about midnight when Dave came to bed. I stirred a little and he wrapped his arms around me. "It's going to be okay," he whispered.

"I shouldn't have…" I began.

"Don't talk."

"We were so lucky to have Neville there."

"Yes. But more importantly, you're safe."

I snuggled a little closer, and comforted, drifted back to sleep.

Chapter 7: Joy

IN NOVEMBER GARY and I celebrated our eighteenth anniversary. Mom sent flowers. Gary's folks called from Florida. For once I was glad this podunk town was not worth visiting.

Eighteen isn't particularly special but it marked being married longer than not. So I got a makeover that wasn't needed but made me feel good. Then on the big day, we went to the club for a lobster dinner. Gary was acting sentimental, murmuring that he wanted to shower me with diamonds, something he'd say from time to time because we married at the courthouse on the spur of the moment. Diamonds hadn't mattered. We knew we belonged together.

Now his hands were on my back, sliding up and down. "I was thinking about a carat and a half, something impressive but not flashy," he said. "Maybe you'd like platinum. I've been looking around. There's supposed to be a year-end bonus."

I hadn't heard about the bonus. But I was never one to pass an opportunity. "You mean like in the movies? You leaning over the counter and trying on the ring while the old guy nods and I say something like, 'Whatever the lady wants…'"

I stopped for a long lingering kiss, giving me time to strategize because he'd really taken me by surprise. "Liz and Marva would just die."

"I'll bet they would."

We visited every jeweler in Worthington, sitting in cushioned chairs while clerks brought out tray after tray. Pretty soon we knew enough to open our own business. I finally chose a blue diamond surrounded by smaller stones all set in platinum.

Meanwhile, I began to plan for the Amity's neighborhood meeting at our house, which I'd scheduled for the Friday before Thanksgiving.

By now Gary was pretty much immersed with his job at *Marty's* and that meant long hours at the office. Whenever Gary gets busy, I get busier, what with the house, the boys and the usual social responsibilities. That was my job and I enjoyed it all.

There would be five couples coming making for an even dozen. Scheduled for seven o'clock, folks could get home from work, grab a quick bite, shower and change into something casual. Why go through the trouble of selecting a second wardrobe if you weren't going to us it?

I laid out a spread of nuts, chips and dips plus two kinds of wine. Elsie, who worked at the Club and helped me whenever I needed her, came to set things up. Gary came home early and we whipped through dinner sending the boys off to a movie.

The first to arrive was a couple I'd never met, Gerda and Werner Stahl, recent transplants from somewhere in Europe or Argentina. He was a physicist working at the research lab that added hundreds of jobs to Worthington, a political pork barrel if I ever saw one.

Gary was at the door to greet them. "Hey, Werner! Long time no see. How's the racket ball?" He turned to Gerda. "You're probably still in bed, looking beautiful while he's knocking his brains out at the club batting the ball around."

Gerda arched her pencil thin eyebrows and cocked her head. "If knowing you proves me to be beautiful, then it serves me well to be your friend." Worthington had gone international.

I took her coat and hung it in the closet. "The bar is in the living room. Can I pour you some wine?"

"That would be nice. It's been a long week."

We went through to where the snack table was laid out, leaving Gary and Werner in the foyer talking about sports. I poured her glass two thirds full, allowing room for the wine's full bouquet like you're supposed to.

Holding the stem, she glided to the couch. "You have a lovely home. I understand you are also new to Worthington."

"Since August."

"We're living in a hotel since September. What a pity. A month earlier and this house could have been ours." She looked around the room, her eyes re-arranging the furniture.

Luckily, the doorbell rang and I got up as more people arrived. Meanwhile, Gerda moved back to the table to pour herself some more wine, blotting the overflow with my best cocktail napkins.

The rest of the group consisted of the Pressers, Paul and Marva, Steve and Mirabelle Rothberg, Nancy Oberman who was Carol's mother and had been a member forever, and Scottie Smythe, a divorced mother of two, the advisor for the Youth Group. Twelve people in a room larger than a three car garage is nothing. We had bought the house expecting to do a lot of entertaining, the furniture arranged for conversation.

By seven-thirty everyone had drunk at least one glass of wine and were seated comfortably. Then someone mentioned Amity and everyone turned toward Bill Presser, as though his takeover was kind of natural. Being board president has its perks.

"Why are we here?" Bill began, his voice booming like it was coming from the pulpit. He turned and gave me a big smile. "...besides enjoying an evening with Joy and Gary." Then his face turned serious. "I'll tell you why." He hunched forward. "We want everyone to be happy. How can Amity send that signal to Dr. Leighton, letting him know our needs, purposes, desires?"

There was an awkward silence. "I kind of miss the Wednesday night prayer meetings that we had when Dr. Walsh was here," Nancy Oberman offered.

"All right. Anything else?"

"We need to spend more time listening to one another," Paul said thoughtfully.

"Neville suggested that it's something we need to learn."

Bill reached into his briefcase and pulled out a legal pad, handing it to Kim like she was supposed to take notes.

"Kids need to be able to explore new ideas. Maybe a class in comparative religion," Mirabelle declared. "Hindu, Muslim... I'd be happy to put the program together."

"And get as many in her class as Nancy gets to her prayer meeting," Marva muttered, "like nothing."

Someone else mentioning clothing boxes for the poor, circle suppers, bridge groups, transportation for senior citizens, all which Kim dutifully jotted down on the yellow pad. After two hours, Kim had three pages single-spaced without one original idea. I wondered what would happen to the yellow pad when we finished. Better to just burn it.

By now the wine was gone and people had switched to the hard stuff. Conversation had run dry, yet no one was making a move to leave and I worried that Gary wouldn't be able to work it into his expense account. Toward midnight, Jason and Matt came home, poking their heads in to say hello, introducing themselves in a casual but friendly way, handling the give and take with charm and good humor, the definition of cool.

Finally at two o'clock we were done. Gerda and Werner were the last to leave and the living room was a mess. Gary and I were desperate for a nightcap.

"Thank God tomorrow's Saturday."

"Tomorrow's Sunday," I said, looking at the clock. "But you can go to the club and work out while I get my beauty rest."

"I didn't think you heard that."

"I pay attention when it counts. I suspect Gerda starts drinking in the morning and has a buzz on all day long. Do you suppose she keeps a stash in her room?"

"Werner thinks she's hot."

"So you think everything went okay?"

"Sure. Bill gave me the names of two more prospective sales reps where I can follow up. The kids got to meet Scottie so maybe they'll join the Young People's group. That should produce more contacts. Kim wrote everything down, taking us off the hook. Let's go to bed."

For a Friday night that turned into Saturday, I guess it went okay. Like I said, keeping Gary happy is my job, and I'm good at it. At least, Gary thinks so.

CHAPTER 8: JAYNE

NONE OF THE kids were in church today so I ended up sitting with Mom and Paul. Dr. Leighton practically puts me to sleep. Then, just as I was ready to walk out, there was Scottie Smythe at the door shaking hands and talking so nobody could get past her.

Scottie's okay I guess. She's young, which can be important for the advisor to a youth group. She gave me a big smile and pulled me into a corner. That always means she wants something.

"Hey, Jayne, how's it going?"

"Okay, I guess. Where's everyone? I'm going to stop coming if none of the kids are around."

"They'll be at the meeting tonight." She smiled. "I just wanted to make sure you'd be there. A social worker from below the bluff will be the speaker. It would help to have a good turnout."

I rolled my eyes. "Sounds like school. How come we can never talk about us?"

"You have officers. Talk to them."

"I have. But every meeting is the same."

"Don't be grumpy, Jayne. If you want change, you have to speak up."

"To Sue? Gimmie a break."

"She's your president. You voted for her."

She was right. Damn democracy anyhow.

"By the way, how is Sue?"

"I guess she's okay. Is she coming tonight?"

"I think so."

"That's good," I lied. Sue's accident was all over school and everyone knew Sue had been behind the wheel when it happened even though her parents kept it hush-hush.

"She's coming with the Volkman kids. They're friends from school."

"I know. Matt has an adorable smile and says cute things around the girls. So Sue's brought him into her crowd. Everyone thinks he's hot. But I happen to know that his parents pay big bucks for tutoring."

Scottie put her arm around me as people kept crowding past. "We all find our place under the sun. Being cool isn't everything."

"Yes it is. But God should strike me dead if I ever giggle over a guy. I'll bet underneath, Matt is a jerk."

Scottie shook her head the way people do, acting like they understand teenagers. "Actually, I wanted to ask if you were busy Saturday night. Can you baby sit like about eight o'clock?"

So that was it. Good old Jaynie, always available. "I'll check with Mom."

"I already have. She said they're going to be home."

"Well then, I guess so." I looked around and saw Mom waving. "See you tonight. I promise." And I hurried over to where Mom and Paul were trying to keep the babies from crawling between people's legs as they moved toward the exit.

After Sunday lunch Mom puts Ashley and Taylor down for their naps while I clean up in the kitchen. I don't know what Paul does upstairs besides waiting, but as soon as Mom is done, I hear them in the bedroom. Whatever...

Mom always tries to talk to me about the you-know-what but I couldn't care less. Anyway, it's gross. I just think studying about it or doing research smacks of porno, even though Mom says if she'd known more, we'd still have Dad around. As far as I'm concerned, he was good riddance.

I'm glad that Matt and Jason are coming tonight. Of course, Scottie could be wrong. But Matt would do anything to be around Sue, and Jason follows his brother around like a puppy, and I do like Jason. I know he's gotta be smart because he's in my English class. It's not exactly advanced placement, but when we're seniors it will be. I plan to take as many AP classes as I can, even chemistry. That way I'll get a leg up toward college. Mom says Dad stopped paying support a long time ago, or maybe that was her way of telling him she didn't want him around. I'm pretty sure Paul would pay for any college I wanted. But there's the little ones to think about. Anyway, I'm hoping that I get a scholarship. I might even get into Harvard or West Point. That would sure make Sue's eyes bug out - but maybe not.

After dinner, Paul drove me to church, dropping me off at the lower level. It was seven o'clock, and we were right on time. I looked at cars to see who else might be there. It was pretty empty, meaning a skimpy turnout – again. No telling how early we'd finish, what with nobody being there. So I told Paul I'd probably hitch a ride from someone else.

My shoes squeaked on the floor as I walked down the hall. Then as I got closer, I could hear kids talking.

Sue was there along with Matt and Jason plus the usual fifteen or so kids who'd been coming on Sunday nights. And of course, Scottie. They all faced the door and wore expressions like I was supposed to be someone else. "If I'm the last one here, does that mean I'm the star?" I asked, trying to act cool.

"We should be so lucky."

I looked at Scottie. "Meaning...?"

"It looks like our speaker has gone missing. We called and there was no answer. So we don't have a program for tonight," Sue replied.

"You mean there's no Plan B?"

"Well, it'll give us a chance to really talk," she said, acting like this were no big deal.

Right. So we can discuss Matt's car and Sue's latest trip to Chicago and the cheerleader's newest whatever. I'd rather have a social worker, thank you. I almost said it out loud but Scottie'd be the only one to appreciate it.

Suddenly there were more footsteps down the hall. Maybe it was the speaker after all. But instead, there was Dr. Leighton framed in the doorway, a big smile on his face. "I was in my study and came to say Hi before going home." I almost didn't recognize him. This minister was dressed in a plaid shirt and blue jeans like an ordinary guy, kind of like the centerfold in a rifleman's magazine.

Above the mumbling, Sue hobbled forward and gave him a hug. "We're always glad to see you, Neville."

He grinned at the rest of us. "Nothing like disaster to firm up a friendship." He looked around. "But where is…"

Now it was Scottie's turn and she explained what happened, or rather, what didn't happen, while the rest of us started thinking about going home.

"Sue is right. We can turn lemon into lemonade. Let's talk." And Dr. Leighton moved toward the side of the room where the tables and chairs were set up conference style, motioning the rest of us to follow. "Ministers are talkers and I've got all night."

"About what?" asked Tanya, a new member whom I didn't really know.

"Don't look at me," he replied. "This is your organization. You're in control. I'm here to listen."

"Then why did you say 'Let's talk?'" I asked innocently.

After everyone stopped laughing, Dr. Leighton turned serious. "Why is talking to one another such a big deal? Is it because it never happens?"

I caught Sue looking at me. She would be the last person I'd want to talk to - I mean, really talk to. "Sometimes there's no point," I said.

He looked around the table. "How many of you have seen people you'd like to know, but don't know how to proceed?"

He was doing it again. "That's not what I said." But no one was listening. Instead, hands came up, then more, and then all of them, even me.

"What do you suppose would happen if you knew the magic formula and could talk to everyone and have them talk to you? What if everyone else also knew how to do this, not just in Worthington but in the whole world?"

"Awesome," Jason murmured.

"Exactly. Religion calls it heaven."

"Well, that's not what we generally do here," Scottie said.

I could have hugged her. At least someone was talking sense.

"Then what? Have you thought about what your purpose is?" It was a question that kept coming up.

"Would you like to see our list?" Scottie laughed. "There's Keeping your Faith Strong, Making Your Commitment in Life, Learning to Share with the Less Fortunate, or Staying on the Straight and Narrow, although I have to admit that last one has the least appeal."

"And with good reason. Too many people go about doing *things* without ever looking at the other person." He sat back and formed a steeple with his fingers like he was getting ready to preach. Bad enough I had to sit through Sunday morning.

"Sensitivity is not on most people's list," he continued. "Yet it should be. Little hurts or offenses can become big ones very quickly. We are taught to be polite but not programmed to be sensitive. So churches should aim to teach us to love one another. It's our mission - or should be."

Religion, philosophy and pop-psychology delivered by the rifleman. I wondered whether anyone understood what he was saying. But everyone's eyes were on him, hypnotized.

Suddenly Rex, whose parents never came to church, stood up. "Let's hear it for Love!" His voice was almost a shout, bouncing off the walls across the room like an echo. He waved his hands up and down, inviting others to stand up and do the same while everyone giggled nervously. Poor Rex. He just didn't get it.

Dr. Leighton walked around the table. When he got to Rex, he touched his shoulder almost as though he wanted to put his arms around him but didn't. "That is exactly what I'm talking about. What this young man says is that he feels enthusiastic, engaged, that he likes what he's heard and wants to be part of it." He turned to Sue. "Isn't that true?"

To focus on Sue, the president, was a perfect first move. But he was taking a chance. If she refused to play the game or just giggled or worse, said something about Rex being a nerd, that would be the end, not only with her, but with everyone else. The first Lemmings on Earth were teenagers.

Sue turned and gave Dr. Leighton her dazzling Miss America smile. But before she could reply, Tanya spoke up. "If Rex wanted to say all that, why didn't he?"

Everyone laughed, including Rex. Sue was off the hook, and so was Dr. Leighton.

"Dialogue is a two-way street. Once you begin really listening, you're more careful in how you express yourself. Pretty soon, you can say what you really mean," Dr. Leighton replied. "Politely, of course. Remember, this is about love."

Suddenly kids were examining what they really meant, and we were off and running.

"Last week you…"

"This is what you said..."

"I could tell you wanted…"

Maybe it was because he'd already landed the big fish with Sue when she was in the emergency room. After that, the rest was easy. Group dynamics with Dr. Leighton, a real pro. I was being suckered in, but it was fun to watch and even play the game.

All of a sudden it was nine o'clock, and then nine-thirty but everyone was still sitting there. Actually, they were yelling, laughing and interrupting each other like in Mr. Bradley's social problems class that always filled up before any other elective. Except that instead of talking about poverty and divorce, we were talking about *us* with Dr. Leighton not leading the discussion at all. Like I said, he's a real pro.

By the time we left, everyone was acting like Dr. Leighton was pretty much okay and maybe our Youth Group could get going again with outings and events the way it did when Dr. Walsh was here. If he could do that, then I'd swallow it. Because this could be the one place in the world where it didn't matter about being cool. At least, that's what I heard him say.

CHAPTER 9: JOY

THE HOLIDAYS WERE creeping up and the weather cool. We had joined in the cultural life of Worthington. That was part of the job. *Marty's* bought season tickets in blocks of four, six and eight to concerts, cabaret performances, and sporting events. The sales department used them to entertain clients, business contacts or other prospects. Gary is in charge of that, so we do a lot of entertaining. But sometimes there are no contacts around so we can use them for ourselves, which helps lock in relationships. Sometimes we'd run into friends, ending up at a jazz joint or piano bar downtown where we meet even more people.

Meanwhile, *Marty's* was growing at a solid ten- percent. If he played it right, Gary might be in line for a spot on the executive committee. Who woulda thought?

Then the holidays came crashing in. Thanksgiving dinner would be at the club, an enormous buffet including all the traditional fixings plus an open bar. It would start a little after noon and continued through the dinner hour.

All the Leightons would be there including the kids, staying with the Pressers. Membership at the club was part of Neville's benefits, so we could expect to see them there.

Arriving a little after noon, we sat with Marva and Paul and their three kids plus the four of us and Scottie Smythe. As always, there was a lot of waving and table-hopping. I usually have a good time, and if things got lame, I could take a walk to the lady's room. So pretty soon I had moved to sit with Carol Stone and her family, tweaking Jennifer and Scott who were happy to get the attention. I talked with Tony, pretending not to notice how he eyed me up and down. Too bad. He's not my type.

Later I followed Gerda to the lady's lounge, ready to pull her head out of the toilet or drag her over to the couch if she'd passed out on the floor. But it was early enough and Gerda was holding together pretty well. So we touched up our makeup, discussing neighborhoods and housing for the dozenth time. Finally I pulled myself away, muttering something about not wanting to miss dessert, even though I never eat sweets. Gerda stayed, dabbing another layer of powder on her face. She was probably there for the afternoon, nursing a private stash from her pocketbook that dangled on the back of the stool.

When I returned, the Leightons had arrived and were seated with Bill and Kim Presser on the opposite side of the dining room attracting a cluster of well-wishers. Ministers reach out to the community every bit as much as salesmen.

I sat down at an empty table sipping wine and didn't see Carol's approach until I caught a hint of her cologne and felt a swish of cool air at my elbow. "It's going to be nice to be back to normal, don't you think?" she asked, taking a seat next to me.

"I have no idea."

Her chuckle was not malicious. "I forgot you were new. Some people fit in so easily."

I wasn't expecting idle chitchat. If anything, Carol was pretty transparent. "And...?"

"Neville is planning a Participation Training session, a weekend program to help people work together. You may remember talking about leadership at the neighborhood meetings."

"But we're not members."

"That's okay. It's open to anyone."

Now I know where I shine, like being organized, running a good show and looking good. But leadership is like golf or tennis. It takes years of practice and I'm strictly a beginner.

She seemed to read my mind. "C'mon, Joy, it's a new world out there."

"Who else is coming?"

"The Rothbergs along with the Pressers and the Stahls. Scottie will be there with her new boyfriend. You and Gary would make ten."

I turned as laughter erupted from where Jason and Matt were with a cluster of teens. "I don't know. Gary's been awfully busy."

"It doesn't start until January. Think about it and give me a call." She patted my arm. "Oops - there goes Jennifer after the desserts." And she rushed toward the buffet table to sweep her daughter into her arms and back to the table where the two-year old had slipped out from under her father's careless eye.

Deserted once more, I was about to take another walk when I saw the group across the room begin to separate, letting me get a good look at the Leighton family. Neville was perfect, as usual, wearing an open-collared shirt and a tan cashmere vest under his sport coat. Sheila resembled a Hungarian gypsy at menopause, her dangling earrings and colored beads jiggling every time she moved. A shimmering satin blouse and quilted vest with matching skirt reached halfway up her shiny black boots. For a costume it wasn't bad, but to carry it off, she needed to be twenty-five pounds thinner or a lot taller. They were deep in conversation with the Pressers. Gary was right there at their elbow, checking things out.

Suddenly Jason and Matt were standing in front of me. "Mom, I'd like you to meet Adam and Hannah Leighton."

I found myself staring up at a Greek god and a red-haired goddess with skin the texture of Ivory Soap. "They're moving to Worthington next semester. Isn't that great?"

Suddenly it was junior high with me trying to think of what to say when facing *them,* the cool crowd, the slick dudes, the ones who could always find the right words, coolest clothes, most current music as though sucking it through their pores. Some feelings never go away. "Well, yes. Will you be in some classes together?"

"Maybe," Jason replied. "Depends on the schedule."

Their lean slender muscles said they surfed the Pacific five times a week and twice on Sundays, radiating that certain air of entitlement like seasonally priced lobster and a room at the Beverly Hilton. Those born rich or beautiful know nothing else.

"Will you be sorry to leave California?"

"Not really. I'll be staying with friends until graduation, then probably go back there for college," Adam replied.

"I've already gone to three different schools," Hannah said. "But it's hard leaving friends."

"Tell me about it," Jason muttered.

"Have you seen your new house?" I asked, making a point of staying in the conversation.

Hannah wrinkled her nose. "Mom says we'd be allowed to store all the antiques in the basement. That way they'd be safe," she added quickly.

Marva had taken me through the parsonage, past the grandfather clock ticking solemnly in the foyer, the scrolled rosewood dining room furniture and assorted oil paintings in gilded picture frames, valuables from years past, but definitely not California. "Not your thing?"

Adam nudged his sister. "Well, we better be getting back to dinner."

"And I must come over to say hello to your parents," I added.

Obviously relieved, they moved toward the buffet, leaving me to work my way across the crowded room toward the Leighton's table.

Gary saw me and like a gentleman, got up to give me his chair next to Sheila, sliding the chair under me. "I see that the kids have already found one another."

Sheila looked up from her plate and smiled. It crossed my mind that her garish clothes might be a cover for a genuinely shy person. Not that I have any sympathy. Life is what you make it. "Adam and Hannah make friends easily, like their father."

"When you're with the right people," Neville added, leaning back in his chair, his plate neatly emptied, his manner relaxed and casual. And once again I wondered how these two ever got together.

"They're very good-looking," I said, and really meant it.

"You noticed."

"Along with everyone else."

Just then the foursome returned from the buffet with their plates mounded. "Hey, full house. We'll find another spot." And they moved back to join Marva and Jayne along with Ashley and Taylor, Paul having gone somewhere else for the moment.

Back to Sheila, I continued talking about the move, offering the help I knew she'd need. "You know, doctors, dentists, hairdresser, dry cleaners, the kinds of details that seem unimportant at first."

"Oh, we won't be moving until January. And we have to get Adam's college settled."

"After that, Amity will keep us occupied with new programs," Neville added.

"Oh yes, new programs."

Was her voice suddenly shrill? The others didn't seem to notice.

Gary gave me the eye that said it was time to go. So we conveyed our goodbyes and Gary went to retrieve the boys while I went for one more trip to the lady's room.

The passageway had walls that arched toward a glass ceiling, each section overlaid with narrow strips of wood and lined with potted plants. Marva said that during Christmas, they would add rows of trees stretching all the way from the dining room to the main foyer, alit with colored lights. Where did the electricity for the lights come from? Marva didn't know. Seeing no one around, I squeezed behind the foliage and there it was, electric outlets cleverly hidden a few inches from the floor. Suddenly I heard voices and ducked down, not wanting to be seen in such an awkward position.

"You could have been more enthusiastic, considering that this is a first impression." It was Neville, his voice sounding angry.

"Please, Neville, not again." Sheila's voice was so soft I had to strain to hear.

"What? Don't do my job? Don't make a living? Don't take care of my family?"

"You know what I mean."

"No I don't."

Then the footsteps faded and were gone.

Peering around the tree, I came out as fast as I could, hurrying to the foyer where Gary and the boys were waiting. Neville and his family were gone.

Back outside, the boys announced that they had decided to join the Youth Group saying that they liked everyone there, but I could tell that the Leighton kids had a lot to do with it. By the time we pulled up into our driveway, I'd lost interest. And January was a long way off.

CHAPTER 10: CAROL

THE TAP ON my office door made Jennifer look up from playing with her blocks on the floor. "Come in. It's not locked."

Neville stood leaning against the doorjamb, a smile on his face. "Good morning. I thought I heard the sound of renovation, a crew of carpenters."

I laughed. "Jennifer's specialty is leaning towers. Do we see a budding architect?" I turned to Jennifer. "Let's switch to the coloring books. You can sit right next to me."

Neville held up his hands in protest. "Let her play. I just popped in to say Hello."

"So have a seat."

He closed the door and sat across from my desk, crossing one leg over the other.

"How's it going?"

Jennifer turned back to her blocks and I leaned back in my chair. "I should be asking you. All set in the parsonage?"

"As much as possible. But I just couldn't impose on the Pressers any more. Things were getting a bit strained."

"In that big house? I'd think you'd be invisible."

"A stranger is always disruptive no matter how hard you try to accommodate. But the parsonage is okay. When Sheila comes, she'll turn it into a real home."

"A woman's touch," I smiled. "And you're keeping busy?"

"Two funerals and a wedding. Then there are home visitations. Baptisms are scheduled..."

I held up my hands. "I didn't ask for a report. I was simply…"

"... being polite. Making small talk."

"I'm glad you've come to Amity, Neville. I hope it's a long and happy marriage."

His smile radiated a blessing. "I appreciate your support." He cleared his throat. "But how's it going with you?"

"You want a confession? Tony hates selling, but there's nothing else out there. Mom never misses a chance to let her feelings out. They don't really get along."

"The eternal mother-in-law. It's their way of being protective." His smile was open and straightforward. "And congratulations in filling all the teaching slots."

"Let's hope it lasts." I looked at the stack of folders on my desk. "My only worry is with the Youth Group. Scottie's doing a good job, but it needs something more and I don't quite know which way to go. My training is with younger kids. Actually, I was hoping…"

"Well, I'm here." Jennifer had moved her toys close to him and now sat on the floor leaning against his chair. He reached down and stroked her hair, then turned back to me. "Go ahead. Ask me."

"Youth membership has never gotten beyond twenty or so, even under Dr. Walsh. A church this size should support four times as many. After all, they are the future. So what does it take to get them to come?"

"For openers, young people need to have a distinct purpose beyond school, sports or the country club. I'm not talking about God or the Bible or any religious orientation, although that should certainly be part of the mix. They also need to work at finding out who they are. For teenagers, that's Job One. If it's a group endeavor, so much the better. Maybe we can find an idea compatible with leadership training but on a youthful level."

It was close to naptime and Jennifer was getting restless. After discarding one toy after another, she moved toward Neville and crawled onto his lap, resting her head on his shoulder.

"It must be time to go home," I laughed. "She's kind of a daddy's girl," I added apologetically.

He wrapped his arms around her. "Kids know where they're welcome. As long as she's quiet, let her be."

I couldn't remember the last time Tony had sat with Jennifer in his arms. With Neville, it looked natural. "Well, if you don't mind."

"I started out wanting to be a teacher, you know. Seminary came much later." He stroked Jennifer's forehead and her eyes began to droop. "I'm also trained in pastoral counseling. I wear many hats. A minister helps wherever needed."

"Thank you, Neville. It's something we all need to be aware of."

"More than that. We need to discard our fears and inhibitions and become more open with one another." He touched Jennifer's cheek as she sat curled up on his lap, now sound asleep. "It's what babies do instinctively."

"You sound like a psychologist."

He smiled. "As I said, a minister wears many hats."

"And who ministers to the minister?"

"You're full of questions today, aren't you?"

"No answer to this one?"

He shrugged. "I suppose it's through prayer or from colleagues. Sometimes ministers have to beg, to ask for emotional handouts, even from a two-year old who wants to cuddle."

"I'm sorry you're reduced to begging. I'll try to be more forthcoming." Jennifer began to stir and he shifted in his chair to accommodate.

"That would be nice," he said softly. "Friends are not always easy to come by, especially in this business."

"Dr. Walsh was a good man, you know. A good pastor. He'd call members on their birthdays. He'd begin by singing happy birthday in his scratchy voice, then spend about five minutes with good wishes. Not just a birthday card, but a phone call and honest to goodness conversation or words of comfort and prayer - whatever was called for. If you were sick, he was there. No invitation needed. If he heard there was trouble, he'd come knocking on your door, asking if he could help. Some people said Amity needed to bring in more members, but Dr. Walsh wanted to serve these already here. I can't see anything wrong with that, can you? Yet there were rumblings."

"You miss him, don't you?"

"Jennifer was still a baby, not even walking, when he died. Mom and I went to the funeral. Tony stayed home with the kids." My voice was getting shaky. "Lots of people came but some stayed away. Factions had become personal."

"Sometimes it takes a while for feelings to heal."

A spigot had been turned on and I couldn't stop. "He wasn't really old, you know. Today, sixty is nothing. He just had a bad heart. He never talked about it. Maybe he didn't know it himself. Some people are like that, never seeing the doctor, assuming immortality." I took a deep breath and smiled. "I hope you see your doctor regularly."

His voice resonated, deep and soothing. "I think you need a hug, but I can't move without disturbing a sleeping child. Jennifer is important too."

I looked at him across the desk, a man of God holding my daughter, and I wondered why holy pictures never had Joseph holding the baby Jesus. "Would it be any less if I came over there to get it?"

"Of course not." He carefully moved one arm from around Jennifer as I leaned down, wrapped it around my waist and for a long moment, we remained together, the three of us.

Then I stood up, my chest pounding. "I'm afraid we're imposing. You probably didn't expect to be trapped here."

"No, please. I'm interested. Is there more?"

I sat back at my desk. "Well, after the funeral, factions really hardened. We'd just moved from the inner city to high on the bluff. New people began coming and were welcome, of course. Money from the highway department had bought land and paid for the building and some of the furnishings. But we needed a much bigger budget to serve the larger facility - salaries, utilities, and so on. And people began to do some serious thinking. What was the role of the church? What was the role of the minister?"

He nodded. "Some want it to be like a thriving business. Others see a different mission. And I'll bet that the Pressers and Stones were on opposite ends of the debate."

"The Rothbergs joined with Kim and Bill along with a few others. But most members wanted what we'd had before, even if it meant having a smaller congregation. Not that we weren't friends. But differences show up when searching for a new minister."

"So you chose Billy Oliver."

"We really didn't know what we were getting. Or maybe he changed after being hired, like some people said. It wasn't what, but how. You know, the kind of person who takes the sweetest wine and turns it into vinegar."

"You've been a member for a long time, haven't you?"

"I grew up here. I want Amity to be here forever."

Jennifer turned her head and opened her eyes, her expression bewildered, first looking up at Neville before squirming to get down, tottering sleepily toward me.

"No matter what, Mom is best," he smiled.

"She'll gravitate to the opposite sex soon enough."

He stood up. "I'd like to continue this conversation but I have an appointment in half an hour. Maybe we should plan on doing lunch sometime."

I nodded, pleased at the prospect. "Mom takes the kids on school holidays to give me a break. We might do it then."

"Sounds good. Just let me know and I'll be there." He tousled Jennifer's hair as she curled on my lap and walked out, calling, "Take care now," over his shoulder as he closed the door behind him.

Left in my chair, I surveying the neat orderliness of my office, feeling Jennifer's soft body melted into mine. My job was still new, and it had taken weeks to classify books, organize files and shift furniture to approximate comfort and efficiency. A modest allowance for draperies and two new chairs turned it into a quiet retreat where I felt competent and safe, today even more so, for it had been a long while since anyone had really listened to me. So I sat still for a long time, feeling my heart beating a song of quiet happiness as Jennifer dozed in my arms.

Chapter 11: Joy

SOME WOMEN WILL spend an afternoon at a matinee or at the museums. Marva and I love to shop. By that I mean finding things for ourselves. Buying for the house or the family, for a party or for a special occasion is not real shopping. That's more like being responsible. Shopping means exploring, analyzing and thinking about what's important, like confirming the self. That's the psychological part. Whatever the season, there is always something to want or need. And each time you find something you want, you learn more about yourself.

My favorite season is autumn. I love the warm muted shades like orange and bronze. My favorite color is gold. That's also my personality. Being autumn means being earthy, subdued and uncomplicated, like the autumn palette. The autumn person is also mature and ripe. My house reflects this. People say I'm easy to talk to. Maybe it's because I'm quiet and move slowly, not like Gerda who slinks around and always looks like she's holding a martini even when she's not.

Marva, on the other hand, is winter, her taste stark, intense, dramatic and modern. She wears a lot of black and white. Her mood swings are also black and white. When she enters a room, heads turn and there's electricity in the air. Their house reflects this, leaning toward the avant-garde. Come to think of it, maybe that's the attractions she had for Paul and vise versa. Architects always like being ahead of the curve.

Marva is also sexy. Right at the start, she'd filled me in about her ex and her life before the divorce, hinting that he was a real stud. After her divorce, she read books and learned that some of his ideas weren't so weird after all, at least not when compared to the French or the Japanese. Then Paul came along and as they say, the rest is history. That's where self-understanding comes along. Gary and I were compatible from the get-go.

So back to shopping. After two hours of wandering through the stores, we went to a pretty little tearoom on the edge of the Mall. The lunch crowd had gone and the room was quiet except for music that's nice if you don't listen too closely. We ordered finger sandwiches and Oolong tea, then settled back to enjoy.

I'd said nothing about the Thanksgiving event at the club with Neville and Sheila, waiting for the moment where I could watch Marva's face while I spilled it out. So now I leaned forward, making sure I had her attention, making my voice sound confidential and important. "I was looking at how they'd connect the lights at the club like we'd talked about, and all of a sudden I heard Sheila begging Neville not to do it again, sort of soft and pleading. Neville kept saying she should be more enthusiastic. Then they were gone."

She stared at me for a moment, then burst out laughing. "Sheila had better get her butt moved here before she loses more than her job." Her red fingernails were curled gracefully on the table. Then she turned serious. "I hope you're not planning to spread this around."

"Of course not. You're the only person I've told because I knew I could trust you," I said, wondering why that mattered.

"It seems innocent enough and it could have been anything. Once the bedroom door is closed, who knows what's going on."

I looked deep into Marva's eyes. "Oh no. Do you think..?"

"Cmon Joy. We're grownups, aren't we?"

I took a deep breath. "I wasn't trying to cause any trouble. You're right. It's none of my business."

It worked. She leaned forward, ready to balance things out. "There were nine people who voted against hiring Neville. I was one of them."

My surprise was genuine. "Why? Didn't you like him?"

"He needed to understand that there was work to be done and it wouldn't be easy." She lifted her shoulders and her voice went up a couple of notes. "It really has nothing to do with Billy. That part is over - at least as far as I'm concerned."

"Isn't he the one who divided the church?"

She frowned. "For your information, Carol was one of his strongest supporters who eventually turned on him. When Billy wasn't interested in her department, she found all kinds of things wrong with him, especially not spending enough time with the teenagers. But he did pay attention. Just not in the way everyone wanted. Others said he spent too much time at the County Hospital and the Veteran's Administration instead of going to the club and hobnobbing with members. It took only a year before they'd killed Billy's marriage and destroyed his career. Old timers are listened to, sometimes more than they should be."

Marva loves the dramatic. Still, I was startled at the intensity of her voice. "So Neville should be..."

"He should be adaptable. The congregation is changing. So is the community."

"That makes a lot of sense. You wanted to remind them?"

"Billy got a raw deal. I voted against Neville, but I do want him to stay. Still, he should know it won't be easy."

"Well then, we'll just think positively." I hesitated. "...and pray."

Then we turned to conversation about fashion, which was good enough but less then what I'd looked forward to. After all, I need to contribute to the conversation and Marva had left me with nothing but a question mark.

She called me the next morning when I was barely out of bed. "I just wanted to say thanks for lunch."

It was her way of checking my pulse, making sure we were still friends. "I'm so glad you called. I was worried I'd touched a hot button yesterday."

"I told Paul what you'd said, and after thinking about it, he called Billy Oliver at the denominational headquarters. Come to find out that Neville has a long history of being involved in church conflict. That's why Neville went back to school. He was out of a job."

I don't believe in ghosts but I was getting goose bumpy. "Isn't that supposed to come out when he candidates? I know they've always looked at Gary's history with a magnifying glass before he was hired."

"It must have fallen through the cracks."

Suddenly there were footsteps on the front walk and muffled stomping as though trying to knock snow off the shoes.

"Someone's at the door, Marva. I'll call you back."

The visitor had turned and was getting ready to walk away as I opened the door. "Good morning. I happened to be in the neighborhood and thought I'd drop by."

I caught my breath but managed a smile. "I didn't know that ministers made house calls. Good morning, Neville. Please come in."

Flecks of snow sparkled on his shoulders under the winter sun. He apologized for bringing dampness inside and apologized again when I took his coat and hung it in the closet. I'd never entertained a minister. Was I supposed to offer him a drink or bring out the Bible and say a prayer? Was it okay that we were alone? Then he gave me his big Christian smile and I wasn't nervous any more. A friend dropping in for coffee. What could be more ordinary. "Sheila and the kids on their way back to California?"

"Afraid so." He stopped, standing in the middle of the room.

"You look cold. Can I get you something?"

"Coffee would be nice."

I went into the kitchen and put a plate of doughnut on a tray along with the coffee. Turning, I almost crashed into Neville, who stood leaning against the doorway. "I though you might need some help," he smiled, taking the tray from me. He appeared taller than when standing in the pulpit, or maybe it just seemed that way because he was so close. "Where do we go?"

"How about the den? The fireplace lights easily and you can warm your fingers around a steaming mug."

"Sounds great. Lead the way."

It was my favorite room, furnished in soft brown leather. Three of the four walls jutted into the back yard. Tall windows exposed the winter sky and a sliding door opened to the patio surrounded by red-berry shrubs that attracted birds year round. Even now, two cardinals were perched atop a snow-covered branch like they were posing for a Christmas card. "You can put the tray there on the coffee table."

He sank down on the couch and let out a sigh. "This is a perfect spot on a cold winter's day. I like your taste."

"Fall colors," I smiled, sitting where I could study his face. "They're warm and earthy. It's where I begin decorating whenever we move."

"Sounds like the life of a minister."

"It does get tiresome, doesn't it? Starting over, making new friends."

His voice got low and husky like when he stood in the pulpit preparing us for the zinger that would fill our hearts and carry us through the following week. "I so want to make Worthington my home, Joy. Can you help me?"

I poured myself a cup of coffee and placed two doughnut holes on my plate before looking up. "Of course. Gary and I can show you where the best restaurants are. His barber is one of the best."

"More than that. I'm talking about your commitment to the church. You listen. You're involved. You're *there.*"

"But we're not even members."

"You will be."

"Who said so?"

"You did."

"When?"

"Call it intuition."

"Is that why you're here?"

"Ministers do more than preach on Sundays," he smiled.

It was a come-on. I'd heard it a million times from guys who'd had one drink too many. Still, I love the give and take, of picking up on clues and tossing them back - your turn, my turn. Of course I always make sure it's at a safe distance, but what could be safer than being with a minister in your own home? I arched my eyebrow. "I'm sure you do."

He played the cards like an expert gambler. "Besides that."

Party talk might be fun, but it was time to shift to safer ground. "How long before the family is here?"

"The week before Christmas."

"If there's anything I can do?"

"I hope you become friends."

That would take some doing. But I held on to my smile, making a mental note to share all this with Marva. "Of course."

"Sheila is my second wife."

"Oh, I didn't know that," I said, startled at the sudden shift.

"My first marriage lasted less than a year. Rachel and I were still in college. Neither of us knew what we wanted." He put down his cup and looked at me steadily. "We all have our peculiarities, our little hurts, our special needs. I'm sure you have yours."

I stood up and reached for the tray, aiming for the kitchen. "I see we need more coffee."

"I just want people to know. Otherwise it might color their perspective." He was following me, and I could feel the warmth of his body behind me, smell his distinctive scent like the interior of a posh hotel.

"Divorce is pretty common. No one is shocked any more."

"I appreciate your understanding. Sometimes people just brush things off with a joke, assuming that takes care of it."

"I'm sure you'll find understanding here at Amity." I backed toward the sink. "So how are things? Are you getting settled?"

"I suppose. But we were talking about Rachel."

I moved to place the island counter top between us. "I didn't mean…"

"No, of course not. But still, you changed the subject when I just wanted to share something with you."

"Neville, you'll have to bear with me. All this is so new."

"That's why I'm here." He looked around. "Could we go back into the den? It won't take long."

I glanced at the clock on the wall. Elsie would be coming soon to do the laundry. "Of course. I'll just re-fill the carafe and creamer."

He took the tray and we returned to the den. "I know there has been dissent at Amity. It's not unusual when going through a lot of changes like losing a minister or moving to different quarters. But I want to be instrumental in the healing process. The first step is to be sensitive and really listen, clearing away hidden feelings and unspoken thoughts. I have put together a program called Participation Training and I want to bring it to Amity."

"Is that the same program Carol was talking about?"

"Probably. She did offer to help."

"And what do you want from me?"

"I'd like you and Gary to participate."

I've never been one to go along with the crowd. Furthermore, I had no particular interest in church beyond the social, which Gary understood even if Neville didn't. But he'd come on a mission and I knew he wouldn't leave until he was satisfied. "I really have to think about this."

"You have much to offer."

"For sensitivity training?"

"You can call it that if you like. I prefer Participation Training."

"I'll have to check with Gary."

"As well you should." The determined look on his face was gone.

"Are you telling me that I'm being sensitive?"

He laughed. "Touché." He put his cup back on the coffee table and stood up. "And now I must go."

Back into the foyer, he retrieved his coat and threw it on in his casual way. Then as a kind of afterthought, gave me a peck on the cheek, opened the door and went out. I watched his descent down the snowy stairs. I'd been kissed by drunks, babies and teenagers but never by a minister. Then I saw Elsie rounding the corner and we were back to today.

CHAPTER 12: KIM

WHEN I WAS asked to chair the program committee, I didn't know whether I was up for it. But it turned out to be relatively easy, a clearinghouse for future events. I'd be a committee of one, something easy enough to handle.

Now, only two weeks before Christmas, everything was under control. There would be two Christmas programs: a children's pageant and a traditional vesper service, both on Christmas Eve. The children had already learned their songs and prepared costumes. The vesper service, a candlelight program of music and readings, would be later that same night. Neville had elicited input from Gerda and Mirabelle to give the program an eclectic air and liven the traditional story. My task would be to arrange for poinsettias and candles to bank the podium, checking for additional seating, making sure there would be enough ushers to handle the expected crowd. I would spend this morning at Amity putting final touches on the two events. Going into the library, I pulled down two anthologies to take along in case they were needed. Then I headed for church.

It was a cold day, with wisps of snow dancing here and there under the bright winter sun. The boys would be home for Christmas. Maggie would be given the holidays off. It would be like old times, just us without strangers' eyes peering around every corner.

I parked the car close to the entrance and picked my way along the snow-dusted walkway, noting shadowy figures moving around inside. Herbie, the custodian, was busy sweeping the floor, helped by his son, a boy of about eight. I went by the staff offices, waving to the church secretary and newsletter editor who were standing at the copy machine, talking. A few steps more and I was in the hall leading to the minister's study.

Neville's office was a large room, accommodating a desk, three bookcases and a conference table flanked by eight chairs along with a couch. New draperies, oriental calligraphy and figurines lent an air of sophistication and richness. The room suited him.

Mirabelle and Steve Rothberg were already there, seated on opposite ends of the couch with Gerda perched on a chair across from them, her nervous fingers holding an unlit cigarette.

"I hope I'm not late," I said, taking off my coat.

"Not at all," Neville replied, half-rising from behind his desk. "I'll get Carol."

When they returned, we moved to the conference table scattered with books, pamphlets and printouts. "We're reviewing some programs done in the past," explained Neville. "But I'd like to try a more original approach - something different."

It was a bad beginning. "But why?" Mirabelle cried.

"Christmas has become a cliché made trite through overuse," he said easily, not at all taken aback. "We'll read St. Luke, of course. That's too beautiful to leave out. But the Christmas story should relate to today. Every birth is a miracle, not just the birth of Jesus. There is joy in bringing forth any new life and offering it to the world."

There was a long silence. Then Mirabelle spoke up, her voice firm. "Jesus was not an ordinary baby. He was, he is, God's son, born to save us from our sins. That's the Christmas message, plain and simple. For God so loved the world…"

"It's the tree, the candles, the poinsettias and smell of pine," Carol murmured.

"Christmas to be likened to Mother's Day or Father's Day? Should we call it Baby Day or Toys for Children Day?" Mirabelle's voice was soft but cutting. "No! We are a church, not a venue for Charlie Brown or the Grinch."

I saw the afternoon slipping through my fingers and I still had to finish Christmas wrapping. "Maybe a different program is exactly what Amity needs." I looked at Gerda, hoping to find support.

"In Germany, Christmas is a religious holiday," Gerda said slowly. "We go to church and then go home. Sometimes there's a decorated tree and a special family meal with wine and a little schnapps but that is all. I know Americans have a big celebration with presents and singing, but that is something I am just now learning about."

Neville leaned forward, his expression earnest. "Think of creating something meaningful."

"Meaningful, yes. But surely more than a baby shower."

"Why not?" Neville cried, jumping up excitedly. "Back then it was the three kings bringing gold, frankincense and myrrh. Today it would be a baby shower. Imagine the joy of a young couple who have spent years yearning for a child. Imagine a single mother who has chosen to keep her baby and now has him nestled in her arms. Or think of the woman caught in the throes of war, giving birth in a bombed-out cornfield. Isn't God manifest in all of them?"

"Two weeks is hardly enough time to change the program," I murmured, wondering how long it would all take. "But I brought a couple of anthologies, just in case."

Neville turned to Carol. "What do you think?"

"If Kim is willing to take it on, it's fine with me. So I'll go back to my office. I still have work to do."

Discussion continued, repeating, paraphrasing, agreeing, disagreeing, including, discarding, and quibbling endlessly. Finally Mirabelle stood up. "Go ahead and do whatever you think is best. I need to get back to work as well. I'm sorry..."

Neville turned toward me. "Your expression speaks volumes."

I hesitated a moment, then pulled out a chair. "I suppose I could put something together. Then we could talk about it."

"That's not necessary. Surprise me."

"But if it were unsuitable..."

"Then let's do it now. I'm ready for lunch. I understand Winslow's is a popular place."

Before I could answer, he'd picked up the phone. "They can take us in a half hour."

I took a deep breath, then nodded. Emerson, Whitman, Frost, maybe Emily Dickinson. It had been a long time.

He squeezed my shoulder. "Give me a minute to check things out with Carol. We'd planned a working lunch, but this is more important."

In a few minutes Neville returned, reached for my books and we walked out to the parking lot. "I have a feeling that there's intense emotion under your quiet exterior just aching to come out." He opened the car door, leaning in slightly as I buckled up.

He was right. These were things I'd been wanting to do for a very long time.

Chapter 13: Joy

I'VE HAD LOTS of practice in moving. It's organize or die. Sheila seemed to approach it from the opposite direction. Let the movers haul the furniture. If they have an eye for placement, God bless them. If not, the pieces would sort themselves out or the family would simply get used to it. Helter-skelter and be damned.

Of course, I didn't learn this until much later. Marva had called to tell me of Sheila's planned arrival. Would Marva arrange for some sort of welcome? After all, she was president of the Women's Club.

"Good Grief, Joy, it's two weeks before Christmas. Let Kim help out for a change."

I decided to let sleeping dogs lie.

Meanwhile, there was the Christmas party at the home of Max Pollack, Gary's boss. It would be my first time there. I'd been to the Presser's house, which was impressive, but Max's had to be ten times more.

I set aside the day to get ready and by the time Gary got home, I was dressed to go.

The boys were in the den watching TV as I stood in the doorway, surveying the decorations. "On your way?" Jason asked.

"As soon as your father comes downstairs. Are you staying in tonight?"

"We might go to the club for a while. Is that okay?"

I nodded. "But be sure to lock the doors and close off the fireplace. Don't come home too late and no one comes over while we're gone."

"Sure, sure. When do you expect to get home?"

"In plenty of time to check on you." I adjusted the sleeves on my Armani dress bought just for this occasion. "You've got the phone number?"

Our talk was interrupted when Gary came down all wired up, ready to help me with my coat. "Kim and Bill Presser will be there, you know. Tonight you circulate with the hoi polloi."

"What's that?"

"People like you and me. We work hard, pay taxes and go to bed with a clear conscience."

Max and Jan Pollack had their spread thirty miles outside of Worthington. It included a tennis court and indoor pool plus a corral and barn with three horses. The servant's wing housed a gardener, groom and an assortment of maids. Max once hired a helicopter to transport his daughter and her new husband to the airport on their honeymoon, the front lawn being the helipad. That was her first wedding. After that she was on her own.

When Gary was first interviewed for *Marty's,* Max let him know that he was expected to handle a three-martini lunch, that being his idea of being civilized. Nothing else interested him. He never pushed people around or made passes at women, no matter how they'd come on to him which was pretty regular, him being so rich and all. He just liked to drink, getting blitzed by noon, earlier on weekends. Throughout it all, he was kind of sweet. *Marty's* could run on its own steam, at least for now. Of course his executives were watching like vultures waiting for the kill, obvious to anyone who kept their eyes open.

There were about sixty people invited, which is perfect for a holiday party. When it gets boring, you can always move to another group. Of course there was the usual pecking order with the more important executives playing King of the Mountain. But by now I'd established my niche among the wives, challenging no one, even though I was younger and better looking than most.

An open house is pretty standard. Dinner is a buffet with people sitting at tiny tables or balancing plates the best they can. Afterward, the men gather near the bar to talk business. The hostess, in this instance, Jan, leads the way into the den or some other open area to hold center stage while the rest stand around with their drinks getting warm because it's impossible to get away. Meanwhile, caterers or servants circulate quietly to clean up any mess that develops. Jan's father was the Marty of *Marty's Quick Stop* and maybe that's what drove Max to drink. But life's a series of trade-offs. You live with what's dished out to you or whatever you manage to grab.

On this particular evening Jan's entertainment centered on stories about living in Texas. She'd shot rattlesnakes and coyotes and helped brand steers while slugging down her own share of hard liquor. Finally she ran out of steam, allowing us to go back to check on the men-folk. By then Max had drunk enough to call it quits so Jan straightened his tie and steered him out the door while we all acted like it was nothing unusual because it wasn't.

I began looking for Gary, the party being pretty much winding down. But instead, I found myself face to face with Bill Presser who blocked my move as he held a drink up high, his face looking jovial, his balance tipsy. He leaned forward, his lips close to my ear. "There's dancing at the pool house. How about you and me tripping the light fantastic?"

"I thought everyone was getting ready to leave," I lied, looking over my shoulder.

He took my arm and steered me toward a tall sliding door. "The party is just beginning. C'mon, I'll show you."

It was a short distance along a covered walkway to a large separate building and I could hear music as we got closer. Gary and I had learned the samba and the cha-cha and gotten pretty good at it before we'd lost interest. But this music was just soft, smooth and rhythmic.

The swimming pool had been covered with plywood, turning it into a large dance floor. Amber lights embedded around the perimeter and mirrored globes on the ceiling revolved slowly like a kaleidoscope. A five-piece combo was at one end of the room, a bar at the other. Jan and Max were nowhere in sight.

As my eyes adjusted to the gloom, I felt Bill's hand around my waist steering me toward the dance floor. "Gary will find you soon enough," he murmured. "Meanwhile, the first dance is mine."

Bill is a very large man, but like some big men, surprisingly graceful. His arms held me close enough to feel the rhythm, and we moved as though we'd danced together for years.

"I'm drunk, Joy. Do you mind?"

I moved my head back a little so he could see me smile. "You mean you're an even better dancer when you're sober?"

"No. When I'm sober, I don't even try."

"It's a pity. What does Kim say?"

"I have no idea. I don't even know where she is." He looked around in an exaggerated way. "Probably in the house commiserating with Jan. Come to parties where you're supposed to have fun and Kim is somewhere pontificating about this and that, always the expert. When she's with Jan, it's AA." He put his face close to mine. "You know what AA is?"

"If Kim can help someone with a drinking problem, more power to her," I said carefully.

"Alcoholics don't want help. That's why they're alcoholics." His lips were close to my ear. "How's that for being profound?"

I laughed. "I wouldn't know. Never had that urge."

He was quiet for a moment, steering us closer to the musicians, then away. "People drink to wash away their masks. I'm drunk, so I can say how much I enjoy looking at you."

My hand was high on his shoulder, feeling the muscles move with every step. "That's a sweet thing to say." And I meant it. "Is Kim the designated driver tonight?"

"For sure. Gotta find some use for the little woman."

"That's not nice, Bill."

"I know. You won't tell her, will you? Honestly Joy, she scares the hell out of me."

His eyes held such a pathetic expression that I burst out laughing. "And when did you begin noticing these feelings?"

"My shrink says it's a mother fixation. All I need is a little TLC." The music had stopped and the dancers were filling empty tables as bartenders came around taking orders. He still had his arm around my waist. But it was okay. Bill was obviously one of those drunks who turned into a teddy bear, a big balding millionaire needing to be cuddled. If he liked me, all the better.

He ordered a Merlot and shook his head reproachfully when I asked for Perrier. "Max has an excellent wine cellar. Aren't you even curious?"

I shook my head. It had been a good evening. I'd met a few more people but not so many as to be a strain. It was almost over and except for Gary being God Only Knows Where, I'd had a pretty good time.

"So how do you like Worthington, Joy?" He leaned forward, his thick fingers stroking the ice filled glass. "I mean, honestly."

"I like it a lot. Honestly."

"And how about your boys. Do they like it here?"

"I think so. They're pretty adaptable."

"They've made friends?"

I nodded. "Sometimes I think they're too busy."

"Kim and I have two boys. They're a little older than yours. A pair of whining dorks, to be perfectly honest. I never got the hang of being a father. Kim didn't either - being a mother, I mean. We tried, but we never got it right. Too many other things kept getting in the way."

"Gary says you have been a big help, introducing him to interesting people, showing him how Worthington does things."

He put down his glass. "Wives have no idea what their husbands do day in and day out. They go to work, they come home. They eat dinner, they go to bed. But let me tell you, Gary is really good. Ready smile, hearty handshake, good at golf, racquetball, tennis…"

It was nice to hear, except that suddenly he was holding my hand. "Gary's a born salesman. It comes naturally."

"And he has a beautiful wife to make it all worth while - naturally."

"Sometimes it's only a matter of practice - like dancing."

He turned his head, looking at the musicians taking their places once more. "Well then, shall we?" He emptied his glass in one long swallow, then led me back to the floor.

It was less crowded, some of the partygoers having moved back to the main house. We glided to a medley of Christmas tunes. They all blended into one another, and we moved to the rhythm.

"So what do you think of Amity?" It was his turn to make conversation.

"I'm still getting used to it. We've never done that before."

"How about Neville's idea of Participation Training?"

"It can be one way of getting to know one another."

"Taking off the mask?"

I nodded. If Bill and Neville wanted to take off masks, more power to them. Let's face it. There are just so many hours in the day.

The musicians were finishing the set, and Bill swung me around, coming to a stop just inside the entrance door. And there stood Gary in his topcoat, hair disheveled, tie askew. "What happened?" I gasped.

"Someone slid into our car while pulling out. The whole side is smashed in." He pulled out his handkerchief to wipe his face.

"Anything I can do?" Bill asked. "Call a cab, drive you home?"

Gary's expression softened. "No thanks. The car's still drivable. If we're lucky, it'll be fixed before Christmas." He turned toward me. "Ready to go? It's after one and it's snowing."

In the living room, Jan and Max were at the door, both of them sobered up, saying goodbye to guests. I thanked them for a delightful party and gave them hugs and air kisses because they're really good and decent people.

Gary brought the car to the door and I slipped and skidded into the back seat, the front passenger door being jammed shut. I tried to make conversation, but leaning forward was a real pain and Gary wasn't in the best mood, which was understandable. So I finally sat back and watched the snow swirl around, praying that Gary wouldn't drive us into a ditch.

It took more than an hour to get home. If he noticed the warm hood as we walked past my car, he didn't mention it, and neither did I. The boys were asleep. I'd find a way to talk to them tomorrow. Some things are better left to be handled on my own.

Chapter 14: Liz

When I learned that Sheila would be moving in, I offered to help, asking whether it would be convenient to come shortly after breakfast.

"Oh bless you, Liz!" Her voice was breathless. "The movers have just left. Could you pick up some bread and milk on the way over?"

"Of course. Anything else?" Suddenly there was a list and I sketched it on a pad next to the phone. I didn't ask about Neville. Obviously, he wasn't there. No matter. Sue and Kelsey were in school and John would be with his playgroup until three.

Traffic was horrendous the week before Christmas with everyone doing last minute shopping. Smack in the middle of the Midwest farmland, farmers used to come to town on weekends, going home by milking time, their lives focused on tractors, pigs and soybeans, serious about rainfall and the Fourth of July. Schools, stores, and buildings were fairly small, so if you had a big house and belonged to a country club that was more like a community center, people treated you with respect.

Then came the Interstate and bang, everything changed. Schools got crowded and housing exploded, along with bars and fast foods. Congestion cut the speed limit to 25mph and people stopped waving to one another along the way.

I turned the wheel carefully, parking along the curb, hoping that the snowplows didn't come by until later. The parsonage was still marked with streaks of mossy green, visible along the darkened foundation, the surrounding trees added to its dinginess. Its price had been a bargain, and

Amity planned on renovating. Then we learned it was a historic site, meaning that even minor changes were strictly forbidden.

Reaching over to grab the supplies plus a package of donuts that had been too tempting to resist, I went slipping and sliding up to the front door. It was opened before I had a chance to ring the bell.

"I'm so glad to see you," Sheila cried, taking the milk from my hand. She was wrapped in a white terry robe. With her head covered in a fluffy towel, her face scrubbed rosy, she looked almost girlish. "I'm all alone with this awful mess." She turned, leading the way into the kitchen. Her gesture encompassed the room. "And the movers just made it worse."

I'd seen the parsonage when the decorating crew arrived to paint the kitchen and bath, wallpaper the bedrooms and wash the walls. Its interior was adequate, but with crumpled newspapers and every surface filled, it was a mess.

Shoving aside some pots and pans from the counter, I made space for the bread and donuts. "Let's begin in the kitchen. Everything is better once you find the coffee pot and toaster." I patted her shoulder. "I'll start on the cabinets while you finish dressing."

"I've never been much good in the morning," she murmured, rubbing her hands over her eyes."

"That's okay. You go on up. I'll get started on my own."

Professional movers sweep up everything in their paths - cigarette butts, burned out light bulbs, even garbage. The trick was to locate something. By the time Sheila returned dressed in a pair of sweats, I had a fresh pot of coffee on the counter along with two rinsed-out mugs. Three small cartons had been emptied, their contents on the sideboard, dishes stacked, waiting to be rinsed and tucked away. One box was now a receptacle for newspaper and packing material. The others had been flattened, leaning against the wall. I'd made a narrow path across the room and cleared a small work area next to the sink. Finding no cleaning rags, a roll of paper towels would have to do.

She sniffed appreciatively. Taking a cup, she poured coffee to the brim, added a bit of milk then making a face. "I usually take cream, but milk will have to do."

"No coffee whitener?"

She shook her head. "Neville is a purist. He won't allow anything artificial around the house."

"Sounds very California."

Her eyes had lost their haggard look as she perched on the sideboard holding a donut in one hand, coffee in the other. "I won't miss it, but the kids probably will."

Suddenly there was a rush of cold air and the front door slammed shut. "Sheila? I smell coffee." It was Neville, his face flushed with the cold.

I coughed and stood up from behind a stack of boxes where I was retrieving another container. "Good morning, Neville. Sheila and I were just going over our plan of attack."

He looked up. "Well, hello there. What brings you out on such a frosty morning?"

"I just thought you could use some help."

Sheila hopped down from the counter top. "She brought donuts."

He looked in the direction of the open container. "How good of you."

"No problem. By the time I leave we should have the kitchen pretty well unpacked."

He laid his topcoat across a nearby stack of boxes as Sheila took another gulp of coffee.

Bewildered, I turned toward Neville, reaching for small talk. "I can't say how much I appreciate all you have done for us. That car incident…"

"I do hope Sue is on the mend."

"Dave was pretty angry when he heard that she'd been at the wheel. But he'll get over it once she gets her license." I turned back to the dishes, rinsing and placing them on the rack. Here in this conservative cow-town, men spent their days in the fields, too preoccupied with work to return mid-day.

I was at the second box when he finished his donut and coffee. "Sheila has a hard time getting started. It was good of you to come by," he murmured. And picking up his topcoat, he was out the door.

"We'll finish the kitchen before I leave, but only if we work together," I said, not looking up. "Why don't you wipe down the cabinets? The dishes on the other counter are washed and ready to be put away."

Like an obedient child, she opened the cabinet next to the dishwasher. "Neville usually comes home around lunch time," she began. "He says it's one of his perks. I hope that didn't disturb you."

"Sheila, are you aware of the dissent that Amity's just gone through?"

She nodded soberly. "Neville will serve this congregation well."

It was new territory and I was not sure where this was going. Sheila had sat on the grass in the parking lot with Sue's head in her lap, soothing and comforting a frightened girl. Neville was with us at the hospital, taking command yet remaining discretely in the background. These were to be the leaders in a church I loved. I wanted them as my friends. "Okay, Sheila. But Worthington isn't California."

Her eyes were luminous. "I so appreciate your help, Liz. I'm hoping we become friends."

Had this been Sue, there would have been a lecture on being indiscrete. "I'm touched, Sheila. But it might be wise to move a bit slower."

She nodded. "Not many have reached out to me, Liz."

I looked down at the last three boxes. "Let's finish unpacking the kitchen. That way we'll have put in a good day's work."

She was as docile as a puppy. Soon we'd established a rhythm, finding the most convenient spots for dishes, cooking utensils and appliances. In little over an hour, the kitchen was free of boxes, the empties stacked outside the door.

"I don't know how to thank you," she said, surveying the room. "I'd never have made this much progress alone."

"No problem. But now I do have to go."

She walked with me into the foyer where I'd deposited my coat atop some folded cartons. Reaching out, she put her arms around me in a long embrace. "I think we're alike, don't you?" she whispered. "I mean, small town girls with solid family values and all that."

Once more I was taken aback. Poor Sheila, moving around the country like a military wife. On the other hand, what had Amity gotten into?

Chapter 15: Joy

KIM'S CHRISTMAS EVE program, if you could call it that, had music ranging from folk guitars to the chancel choir and everything in between. The readings sometimes made sense and sometimes didn't. I mean, what does a welfare mother living in the ghetto have to do with Christmas?

After a while I stopped listening. Instead, I sized up the visitors who only attended on Christmas or Easter, putting a dollar in the collection plate and going home feeling holy. Some were even dressed in sweats or blue jeans, gawking at the decorations like a bunch of hayseeds. Others were the college students home for the holidays, people like Adam Leighton or the Presser boys who, like Bill said, were pretty dorky, all of them jammed elbow to elbow in a room filled with poinsettias and flickering candles that consumed every last bit of oxygen until everyone was about to faint.

But Christmas Day was nice. We opened presents in the morning and had a kind of open house in the afternoon with people nibbling on canapés and tiny sandwiches that Elsie had made the week before and stored in the freezer. And of course there was holiday punch and the open bar.

A few days later we had a party for Matt and Jason's friends, most of whom I already knew. It lasted until two in the morning. I'd hired Elsie for the day. Marva and Liz showed up with Jayne and Sue, and I talked them into staying. It made the evening bearable.

But now the holidays were over. I'd taken down the decorations. The parties, concerts and gatherings that had kept me so busy were happy memories. School was back in session. Gary had gone to the office before anyone else was up. It was time to get back to normal.

I went into the den and picked up the phone, thinking Marva and I might go to lunch and catch up on all the happenings, especially what was happening with the Leightons. Then I remembered how I promised Sheila I'd call. That was three weeks back. Why pick Marva's brain when I could use the direct approach?

Sheila answered after three rings, her voice fuzzy.

"I hope I didn't wake you," I began, keeping my tone light and cheerful.

"Not really."

"I'm kind of at loose ends, what with the holidays being over," I began. "How about lunch? It might be a nice break."

She cleared her throat. "Oh dear, I'm not even dressed."

"That's okay. It's still early. I'll pick you up at eleven."

"I'm not very spontaneous, Joy."

Now I hardly know her, but once I make up my mind, these things are supposed to happen because I have a Positive Mental Attitude. Of course Sheila didn't know me that well either, but it might be a good thing for her to practice PMA, since she's with different people day in and day out. So I coaxed. "We could just go to the club. I'll call and make a reservation."

"I'd need to check with Neville first."

"Oh come on, Sheila. This is the twenty-first Century. Live a little."

"Could I call you back in about ten minutes?"

"Sure. My time is yours."

Her ten minutes turned into a half-hour. By then I'd written three thank you notes and addressed a card that said *Sending Friendly Thoughts Your Way* to Mom, hoping that would satisfy her until I could call.

"I'll meet you at the club at eleven thirty," she began.

"Oh, that's all right. I'll pick you up at eleven. It'll give us a chance to talk."

"About what? Is there something...?"

"Just things in general. Like getting to know one another. I don't know - just things."

"Oh. I thought there might be something special."

"Sheila, go and get dressed. I'll be there in an hour."

After finishing two more cards and checking the mail, I got in the car and pulled up at the parsonage promptly at eleven. When she didn't answer my ring, I tested the doorknob. Finding it unlocked, I stuck my head in just as she came clattering down the stairs.

"I'm ready," she cried. "I just need to find my gloves." She was dressed in a navy blue pantsuit with a multi-colored blouse in an abstract pattern. Her hair was brushed away from her face and hanging loose above the collar, looking better than expected. Moving toward the front closet, she pushed aside an assortment of jackets, pulling down a tan camel hair coat.

I led the way outside and waited as she tried out several keys before finding the right one, then holding onto the railing, stepped carefully around the icy patches and into my car.

"Gary got the car fixed." Her statement was a question.

I nodded, easing into traffic. "Lucky for us, it was all body work. How did you know?"

"The kids were talking. It's too bad that had to happen. And right around Christmas, too."

"It's a company car. No big deal."

"That sounds better than a car allowance."

"Like Neville's?"

"We're hoping to buy a second car soon."

It wasn't the kind of conversation I'd had in mind. But maybe once we'd gotten to the club and sat down...

The parking lot was clear with only a trace of moisture on the blacktop. We checked our coats and found a table at the windows facing snow-covered trees and the golf course beyond, actually kind of pretty. I ordered a carafe of wine the way the businessmen do, and we sipped comfortably as we waited for our salads. "I had a feeling that we'd have lots in common," I began.

"Oh yes. Two people who like anchovies says a lot about them both."

"I meant like moving around so much, because Gary and I have been gypsies too. Are you getting settled all right?"

"Little by little. I've taken the third floor in the parsonage for my studio. There are windows all around. I go there when things get hectic."

"Good for you. I've often thought I'd like something like that." I smiled politely, wondering why on earth she'd want to escape just when things were getting interesting.

"But the trees practically cover the windows. I asked Neville if we could trim them back and he said he'd ask." She took a sip of wine. "Painters need lots of natural light."

"Oh yes. You did say you were an artist. How fascinating!" I suddenly realized that the print on her blouse was flecked with dabs of paint. "What kind of art do you do?"

"Mostly collages and sometimes fabrics. I've done some wall sculptures but I'm still learning. Basically, I paint." She followed my eyes and tugged at the front of her jacket. "Are you into art?"

Our salads had arrived, which allowed me time for an answer. "I enjoy looking. But I also like music. People usually don't have time for both, don't you agree?"

"What kind of music do you do?"

"It's not fair to answer a question with another question," I said teasingly. "Anyway, we were talking about you. What are you doing now?"

"Once the house is in order…" She took a bite of salad and another sip of wine. "Neville doesn't want me to get a job, so there'll be time."

We chewed in silence and I searched for something more to say. *Sheila, can we talk about where you won't work? Sheila would you describe how you are you putting your house in order? Can you tell me what you think about the spring fashions?* "I hope we can get together more often," I lied. "I know how lonely things can get when you're new in town."

"Yes. I don't want another baby. Maybe we ought to get a dog."

"What?"

"Kids and dogs help you meet people. Except that our kids are pretty much grown."

"I don't think you need to go that far," I laughed, "seeing you have the studio retreat when things get hectic."

"I know. But like everything else, it takes time for friendships to build."

"Of course." I waited for her to continue, but she only stared with a fixed smile, her fork dabbling on the edge of her plate. I glanced at my watch. We'd been here thirty-eight minutes and everything I said had led to a dead end. I poured more wine, which took care of another minute. The room was beginning to fill, the noise level increasing. I cleared my throat and moved closer. "I'm planning to attend Neville's Participation Workshop. Will you be there?"

She leaned back, body language cautiously alert. "I've attended a number of them. So there's no need to take up space."

"Oh, then you can tell me all about it. What do you do for a whole day? Neville says it's a way to connect. So what happens? I mean, do you work together in groups or listen to inspiration talks or play games?"

"There are examples of how people solve problems. You discuss things like church membership and committee work. Then you do a little role-playing and talk about interactive styles. You'll see for yourself."

"Gary has a meeting downstate. But I plan to be there." I swallowed what was left of my wine and topped off our glasses, emptying the carafe. "Will Neville have a program like this for the young people? I hear he's made quite a hit with them."

"If he does, it'll be a first."

"I'm so impressed. Where did Neville get the idea?"

Sheila's expression was still guarded. "I don't know. Neville is the only minister I've ever been married to."

I couldn't tell whether she was being funny or that it had just came out that way. "Gary has lots of associates he shares things with. Our dinner table conversation is full of stories."

"Neville's work is personal and private. We don't talk shop."

"I didn't intend to pry." Sometimes getting to know some people is more trouble than it's worth. "How about dessert? I saw some yummies on the cart."

By the time the server found the cart, brought it over and explained each selection, we'd used up another ten minutes. Sheila chose a tiramisu and I settled for coffee. I took another look at my watch. "It's after one! My goodness, how time flies. I guess it's time to go."

We drove the short distance back in silence. Then as we pulled up in front of the house, she turned toward me. "Would you like to see my studio? I've unpacked a few samples of my work."

My curiosity got the better of me. "Why yes. I'd like that very much. I promise not to stay long."

"That's okay. It's early."

I eased the car into a parking space and we walked up the steps into the drab and silent house. Although I hadn't been up there before, I was imagining the third floor as a ballroom, its hardwood floor and narrow windows open to the summer air. But it was musty and cold, its floor streaked and uneven, its windows dirty and frosted around the edges.

There were four large tables, actually slabs of plywood supported by sawhorses, arrayed with paints, brushes and jars containing brownish liquid that smelled like turpentine. Boards on concrete blocks held boxes, file folders and other odds and ends. Scattered around the room were squares of color that I assumed represented Sheila's work. Some were colored shapes like the Picassos or Dadas you see in modern interiors. Others were textured, reminding me of kindergarten collages where the teacher made us use every last bit of colored paper before getting more. A small radio was on the floor connected to an outlet half way up the wall. There were a few folding chairs leaning against the wall and some scattered here and there, all too dirty to be of use.

"So this is home," I smiled, pulling my coat tightly around me.

"Do you see what I mean? If we could cut back some of the trees, the light would be so much better."

"A window washer would help even more."

"Maybe Marva could talk to Paul?"

I studied her face, so childishly hopeful. "Sheila, you're entitled to ask this for yourself. No, not ask -- demand. You're the minister's wife."

We were interrupted by a door slamming below and Neville's voice echoing up the staircase. "Sheila? Are you up there?"

"Neville likes to come home during the day," she murmured. Turning toward the stairs, she called out that we would be coming down in a minute.

"I don't want to keep you," I said, grateful for an excuse to leave.

"It would be so much easier if you'd talk to Marva about the trees. Sometimes Neville forgets," she pleaded.

Another niggling task to add to my list. "All right. I'll give it a try."

Neville was in the living room when we came downstairs. Seeing him among the clutter was unnerving, this fastidious gentleman so out of place in the middle of yawning boxes and stacks of books piled every which way. He'd reorganized his church study within weeks. Why was it taking so long for them to move into the house? "We went to the club for lunch. Then Sheila gave me a tour of her studio."

He returned my smile and it was as though Sheila was invisible. "Hey Joy, nice to see you. Survive the holidays okay?"

"Oh yes. Tree is down. Decorations put away. I'm back to normal."

"I noticed you on the list for the Participation Workshop. Carol will call to remind you."

Neither had invited me to sit down. "Well, I guess you have things to do."

They didn't protest. Instead, Neville held the door and waved as I pulled away.

Elsie was scouring out the kitchen sink when I drove into the garage. She met me at the door, wiping her hands on a towel. "We've been trying to reach you for an hour. They've taken your mother to Prentice Hospital in Pittsburgh with a ruptured appendix."

When faced with bad news, I prefer that it's more gradual. So I had to sit down a minute and pull myself together. "Why didn't you call the club? You knew that's where I'd be."

"They said you'd already gone." Then I remembered I'd left the phone in the car.

It took a dozen phone calls, but I finally reached the doctor in Pittsburgh. Mom was doing fine but was asking for me. Would I come?

By five o'clock I was on a plane to Pittsburgh. For now, nothing else was more important. Worthington, *Marty's Quick Stop* and Amity Congregational Church were wiped from my mind and all I could think of was that I was needed.

CHAPTER 16: JAYNE

HOLIDAY PARTIES. I'M always glad when they're over. You have to keep smiling so you don't look like a dork. It's worse if you don't go, because then people think you weren't invited.

Still, the open house at the Volkmans was the best. First off, it was big, with lots to do. Most of us kids stayed downstairs at the pool table or playing video games. That way we didn't have to hang out with parents like Mom and Mrs. Mason, who said they'd come for just a little while, then stayed the whole night. Second, there were a few new faces, including Jason and Matt. At least, they're new to us. And there were Hannah and Adam Leighton, who happen to be way cool. Sue Mason arrived seriously overdressed, and that turned Matt on all the more. They'd gotten to know one another pretty well the night of the big snowstorm. Now they were a pair.

I talked mostly with Adam who is way older but really neat. He's a senior, finishing school in California so's not to kill his GPA and class rank because he has huge aspirations, like Stanford or Berkeley. I didn't think I'd ever get to know him. But here he was, asking me all kinds of things about Worthington as though he was really interested. That's what happens when you're new in town. I didn't mind. I told him about the people in the church, being sure to say nice things since I knew it would all get back to Dr. Leighton. Adam's into meditation and Zen. I gave him the Worthington version of Zen which I'd learned from my Comparative Religion class. That impressed him.

We also talked about gays in San Francisco. He'd thought about it a lot. We agreed that you don't have to be queer to be queer. But still, it was San Francisco…

Adam said he'd call me later in the week. I didn't expect it but he did the very next morning. We talked for a long time. I think I've found a new friend. Mom will be ecstatic.

I didn't go to church today. Actually, I haven't gone for a while but that's okay with Mom and Paul. They say that after ten years of Sunday school, I've put in my time.

Adam and Hannah are going to pick me up this evening and we'll go to the Youth Group together. It'll be a kind of farewell party with the homies leaving after the holidays, including Adam.

On our way, I tried to prepare them. We do things different than Californians. But they were cool. Having lived all over the country, they understood cultural differences.

I know adults have their own ideas about parties, but this was something else. The room was decorated like a junior prom from the 50's with red and green crepe paper swaging out from a bunch of mistletoe in the middle of the ceiling. I think every Mom within five-states decided to use the year-end to dump their leftover refreshments. I even saw a dish of candy corn. Nearby, chips and dips spilled over plates of cookies and brownies, and candy pieces splashed with punch were making a gooey mess. They'd covered the lights with red and green see-through stuff, so everything look moldy. There was a DJ, but the music was the kind no one could dance to. Jason Volkman was right there in Hannah's face like he'd been waiting all evening. It's obvious to everyone that he's got a king-sized crush on her. Then before I knew what was happening, Adam walked me up to the DJ and we were in the middle of the floor dancing. Pretty soon there were others, and the music got louder along with the kids who were trying to act like they were with it. Sue and Matt were dancing nearby and then we were bouncing around, trading partners, in and out and around. I would have been embarrassed except it was Matt and Adam's idea in the first place, with both of them jumping up and down and swinging their butts like on MTV.

Now I don't know what it takes to be cool, but right then I was. Maybe it was because Matt and Adam were older and came from someplace else. Maybe it was that Sue was president of the Youth Group along with being a cheerleader at school. All I knew was that I was right there, in front of God and everyone.

By the time the music stopped, I was totally out of breath. I'm not a bad dancer, but I don't get much practice because dances require having a boyfriend. That's Mom's idea, not mine. She says nice girls don't attend public places alone. Really retro. Even if I wanted a boyfriend, which I don't, I can usually find better things to do with my time, leaving all that jerking around to the losers. "I think I'd like something cold," I said good and loud because everyone was competing for decibels.

Just then Scottie walked up and started making a big deal about Adam leaving, then asking about Matt's grandmother and her ruptured appendix going deep into scientific detail and medical terminology. Scottie's a surgical nurse and likes talking shop. I suppose that's expected since she's at the hospital more than not. But it was her idea to get a divorce. Now she says she *has* to work, but I don't believe it because her ex is in the army, so she'll get child support forever. My mom should have been so lucky.

Other kids were crowding around the refreshment table and there was no end to Scottie's interest in the rotten appendix even though Matt reported that everything was fine. So Adam and I moved toward a couple of empty chairs. I hadn't seen Adam's father standing off to the side with the Pressers until I looked down from a long swallow of lemonade. When Dr. Leighton saw me looking at him, he walked over.

If a grownup could be considered cool, it would be Dr. Leighton. I guess that's where Adam gets it. No matter where or when, these guys are always in control, but in a nice way. I heard Mom telling Paul that Dr. Leighton was too slick for her taste, but now that we're getting used to him, most of the kids think he's okay.

"Kim and Liz spent all afternoon on the decorations." The look on his face said we should go over and thank them.

"It's been a great party." I wrinkled my nose the way everyone says is so cute when Sue does it. "I can stay to do cleanup if someone gives me a ride home."

"The DJ will be here until nine. If everyone pitches in, it should get done in no time." Like I said, Dr. Leighton has a way of taking control.

So we went back to what was supposed to be the dance floor. By then the lemonade was gone and the food dishes were either empty or spilled on the floor. I danced around Matt and Jason and even goofy Rex, but that was okay because cool people can afford to be generous.

At nine the DJ packed up and the grownups took off. By nine-thirty, we'd filled seven garbage bags with wilted chips and crepe paper, carrying them to the furnace room for disposal. The lighting was uncovered, the floor swept clean. By ten there were only the six of us left. Totally exhausted, we flopped down on the last of the folding chairs and stared at one another - Matt and Sue, Jason and Hannah, Adam and me.

"Time for the good stuff," Matt said with new energy, running around the room to turn out the lights. Pretty soon the room was as dim as a Halloween spook house. "Too bad we don't have floor cushions like in the 60's." It was like they were planning an orgy.

"There's a couch in the study," Sue offered.

"No way! Aroma lingers." Adam turned to me. "You with us? It's okay if you don't want to."

"No hard feelings, Matt agreed. "Little brother is still waiting for the right moment."

"What better place than at church," Sue giggled.

I trusted Adam. "Sure. Why not?" I'd been invited to pot parties since fifth grade but up to now I wasn't interested. But like with Jason, it was only a matter of time. I'd been waiting for the right moment.

It was like in the movies, squares of thin paper sprinkled with weed, rolled and lit, then passed around like a peace pipe. I took a small hit and held it, glad the lights didn't show my face, glad I didn't cough. First my head slowly clouded up, then I felt it in my stomach like a shot of adrenaline. Jason was across from me and I squinted, pretty sure he'd taken a drag. Then Adam, his eyes meeting mine, his smile reassuring as he breathed deep, holding it in for a long time then easing it out ever so slowly. The circle was complete.

Now I was mellow, here with all my friends and good buddies. I slumped down like a rag doll, legs spread out, arms dangling, my head resting on the back of the chair, comfortable as sin, waiting for the high.

"Heard about the three holes in the ground?" Matt asked of no one in particular.

"Well, well, well..." Hannah replied, and everyone burst out laughing.

"Were you there when Troy got a hole in one? He dropped a match and put a big hole in one" Sue said.

More laughing.

"Do you remember Reverend Oliver? You could tell he smoked a lot because all his clothes had tiny cigarette burns all over them," I said. "Even his church robes."

"Holy smoke!" Hannah muttered, and everyone doubled up laughing.

"Stoke the toke," Matt cried, his voice echoing in the empty room as he rolled another joint. Then there were two being passed around with a blue cloud hanging over our heads, a halo of bliss. "How's your grandmother doing, Matt?" I asked, feeling warm and friendly-like.

"Are you asking when my Mom is coming home?"

"Well, that too," Sue answered.

The others laughed. I didn't get it.

"Mom's staying until Grandma's back on her feet. That could take a very long time."

"California East," nodded Adam. "I should be so lucky."

"Lots safer than in the car," Sue agreed.

"Won't your dad be home?" I asked.

The others laughed again.

"We need to have a little talk," Adam said, his chin nuzzling my shoulder.

I smiled, hearing my inner voice, the one that says *You're okay,* saying I was cool.

"It's still early. How's about a trip to *Topper's?"* Sue was running her hands through her hair. "I'm getting hungry."

"But we just ate…"

"My Lord, you do have a lot to learn," Sue muttered, and for a minute I was back to hating her.

"Why not?" Adam said. He took my hand and pulled me to my feet. "You okay?"

"After I make a pit stop." It was probably another side effect but decided not to ask.

The hall was dimly lit but I made it to the bathroom without stumbling. Flipping on the light, I finished my business looking in the mirror to see a new Jayne. But it was the same old same old. Somehow that seemed terribly funny and I giggled to myself for a long time.

When I came back, it was icy cold from the opened windows. Sue was in the process of bossing people around. "I guess we'll need both cars," she said. "Who's riding with who?" She looked at Jason.

"We can sit in the back seat." Poor Jason. Always the little brother.

Sue's face said it was okay, so we all went out to the parking lot with Adam first checking to make sure the church door was locked.

Driving to *Topper* was my first time being alone with Adam, not counting our talk on the phone. He apologized for the car being cold. He asked what kind of food I would be ordering, as though he was really interested. He promised to call me from California. And it was all fine with me, especially that last part.

The others were already seated when we arrived and I made a quick call home before joining them. Mom said she was worried because it was really late, but when I told her I was with Adam, it was okay. I guess she likes him too.

It was the end of a perfect evening. Food had never tasted so good. Conversation had never been so animated where each minute there was a pause, another would jump in with a story or a joke. I'd watched party tables at restaurants before. Now I was part of the party. Another first.

It was close to one when we left, with Hannah almost falling asleep in the back of Adam's car. He didn't see me to the door, but I didn't expect him to. After all, this wasn't a real date. So I just waved as the car pulled away and hurried to bed, not even bothering to wash my face or brush my teeth. Tomorrow would come early with school back in session. I'd be getting my English term paper back, which normally would be a major event. But somehow, all I could think about was whether Adam would call.

Chapter 17: Joy

PEOPLE AREN'T SUPPOSED to die of appendicitis, but according to Mother, she almost did, at first saying it was only a stomachache, then blowing it up dramatically as though it was front page news. Some people are like that. I'd rented a small car at the airport and stayed in her apartment, giving it a good cleaning between visits to the hospital. That took a week. Then the doctors let her go home, knowing I'd be staying with her. That added another two weeks. Meanwhile she talked constantly about laxatives and arthritis pain relievers and kept the TV on from morning until night. And I don't care if I ever see another deck of cards.

Pretty soon I was desperate to go home and begged her to hire someone so I could leave. Too much money, she said. Of course my being there was a bargain, paying the phone bill, the car rental and buying the groceries. And when I'd call Gary, he was no help, saying that everything was fine and I shouldn't worry. I knew he'd scheduled a couple of business trips downstate, leaving the boys alone and acting like it was no big deal which bothered me big time. I'd also called Marva to get the scoop on Neville's workshop, but she was totally vague, which sent my antenna twanging, another reason I wanted to go home.

Finally Mother was back on her feet, going up and down the stairs like a pro. Mrs. Hadda from next door had been coming to visit and said she'd keep an eye on her. So I packed my things, gave Mother a hug and promised to call every day. Then I got into the car and drove to the airport.

The plane touched down at seven-thirty and Gary was there waiting. I love the feeling of coming home when everything looks different, a familiar picture in a new frame. I'd done a quick touch up on my face and run a comb through my hair, because I wanted him to see me in that special way too. He kissed me on the cheek and hoisting my bag, and led me to the car. Then he leaned over and really kissed me and everything was back the way it's supposed to be. "We'll meet the boys at the club before going home if that's okay."

It took only about twenty minutes to get there, the roads clear of January snow. In the dining room, we found them at a table crowded with young people.

Matt gave me a hug, then pulled out a chair for me. "How was your trip?"

"Good," I smiled. "Did everything go well or should I have a drink first?"

"How about two drinks? One for each of us."

Everyone laughed.

I looked around the table. "Been here long?"

"Since about six," Jason replied.

"Is my car all right? Has it given you any trouble?"

"Just a small fender-bender. Just kidding," he added quickly.

"I think I'm ready for that drink."

They laughed politely but seemed relieved that we'd be moving on.

Gary ordered wine and we lingered in the bar for about an hour, catching up on events, talking mostly about *Marty's* and how everything was going at work. Max Pollack had gone to a rehab center for a week and to AA for two. Then he was back to his old ways. Meanwhile, each of the executives was trying to get a toehold. Gary was definitely in the running. We also talked a little about the boys, about Amity and Bill Presser.

At about nine-thirty we left the club, crossing the empty dining room, the kids having long gone. By the time we pulled into the garage, it was close to ten. My car was safely nested in its proper place. I ran my hand over the hood noting it was still warm to the touch. Matt and Jason must have just gotten home.

Gary took my suitcase up to our room while I looked in on the boys to say good night. We didn't talk much since I was anxious to get to bed myself. It was good to be home. A month is a long time.

I woke up early the next day and after a quick shower, got dressed and went downstairs, energetic after a good night's sleep. Gary had begun hitting the club for breakfast and a workout before heading to the office. The boys had grabbed some toast and juice, then dashed off, so by eight o'clock I was alone. A little at loose ends, I called Marva.

"Hey, you're back! Come on over. The coffee's still hot. The kids are watching TV and we can talk."

I stopped at the drugstore for some picture books for the little ones and after big hellos and hugs, I went into the kitchen with Marva while the kids turned back to the TV. "I just spent a month with people who were still fighting World War II. Please let's talk about something else."

She laughed. "So you didn't have a good time."

"I didn't expect to. What they say about mother-daughter is baloney. Thank God I had sons."

She nodded. "Still, Jayne and I are close." She leaned forward, her face inches away from mine. "Guess who's been calling her?"

Now I like Jayne a lot. But she's been Plain-Jane since kindergarten, and with good reason. "I can't imagine." I caught my breath. "I mean…"

"Adam Leighton's called her twice, all the way from California."

Adam and Jayne. Not exactly beauty and the beast, but close. I raised my eyebrows the way she expected, giving her a big smile. "How nice. Have Neville and Sheila said anything?"

"Why should they?"

I studied her face, so beautiful with its high cheekbones, smooth skin, and thick lashes. Poor Jayne must have taken after her father. "Jayne's a wonderful girl." It was the best I could do.

"I know she's no beauty. But she's smart enough to see through a fake. I've taught her that much."

"Marva, if I had a daughter, I'd want her to be just like Jayne. And if you can't trust a minister's son, then I don't know who." I couldn't think of anything else to say. "So how did Neville's workshop go?"

Her smile disappeared and she looked down, taking a long sip of coffee. "It was okay."

"No, seriously. I want to know if I missed anything."

"I shouldn't be saying anything. After all, you might have seen things differently."

"Marva, don't I tell you everything? Like remember the time…"

"Well, okay. So here's what happened. At first we all just sat around the conference table in Neville's office and did the usual debriefing thing. Then people loosened up a little and some moved to the more comfortable chairs or sat on the couch. The lights were kind of dim - you know how his office is set up. Neville began talking about interaction and listening to others and to your inner voices – you know, his usual shtick. Then he invited us to think of concepts. We examined words like patriotism, love and God, sort of like free association. It sounds cheesy but after a while it clicked as people moved deep into their personal stories.

"Pretty soon Kim told everyone that she never feels appreciated and Carol said she wanted to be a ballet dancer until she gained too much weight. Scottie had brought her new boyfriend, Herb Meyer, and they were looking all moony eyed at each other even though this was maybe only their third date. Bill and Kim Presser hardly spoke to one another, but then what else is new?"

She picked up a napkin, and began rolling the corner between her fingers. "At lunch time they brought in sandwiches and veggies with dips - you know, the usual. There was cold beer and wine carafes along with soft drinks. Everyone was feeling pretty loose - especially Gerda and Werner Stahl - you know, the physicist and the gal who thinks she's Marlene Dietrich. Then suddenly Gerda started coming on to Paul big time. Paul began giving me the eye like he wanted someone to peel her off. Neville was totally clueless and I didn't want to make a scene but I thought Neville should have done something about it, at least moving her to the other side of the room."

She was becoming agitated and I was stunned by her fury. "Maybe she was just being friendly."

"Joy, when a woman sits on the floor and practically puts her face in a man's lap..." She took a deep breath. "And Werner just sat there. I guess he assumed Neville was in charge. Or maybe he's used to it."

"But why didn't Paul...?"

"I called Neville the next day and told him how I felt. He said we should be more sensitive to the way Gerda expressed herself and be more inclusive. Sensitive! Hells bells, what else could you call it?"

"Is it possible you were imagining..."

"No way. Paul was her target." Her eyes blazed in a way I'd never seen before. "But if Gerda thinks she's going to move in on my man, she'd better be ready for battle. Once burned, twice shy. And if Neville wants to implement this kind of goings on, he's going to have to deal with me."

"Is that what you told him?"

"Of course not. But I'm beginning to wonder what Neville is getting at."

I did too, but this wasn't the time to get into it. "What did the others do?"

"Mirabelle and Steve Rothberg sat back with disapproving expression on their faces. They left early which was just as well because Mirabelle is totally full of herself, a real religious nut. And Steve's got a ring through his nose. I wouldn't call him whipped - just useless. Carol and her mother were there. She was fine but Nancy kept whispering to Mirabelle and Steve, annoying everyone. I mean, if we were supposed to be reaching out to one another, what's the whispering all about?"

"All in one afternoon?"

"Let's say you didn't miss a thing." Marva was on a roll. "Bill Presser's commissioned a study, analyzing our finances. The report says we're on the brink of going broke. Oak pews and choir robes hide a huge mortgage and a three year deficit from ministers coming and going."

More in-fighting and griping? This was not why I came. I looked at the clock over the stove. "How about going to the club for lunch? My treat."

It took a little to pull Marva down from her fury but seeing the little kids calmed her down and by mid-afternoon, Neville, Amity and Gerda were sent to the back burner, at least for a while. And I had plenty to discuss with Gary.

CHAPTER 18: CAROL

THERE ARE ADVANTAGES to being a teacher. For me, the holidays enable Mother to baby-sit Jennifer and Scott, something she loves to do anyway.

I'd set the alarm for six o'clock but awoke beforehand, tiptoeing downstairs to get dressed. I was to meet Neville at the office at seven. From there we would go to the university. I had no idea what plans he had in mind. It only mattered that we would spend the day together, Neville Leighton, my pastor, advisor and now a special friend. Better yet, I'd be paid.

In my car, I muttered a prayer and turned the key causing the engine to sputter before it caught, throwing frost onto the windshield, arriving at the church in record time, pulling up next to Neville's car in the parking lot, its engine still running. He smiled as I settled on the seat next to him.

"We'll be meeting with Ken Jones," he began as he pulled out to the street. "He's the dean of Community Ed and an old friend back from our days in grad school."

We turned from the highway and were halfway up the bluff, driving past faded farmhouses, a reminder of Worthington's rural past. They'd been converted into apartments or single room occupancy, rented to street people and college students. Down below were tiny cottages sporting trees and shrubs and an occasional flagpole in their postage stamp yards. Amid all this was a six-story high-rise, Worthington's answer to public housing, once heralded as cutting-edge and innovative, now a festering eyesore ready to be torn down. This was the area that had fascinated Billy Oliver and was such a turnoff to Amity members. Not that they - and I counted myself among them - were opposed to helping the less fortunate. Rather, it was Billy's attitude of righteousness, of being holier-than-thou that was so offensive. I stole a look at Neville and saw no change in his expression. If he had aspirations as an evangelist, it was well hidden.

Midwest University was originally a college for farm kids. Then came the Interstate bringing tax money to expand the foundations and endowments that kept it running. Within five years, Midwest was a university. Tucked in a residential neighborhood with winding streets and clipped lawns, it was a green oasis within a sturdy but inelegant past, a school where farmers sent their daughters to be wooed and wed by upwardly mobile professionals, a haven for those with high SAT scores but poor grades, or the reverse, repairing what should have been done in high school, grade school or before. It sported six sororities and fraternities housed in stately Victorian mansions, their broad verandas speckled with wicker chairs, ripped book bags, and embroidered flags that said things like *Welcome to the Monkey House* followed by Cyrillic Greek lettering in silver or gold. Though mostly new, it reeked of old-fashioned academia. Neville would fit in nicely.

He pulled into a parking spot marked Visitors. Coming around, Neville opened the door, his hand lightly on my elbow to help me out.

The short path into the building was dry and broad and we walked easily side by side. In a few weeks there'd be crocuses and snowdrops, the early signs of spring. Inside, the atmosphere whispered of intellect, collegiality and learning. A receptionist led us through a hall into the office of Dr. Kennedy Jones, Dean of Continuing Education. Then she disappeared.

Dr. Jones could have been Neville's brother. About the same height and equally slim and fit, they shared not only physical features but wore the same clothes, each with exquisite taste worn casually as though money were no object. "And this must be Carol," he murmured, holding out his hand. "Neville tells me you're his right hand."

"Ken was my mentor at USC," Neville smiled. "So imagine my delight when we ran into one another in Vermont last summer."

"It was *my* pleasure," the dean insisted.

"And mine as well," I said.

"So let us proceed." He moved toward a large mahogany desk at the far end of the room flanked by several chairs. We followed and sat down facing him. "I've prepared a packet with a handbook and campus map plus other relevant material. You're welcome to wander about. Just don't interrupt a class in progress." He handed us each a binder. "I assume Neville has filled you in. You'll be working from this building. If you have any questions, I'll be here all day." And with that, we shook hands and left.

Back in the hall, I looked at Neville questioningly. "Am I missing something?"

"We can talk while we walk around." And touching my arm, Neville steered me into the hall.

It was early and classes had not begun. The first floor held offices for administrators, staff and faculty. The second contained labs - cooking, hairdressing, photography, ceramics and so on. The third floor had a completely outfitted gym, with exercise equipment occupying one half. We ended up on the top floor comprised of classrooms plus a few storerooms, a haven above the clatter. We stepped on the carpeted floors into a large empty classroom and I moved toward the window looking at the early morning sky, pink with promise.

Neville stood at the door watching me, then walked to my side. "I'm planning to teach a couple classes in my spare time. Amity needs to connect to the community and this is a good place to start. What do you think?"

"Who would use these facilities? The wealthy belong to the country club. The poor don't have the time. As for Amity, you remember how Billy Oliver…"

"People need people. Everyone searches for ways to connect. That's part of the human experience. I'm an educator as well as a minister. This could be a way of Amity giving back."

"I don't understand. How could this…"

"People reaching out to one another could change the world. But our society has become stiff and formal. They need to learn how to really love one another.

"I told Ken that you'd be a big help," he continued. "I've watched your organization and skill with people. We're putting together a class in Sensitivity Training beginning in March. Also a teacher training program and some training for fair housing." He paused. "You are someone who can take charge, Carol. So would you be interested in being my assistant? It would add hours so you'd be full time."

I caught my breath, feeling suddenly light headed. He was offering more than a steak dinner. "I think I can work it out. But first, I'd need an outline, a description of responsibility, of hours…"

"I knew it," he cried, throwing his arm around me and squeezing my shoulder. "Already you're asking the right questions. So how about getting some coffee where we can talk – informally, of course?"

There was a coffee shop on the edge of the campus, now empty. We ordered coffee and sweet rolls but I couldn't eat anything. He leaned forward and put his hand over mine. "Not hungry?"

"I'm sorry. I thought I was."

"You seem tense. Is something wrong?"

"Just a twinge. It'll pass."

His voice was almost caressing. "I want you to know that I'm here for you. You don't mind that, do you?"

I took a deep breath. "I do not feel compromised, sir. This is not Victorian England. We are simply having coffee together. What could be more innocent?"

He chuckled. "Good. So let's go on. We can drive down to the public housing office and talk to them there." He signaled for the check. "Will it be okay if we're a little late?"

"No problem. Mother loves her time with the kids."

Back at the university, we spoke briefly with Dr. Jones and by the time we left, it was Ken and Carol, as though we'd known each other forever.

Driving down the hill, Neville and I began reminiscing about our own college days, reflecting on how we'd changed. "You're feeling better." It was a question.

"Yes. I guess I just needed a little nourishment."

"In more ways than one?"

I could feel myself blush. "You're different from Billy Oliver."

"So they say."

"Did you know him?"

"Slightly. After all, we're colleagues."

"Did you know Dr. Walsh?"

"Yes. He was an icon. They don't make them that way any more."

"Yes they do." I blushed again.

"I'll take that as a compliment."

We were now at the housing project and Neville pulled up in front of a sign that said Building Manager. It was almost one o'clock and the winter sun was bright against a brilliant blue sky.

Inside, the office smelled of Monday morning disinfectant, its floor freshly washed. We sat for about an hour talking with the manager and her secretary who'd silenced the phones' constant ringing, basking in Neville's charm. We would meet once a week for four weeks of training, then once a month for the next six as follow up. Afterward, Neville and I walked around the complex, returning full circle to the car. The crisp air provided new vigor and I once more felt light and energetic.

"Efficient management is priceless."

I nodded.

"So now for a rough agenda. Maybe we can do that when we stop at the club. It's more or less on the way back."

We opted for the deserted bar, sitting at a corner table. Neville ordered wine and an appetizer plate. We toasted the university program, the teacher training stint and independent housing in the valley. With the second glass we celebrated the new year, the new face of Amity and all the mothers in the world, especially mine for enabling me to be there. I took another sip of wine, running the tip of my tongue over the rim. Then I lowered the glass and tossed my head. "Life begins a forty. Well, all right -- thirty-six." I leaned forward. "Can't lie to a preacher."

He laughed. "But preachers do lie."

I opened my eyes in mock amazement. "A man of the cloth? How so?"

"In the ways we present ourselves."

"Including you?"

"Sometimes."

"Like now?"

"No. Now I'm being myself."

I stroked the stem of my glass. "Then what about the other times?"

"I'm either trying to impress others or rescuing my faltering ego."

"I never thought of that. Then who ministers to the minister?"

"Those who love him, I suppose. Unless they are also trying to impress others or rescuing their own egos." His expression turned serious. "That's why people at Amity need one another. They need the Bill Pressers and Gerda Stahls and Mirabelle Rothbergs."

"You'll never know how much that means to me."

"Yes I do. I've seen it in your eyes. It was there the very first day we met. I know when someone is hurting. You can't hide pain."

"I get by."

"Don't be a martyr, Carol. There are easier ways to deal with things."

I couldn't think, only absorb, like osmosis.

By the time we returned to the Amity parking lot it was almost five o'clock and getting dark. I'd become a little woozy so Neville insisted on following me home, tapping his horn cheerfully and waving goodbye when I turned into the driveway.

Jennifer and Scott greeted me at the door. Tony had picked them up and all three were ravenous. Where had I been? What had kept me?

It was too late to cook. Maybe a treat -- McDonald's? Tony's peck on the cheek turned sullen as he sniffed my breath. "Not exactly espresso…"

"I was celebrating. Neville gave me a job."

"You have a job."

"This is full time," I said as I helped Jennifer put on her parka. It was all I needed to say.

It was past seven when we returned home and almost eight when the kids went to bed. Then it was time for Tony and me. I explained everything that had happened but once I'd sketched out the basics he lost interest. Plato listed three kinds of love. I made a mental note to look it up in the morning. Then exhausted, I turned over and went to sleep.

CHAPTER 19: JOY

AFTER MAKING ALL that fuss about Neville's workshop, Marva still went ahead and committed herself to chaperoning the young people's weekend retreat. Then she came down with the flu and passed it on to Ashley and Taylor. I agreed to take her place before I knew what I was getting into. Frantic calls at midnight have a way of doing that.

The retreat would be at Summit South, a big log cabin surrounded by smaller ones, each with fireplaces and rag rugs to add to the authentic look. The original owners started to build a ski resort, but the Midwest is stubbornly flat and they ran out of money before their bulldozer could create the necessary hills. After foreclosure, a bunch of locals bought it, thinking they could turn it into a conference center. When that didn't catch on, it was rented out to anyone willing to use it at a modest cost while the owners tried to figure their next move.

Carol had given me a quick briefing, saying that the workshop would explore human potential. It would help the kids connect although I thought they'd done a pretty good job of connecting on their own.

Neville would be there, of course. The theme would be called *Possibilities,* which had something to do with self-actualizing, whatever that means. I was surprised that Jason and Matt had planned to go but you can never tell about teenagers. Lucky for me I had a brand new ski outfit in my closet, so I pasted on a smile and proceeded to pack. Elsie helped me load the car and I made out a list of instructions for her to follow while

I was gone. By mid-afternoon, I was ready to pick up the boys from school, and we arrived a little after four.

The inside of the main building looked like a Western movie scene with rough-hewn tables and chairs and fringed lampshades dangling from the ceiling. Matt and Jason were met with a welcoming whoop and I was left to work my way toward the adults near the registration desk at the far end of the room. Carol was leaning against the wall, counting the turnout.

"Where did everyone come from?"

"Isn't this great?" she cried. "I think Neville is developing a following."

"Where will you put them all?"

"Oh, there's plenty of room. Each cabin sleeps six with an adult in calling distance." She looked at my suitcase. "Let me show you your room. You're bunked right upstairs. I hope you don't mind. The bathroom is just down the hall."

"I should move the car first."

"The boys can do that for you."

We mounted the wide staircase next to the reception desk, leaving behind the patchwork of bright green, yellow and red outfits framed against the knotty pine. The hallway was quiet and dimly lit. "This level is in the shape of a horseshoe," she explained. "The open part creates the high ceiling for downstairs."

I peeked through an open door. The corner bed had a comforter and was piled with pillows. Across was a dry sink holding a pitcher and basin over which was hung a small mirror. An armchair in faded paisley and a three-drawer chest completed the decor. My suitcase was leaning against the wall, waiting to be unpacked. "How did that get up here?"

"There's a back stairway leading to the kitchen. One of the kids must have brought it up."

We continued left, past a series of classrooms, then left again. Two closed doors completed the U. One had the word *exit* flickering above in red fluorescence. Carol pointed to the other door. "Neville and Sheila are staying in the room opposite." She looked at her watch. "Dinner's at six. You might want to use the time to unpack."

A weekender doesn't hold much and I finished unpacking in less than fifteen minutes. With time to kill, I wandered through the classrooms, running my hands over tables and chairs made of the same knotty pine as those downstairs, a shade lighter than the planked floors, faux wilderness for the privileged few.

Coming to the end of the hall, I noticed a streak of light under Neville and Sheila's door and heard muffled voices. Smiling, I tiptoed past.

Down in the kitchen, three women moved from stove to fridge, filling oblong trays on the counter. "Hello Joy. I'm glad to see you." It was Sheila, mopping her brow with the corner of a red bandana around her neck.

"What are you doing here?"

"When all else fails, call the minister's wife," she laughed. "The staff was overwhelmed with the big turnout. I'm not much of a cook, but I can follow directions. So here I am."

"That you are. And a good sport as well." I tried to measure how long it would take to work up that kind of a sweat. "Did you drive up with Neville and Hannah?"

She nodded. "Neville was out late last night dealing with old Mr. Webb's funeral so he's taking a little nap. I'm supposed to call him when dinner is ready."

"I can do that for you."

"Oh, would you? It's time. Our room is right at the top of the stairs."

"I know. Carol showed me."

Halfway up the stairs I almost collided with Carol. "Sheila asked me to call Neville," I said, catching my balance.

"Don't bother. He'll be down in a minute."

"Oh?" I gave her my fish-eyed look.

"He wanted my input. After all, we work together." Her voice was like ice.

I resisted looking over my shoulder toward Sheila. "I'm sure you were a big help," I muttered, getting in line for dinner then pulling up a chair next to Liz. "Seat taken?"

"Just waiting for you," she smiled. "You were a good sport to fill in for Marva."

"Don't mention it," I said, glad she was being friendly.

"Teenagers! They've already been through the line once and are getting ready for seconds." It was Carol as she plopped down on the seat next to me, her plate filled to overflowing. "So have I missed anything?"

"Clearly not dinner," Liz laughed.

"I really don't understand the program. But you seem to be one of Neville's fans," I began.

"I want Amity to prosper," Liz declared.

There was a fierce edge in her voice and I wondered how far Billy Oliver's report had been circulated. Just then, Neville appeared at the podium, motioning everyone to be seated. It was time to begin.

He started with a joke, made a comment on the weather and added some self-deprecating remarks before beginning with the main idea - Possibilities.

I leaned over and whispered in Liz's ear. "What did you mean about wanting Amity to prosper?"

She turned her head away. "Not now. I want to hear this."

So I sat in respectful silence, catching a word here and there, most of it like the sales pitches I could recite by heart. *Inner beauty. Hidden ability. Passion for life.* Switch some of the words and I could be at Junior Achievement hearing a promotion for potholders and plastic cups. Like with a million inspirational talks that cost big bucks, the audience was prepared to listen. When he finished, there was lots of applause.

I looked over toward Matt with his arm around Sue, Hannah with her head leaning on Jason's shoulder. Group psychology. Put a bunch of people together and they feed on one another, like following the Pied Piper or joining a voodoo cult.

Then Scottie appeared front and center. "I want everyone to count off to ten. All the Ones will go to room 201, the Twos to room 203 and so on. When you get there, you'll elect a facilitator, record keeper and spokesman. There'll be ten minutes to answer a list of prepared questions, then forty-five minutes for discussion. We'll reconvene here in an hour. Got it?"

I turned to Carol. "Where do you want me to go?"

She was all business. "You and Liz will be upstairs to facilitate distribution of tasks or encourage discussion. Just be there."

I nodded. *Toastmasters,* here I come.

The upstairs hall was now brightly lit, each classroom occupied with seven or eight kids. Matt and Jason were taking charge the way they always do, ordering one to sit here, another to fill out the forms. I smiled and waved as I walked by, then took a questionnaire into the hall to read. *Write down your feelings when you see the following words: Nerd, dark, Angry, Queer, Jerk...* There were fifteen in all.

"I'm hot." Liz had come from around the comer, her sweater tied around her hips. "It must be the press of bodies."

I waved the paper at her. "Did you see this list?"

She studied it over my shoulder, then shrugged. "Mind games. The kids are used to it."

"My boys never mentioned this."

"There are lots of things your kids have never mentioned. If you're lucky, they never will. Neville knows what he's doing."

"I hope you're right."

Now the hour was up and the kids had identified the words, pretending they were examining vocabulary in some far off venue, knowing it wasn't really a game, that once someone was called *nerd* or *dork,* it would determine his life for the next four years or even forever.

They trooped back into the dining room, each group ready to report. Hannah was first. "We wanted the answers to be anonymous so we jumbled them up and threw them in the middle of the floor. Then each person picked one at random and read it out loud."

There was a murmur of approval. Hannah's group had identified one of the hazards in the game.

Then Rex, the pimple-faced kid from down the hill whose parents never came to church, stood up. "People in our group thought this exercise was incendiary." He pronounced his words carefully, drawing them out for maximum effect. "We thought there should be some positive terminology to balance the negative ones. After all, Dr. Leighton began with a talk about Possibilities." He looked around. There was no visible reaction from the group except for a few sneers. Kids know a nerd when they see one. He sat back down.

Tanya was next, relishing her fifteen seconds of fame. "We thought this was a good way to help kids who don't know how to, you know, kinda make friends."

There were ten groups in all.

Now it was Neville's turn. "What effect did this have on you? Does name calling enhance or limit your possibilities?" First his voice was tender and cajoling. Then the question were barked out making everyone jump, then giggle nervously. He paused as tension mounted. Then his voice softened. "Now let's look at another list. I want you to connect one or several of these positive words to a specific member of your group and tell him why you think it's true. We'll do that right here. You have fifteen minutes."

The words turned the evening into a love-fest, with hugs, tears and kisses of affirmation. *Cheerful, Friendly, Helpful, Good Sport...* I wondered how many had actually earned the title. No matter. They were on a rapturous high. More voodoo. Liz gave me a smug look that said I told you so.

In the middle of all this, Neville stood up again. "How many of you are up to a trust walk? You know, leading a blindfolded partner back to the cabins."

Teenagers are unpredictable. Sometimes they'll go along with the weirdest ideas. Other times they can be unbelievably stubborn. I held my breath, wondering which way it would go. But this was Neville's night. After a flurry of jostling and self-conscious giggling, the pairs were established and after Neville offered a final blessing, they left, two by two.

I turned to Carol. "Are we covered for liability?"

She laughed. Then her expression changed. "You're serious, aren't you?"

"I haven't seen as much as a first aid kit. Is there a doctor in the house?"

"Oh for God's sake, lighten up, Joy."

"Something *could* happen," I insisted.

Her voice turned sarcastic. "We could form a posse and check the territory if it'll make you feel any better."

I was sorry I'd come. "Never mind. Scottie's a nurse. That should cover it."

Back in my room, I looked through the window, watching the twinkling lights from the cabins. Midwestern kids - salt of the earth, my boys among them.

I undressed in the dark and sank down on the bed. From time to time I'd get up to see cabin lights and shadows well into the morning hours. I finally drifted off to sleep and was awakened by the alarm at seven. An earthy smell drifted up the stairwell, like bacon frying or hickory smoke from the fireplace. Groggily, I made my way to the bathroom, and into the shower, allowing it to run for a long time. Another whole day lay ahead.

Breakfast was over at nine, followed by something related to being your brother's keeper. Watching kids stumble through role-playing was not my idea of how to spend the morning. But there were a few bright spots, like when Jayne, in a total role reversal, pretended to be the cheerleading captain, talking her friends into inviting Sue to the movies. And Hannah was totally convincing as a new girl, trying desperately to fit in. That Jason was the one to rescue her from being a wallflower brought down the house.

After break, groups were divided into workshops, exploring how each person could help enrich another's "Possibilities." So once more I was there to monitor, adding an idea here and there, establishing that Matt and Jason's mom was cool.

Afterward, I sat with Liz and Carol at lunch, making conversation as though I was having the time of my life. A break while the room was prepared for a video and everyone used the time to pack because we'd be going home right after supper.

Once back together, Neville was center stage. Standing at the podium, he motioned for silence. "Reaching out to one another, building trust and understanding and finding one's sense of affirmation is a learned skill. It can lead to an expanded humanity and deepening spirituality, communing with the godliness that lies within us. This weekend we have experienced a few of the exercises that show how, through practice, it can be learned.

"This film will show you what happens when these skills are not learned or are learned only half-way," he continued. "It shows that in our shrinking universe, you are indeed your brother's keeper."

The film began by showing the effects of anorexia and bulimia, young people with skeleton bodies and skin as white as alabaster, their enormous eyes staring at nothing. When should there have been help? Next the camera panned along a playground with happy laughing children who were ignoring two others huddled next to the building, separating the sheep from the goats. Then the bullying, something not intended for recess, especially when there was no rescue. When should there have been help?

I looked away, feeling the hairs on the back of my neck tighten. Tanya and Rex sat with their chins in their hands. Matt was whispering something to Sue, his face earnest. Jayne was alone and unmoving at one end of her table staring at the wall above Neville's head. Most were inert, their expressions frozen. Whether this was something they understood or not, it was far too much for a weekend afternoon.

When the lights came back on Neville was back on his feet. More pacing back and forth from table to table. More talking about the people in the film - What should have been done? What could have been done? Needed to be done. Some of the girls were crying. Three had left the room. My eyes searched for Liz. So much for personal fulfillment. It was only three o'clock. There was another workshop and then supper. After that we could head for home.

Back upstairs we were given another list. Write down the names of three people who aren't here. Write three positive things about them. Neville was getting ready to close the deal. What better way to fill the pews than to invite someone to church? Some were now saying this was hokey and stupid. Others wanted to wallow in the drama, the excitement. And there were more tears. Moods can be contagious.

After an hour of sniffling, with the bathroom awash in soggy Kleenex, we went back downstairs. Neville went into an explanation of *empathy* and really *experiencing* the other's feelings. But there was only politeness and weary affirmation. The kids were wrung out and so was I.

Supper was gravely quiet and much of the food untouched. Matt thanked Neville for a wonderful weekend. Sue echoed her appreciation, waving her hands to generate an enthusiastic response that was half-hearted and lame. Neville gave a short prayer of thanksgiving. It was finally time to go.

Matt and Jason slept all the way home - or at least, pretended to. It was just as well. I needed to sort things out beginning with how much to share with Gary let alone anyone else.

Chapter 20: Kim

SPRING. THE EARTH'S annual housekeeping, flushing rivers, awakening bugs and beasts, prompting birds to nest, singing as they go. It's understandable for humans to yearn for that indefinable something.

Meanwhile, things at Amity have taken an interesting turn. Neville Leighton invited me to come and observe his class at the university. I must confess that psychology has never been my field of interest. On the other hand, I'm ready for a change.

The class was an extension of Neville's Participation Workshop. I hadn't benefited much from the January session, mostly because Bill was there and he tends to dominate. Still, the discussion and activities were enough to pique my interest, namely that pure honesty be acceptable and safe.

I plunged into research beforehand because that's my nature. Once exposed to new ideas, I'm driven to follow as far as time or energy will allow. Soon I was devouring everything, spending hours on the Internet, reading, participating in chat rooms, writing to scholars in the field. Neville applauded my interest. Maybe that was why he invited me to come and observe.

I arrived a little early and ready as usual. Neville handed me the syllabus to read while we waited. Class exercises were geared toward leadership while at the same time respecting the autonomy of others.

When students came in, I moved toward the back of the room prepared to take notes. But that wasn't Neville's style. Participation

Training was meant for everyone joining in. The first was an exercise in values. Small groups were given an ethical dilemma to solve. *Doris, age 50, has a 22 year-old son Donald who was horribly burned in a bonfire. The treatment, proven successful, is painful beyond words. After four treatments, Donald wants to have them stopped. To do so would leave him scarred for life. Doris has the option of having her son declared incompetent and ordering the treatments to continue. What should be done?*

I immediately saw it as an exercise in logic between the greatest good and the least harm. In the group, I phrased my suggestions carefully, knowing I was among simple, unsophisticated people. Pretty soon we were creating lists: pro and con, Donald and Doris, tactic and strategy. One person acted as secretary, writing ideas on an easel. I was facilitator pro tem. After an hour we took a break, followed by the entire class reconvening to compare notes.

A consensus had emerged, that since there was no mortal threat, Doris should do whatever it took to continue Donald's treatment, going as far as declaring Donald incompetent, not just because she was his mother or because he would eventually thank her but simply because it was the right thing to do.

"Now let's tweak this just a little," Neville said with a twinkle in his eye. "It so happens that this problem is based on an actual court case. You were correct in guessing that Doris would do what was necessary to continue treatment. But imagine it's five years later. Donald has graduated from college and is about to marry. He is bitter and blames his mother for all his pain and suffering. He is so angry, he hasn't spoken to her in years. He even refuses to invite her to his wedding. Is it possible to bring them together?

Everyone groaned. We went back to our small groups and followed the same process, listing the greater good and the least harm. We concluded that the guest list for Donald's wedding was a red herring. The real issue was that of alienation. Why hadn't Doris done something sooner? As for Donald, was his alienation having special impact since he was an only child? More importantly, what might make the parties *listen* to one another?

Once more the class reconvened. We agreed that first of all, Donald needed help in dealing with his bitterness. Second, the prospective bride should be brought into the picture. Perhaps family counseling. And that's exactly what happened to the real family.

By now I was so exhilarated that it was a jolt when Neville said, "So until next week..." and began to collect papers and make room for the next instructor.

It had been my practice to find an excuse to chat for a moment with my instructors after class. Certainly that should be possible since my attendance here was by personal invitation. But six or seven students had the same idea. Then there were other students coming in. So I allowed myself to be swept through the doorway, finding myself back outside with the spring air playing around my collar, watching the breeze turn the willows into pulsating hydra as the golden branches lifted in rhythmic accord.

Suddenly I felt Neville standing next to me. "The sky is seductive, isn't it? It's almost a shame to go home." He looked at his watch. "How about joining me for some hot chocolate and a sandwich? There's a small tea room about a half-mile down the street."

I couldn't have asked for more.

The café looked like the inside of a British movie and smelled of freshly baked bread. I chose a seat next to the window and shrugged off my coat, draping it over the back of my chair. The server came promptly and stood with pencil poised. "Hot chocolate and tuna salad on whatever bread that smells so good."

Neville nodded. "Make mine the same."

The food arrived promptly and I wrapped my hands around the warm mug and took a long swallow. "My family was instrumental in the university's growth, you know. My uncle is president of the board."

"I know."

"I've met Ken Jones. He's your friend?"

He nodded. "From college. He had a wife and a couple of kids to support. So he turned to administration."

"Poor man."

Neville laughed. "Don't waste your pity. Administration deals with people, so he's using his skills."

"I guess I'm being sentimental. It's spring and the campus is lush, so reminiscent of bygone days. I look back at my college days as being happy."

He studied my face, his expression serious. "Tell me about it."

"Oh, it's really nothing."

"Really?" His voice was warm and insistent.

Suddenly my words came in a rush like a spring cloudburst. He'd already known about Vassar. He'd guessed the rest. So I told it like it was, all of it, with neither passion nor guilt.

When I was finished, Neville reached over and put his hand over mine.

"Thank you for sharing. It couldn't have been easy."

I took a deep breath. "It's in the past. I've never told anyone."

He smiled. "You're one strong lady. How come I haven't seen that side of you before?"

"It's been hibernating. Another aspect of spring."

"And now you're drawn to study psychology?"

"I think so. Oh, I don't know." I bit into my sandwich, suddenly uncomfortable.

"If you did, would you enroll here or go back East?" he persisted.

"I hadn't thought that far ahead."

"And what do you suppose Bill would say?"

The sandwich was a hard lump in my throat. "Who knows?"

"Who cares?"

"Sounds like you've been talking to him."

"About Amity. He's a very interesting man."

"I suppose it was about money."

"It's always about money," he said ruefully. "I'm hoping that Amity's new direction will stem the flow." He sat back. "What do you think?"

"It depends. I could present a series of reasons such as the obvious tie between the spirit and psyche that makes a church an appropriate venue to explore self-awareness. We could talk about how the acceleration of events underscores individual needs to interact. I could mention Amity's changing life in the community." I paused. "But at the gut level, I think this new direction is right."

He laughed, then turned serious. "Thank you for your support. I can't tell you how much that means to me." He paused, tracing a small chocolate spill on the white tablecloth. "Sometimes I, too, feel alone."

I remembered the expression on Carol's face every time she looked at him. Years before I'd told her that Tony was a loser and history had proved me right. "You have a following at Worthington. Use it."

"You're right. I'm a very lucky man."

"My time will come as well." I looked outside at the sun inching toward the horizon.

"Meanwhile, it's getting late. We'd better leave." He withdrew his hand from mine, but the warmth lingered.

Outside, the wind had turned sharp and I pulled my coat close around me. We walked at a brisk pace and arrived at my car just as I was beginning to feel chilled. As I got in, he leaned forward and squeezed my shoulder, his lips brushing my cheek. "It was a good day, wasn't it?"

"Yes. I hope we can do this again."

"You can count on it." Giving a thumbs up, he stepped back and waved as I pulled away.

It was almost five o'clock, too late to cook dinner. So when I arrived home, I went upstairs and ran a comb through my hair, added a little lipstick and settled in front of the TV to watch the news and wait for Bill.

He arrived in a horrible mood and burst out angrily when I laid out my plans. "If you'd called, I could have worked another hour or two. Now it's rush hour…"

"Each time I call, you find something to criticize."

"If the shoe fits…"

"Well then, I'll go by myself."

He shifted his weight, leaning forward. "What in the hell is the matter with you? Do you always have to be bitchy?"

"Me?" I laughed bitterly. "I was looking forward to going out to dinner with my husband. Note the lipstick. I also applied fresh cologne. I don't know why I bother."

"Oh, for God's sake, Kim. He moved his briefcase to the other hand. "Just give me a minute to go upstairs and then we can go. Let's hope they haven't run out of the catch of the day."

That last was a flat-out invention since Bill hates fish or seafood. I bit my tongue and got up to call in a reservation.

Weeknights are not busy, so when we arrived we were promptly seated. Bill ordered a bottle of wine and after downing two glasses, was reasonably pleasant, telling me about his day at the office, inviting a report about mine. At first I hesitated. But after a long sip of wine, I began, describing Neville's class, and then taking a deep breath, about going back to school.

"Well I'll be damned. An intellectual itch that needed to be scratched."

Just then the server appeared and he turned toward her. "I suppose you're all out of the catch of the day."

A smile tugged at the corners of her mouth. "I'm afraid so, Mr. Presser. If you'd come in a little earlier..."

"Blame it on my wife. It takes her forever to get ready."

"But we do have some T-bones that will melt in your mouth."

"He'll have a large Greek salad. Hold the anchovies," I said, my voice louder than intended.

".. .along with the T -bone. Make it rare." He winked at the server.

"Suit yourself, I shrugged. "I'll take the vegetable plate." The server collected the menus and retired to the kitchen.

"Jack Sprat," Bill said, pouring more wine from the carafe.

"Your arteries are going to kill you."

"Will that make you sad?"

"Never ask questions that might elicit a negative response."

"Very good, my dear. You've been listening. Are you sure you want to be a psychologist? You'd make a fine lawyer."

"And compete with you? No thanks."

The server arrived with the food and Bill gave it his undivided attention. I watched as he stabbed the crusty meat close to the bone, releasing the succulent juices.

"Just the way I like it." He looked up at me. "Sure you don't want some?"

"Do you mean to share?"

"You're welcome to order your own."

I shook my head. "Neville and I had a wonderful talk, repast for the soul. So I'm not hungry."

Bill rolled his eyes and took another bite.

"You have something against metaphors?"

"How often do you suppose Neville has whispered wonderful words into some other parishioner's ear? It's all part of the pitch."

I could feel indignation swirl to the surface. "Neville is the most sincere, understanding, helpful… But you're always looking to find fault."

"Don't be so sure. It so happens that I had my own little talk with Neville." He leaned forward and lowered his voice. "Would you like to know what it was about?"

"Money, no doubt."

"Ah, this time you're wrong. Guess again."

I put the fork on my plate and sat back. "I'm really not interested, Bill. So whenever you're finished, I'm ready to go home."

"Don't want to play? Well then, I'll tell you. We talked about personal fulfillment."

I looked around for the server. "You've had too much to drink, so if you don't mind, I'll drive home."

"You should be pleased that Neville and I have a great deal in common." He reached for the wine carafe but it was empty. "So you can say that I am also the most sincere, honest, understanding…"

I stood up and dropped my napkin on the chair. "Shut up, Bill."

The server walked over with the check. "I hope everything was all right," she said, smiling at Bill.

"It was great, Katie or Maria or whatever your name is. You're a good cook. Maybe you can give my wife some pointers."

"It's Katie, Mr. Presser. How did you know?"

"You just look like a Katie." He scribbled his name on the check, handing it back to her. "So tell me, Katie, do you ever go swimming?"

"Only in the summer," she laughed. "I leave the winter swimming for the polar bears. There is such a club you know."

He stood up taking the coat check from his pocket. "My own preference is to swim in the heat of the summer in the moonlight, butt naked." He tucked the pencil in Katie's apron pocket. "I'll bet that club would be a huge success."

"I'm sure. But not for long," she laughed.

"You're probably right." He turned to me. "Ready?"

We retrieved our coats and moved toward the door. "I'm driving," I repeated.

"Sure, sure." He held the handrail as he navigated down the steps to the parking lot. "You know, we might be able to sink a swimming pool in that flat stretch behind the house and go skinny dipping in the moonlight."

"Right. You'd get premium prices for grandstand seats."

He took my arm and nuzzled his chin in my hair. "We could invite our friends. I'll bet Neville would cut a fine figure. He works out regularly."

I pulled away and increased my pace, opening the car doors ahead of him. "You're disgusting. Just because Neville is close to our age, just because he's slim and attractive, not like…"

"Guys are guys, Kim. I'm telling you, when we talk man to man, there's no difference. As a matter of fact…"

"I don't want to hear it," I said. "You're a lawyer and he's a minister. There are rules."

"Have a heart, Kim. Don't you think Neville needs a shoulder to cry on?"

I didn't answer. Instead, I pulled out and drove home in silence. Maybe going back East wouldn't be such a bad idea after all. Alone, I could immerse myself without distraction. There would be time to sort things out.

The garage door clanged down behind us and Bill got out of the car, steadying himself. "Let me show you where we should put the pool. It's right past those trees."

"We don't need a pool, Bill. We belong to a very acceptable country club and can swim any time we want, indoors or out." I picked up my purse and moved toward the kitchen door.

"How about just going back there to see? There's a bright moon and the air smells like spring. C'mon, Lit Lady. Together we can revel in Mother Nature and you might even be inspired to write a poem."

"That's okay. I'll just go inside and read for the rest of the evening." Without turning my head, I walked into the house.

"Oh-h Kimmie," His voice was a drunken wail.

I was at the computer when he came in, not bothering to look up as I heard him trudge heavily up the stairs. There was work to be done. Most students had already submitted applications for fall enrollment. I hoped I wasn't too late.

Chapter 21: Joy

LENT HAD BEGUN and people were walking around with ashes on their foreheads. Marva said it didn't mean anything unless you were Catholic, which we weren't, so I didn't bother to look further.

I'd told Marva about the high school retreat and I wasn't sure whether or not she reacted but she'd just gotten over the flu, so it was hard to tell. As for Jayne, every time I visited, she was either out or busy with homework.

Going to church was still a Sunday morning ritual, even though attendance was falling off. Coffee hour was the place to meet and greet people, allowing us to rub elbows with executives and professionals, proving that we could hold our own. Everyone at *Marty's* was waiting for Max Pollock to be put out to pasture and Gary was right up there jockeying with the best of them, so this was good practice.

We'd been thinking about if for a while and after adding up all the advantages, we decided to join Amity which would be a lot different than becoming Mormons or Catholics. At Amity, there was only one requirement, and that was to be baptized to wash away your sins. We'd already been baptized as infants when our sins were pretty ordinary, our parents wanting to give us all the advantages. Neville asked us whether we believed in God and in Jesus Christ and we answered that of course we did. I mean, what else can you say to a minister? And that was the end of it. Later there would be a big ceremony on Easter Sunday welcoming all the new members that year in front of God and everyone. I was already planning what to wear.

Meanwhile, I needed to prioritize my time. I liked the Women's Guild especially since Marva was both president and also my best friend. They sponsored things like inter-faith teas and bridge luncheons and did other serious things like fund-raising auctions. This particular spring, Marva had put together a program about stained glass windows. Women from all the churches in Worthington attended, most of them of the old and rich persuasion.

I came to help even though I didn't have any particular job, and Marva was pleased as usual because she and I work well together. The program involved touring the church buildings in and around Worthington and then coming back to Amity for lunch. That was followed by a video show of stained glass windows around the world, places like Notre Dame or the cathedral in Rome.

The day turned out to be a real winner. By renting a bus and getting some of the women to bring their vans, we were able to accommodate a large turnout. Marva even got Paul to give the lecture which he could do off the top of his head, this being his profession after all. But more than that, anything to do with architecture gave him a real turn on.

At lunch, Neville and Carol, who were working in their offices, came in to say hello and join with the women, a salad affair that was simple yet satisfying. Neville turned on the charm, saying how happy he was that such delightful ladies found time to attend. Then he and Carol took off to self-actualize the inner city.

The screen and projector had been set up and Paul began to narrate. Architecture - solid stuff like steel and plaster, something you can grab onto, not that highbrow, pie-in-the-sky stuff that fades away the minute you get too close. None of that Brother's Keeper business that takes hours to get to nowhere and leaves you with an Excedrin headache.

The audience must have been on the same wavelength because they gave Paul a standing ovation just like in the theaters or concert halls. The question and answer period that followed lasted an hour. Then it was over.

The bus came right on time, and one by one the vans pulled away, leaving us to go back inside where the caterers were cleaning up the last of the mess. "Good show, Paul," I said, and meant it sincerely.

He was really wired. Some men never get enough of the limelight no matter how important they are. "Let's go to the club and celebrate, make it a foursome for dinner. Jayne won't mind."

There was no stopping him. So I called Gary, telling him to meet us at the club.

When we arrived, Gary was already waiting in the bar. "Hey there, professor."

"A star is born," Paul grinned. "They loved me."

Gary held up his glass to summon the server. "I'll drink to that."

"The house was packed and they gave him a standing ovation," I added, knowing Paul would have mentioned it himself if I hadn't.

"Was Neville there?"

"Oh yes. This was his domain and he never misses a beat," Marva replied.

Marva and I hadn't had much chance to talk about the retreat or anything else what with her having the flu and then being busy with the Women's Group program. So now I leaned forward waiting for the rest to come out. "I guess the minister is always the host, no matter what."

"It's not *his* church," Paul declared. "It belongs to all of the members."

"Isn't he a member?" I asked, acting like someone eager to learn more about church organization from the master's feet.

"Of course. And so are you. But do you stand up on Sunday morning, saying you're happy people could come and invite them to stay for coffee?"

"That's exactly what Carol did the first day we came to Amity," I said, gesturing the way executives do when they're making a point. "And look what happened. Two new members *and* regular contributors."

"Not quite. She spoke to you personally. She didn't get on a soap box and address people as they walked in the door."

"You're pressing the wrong button," Marva sighed. "Paul's taking his job as new president very seriously."

"So Neville wasn't supposed to be there?"

"That's not what I said," Paul answered.

Just then Bill Presser stepped out of the shadows, his bulk towering over our table. "Fancy meeting you here."

"Well whaddya know. Fancy meeting *you* here," For once I was glad to be interrupted. "Where's Kim?"

"At home with her vegetable plate, or maybe on the phone to Neville or on the Internet. Welcome to my second home. At least here I'm allowed to eat in peace."

"Well pull up a chair and join us," Gary urged. "We're talking about stained glass and Gothic cathedrals. Maybe Amity can invest in a few."

"…with no money to pay for them," Bill said, sitting down next to me. He leaned forward, resting his arm on the back of Marva's chair.

She scowled. "It never goes away, does it?"

"And it's getting worse," Paul added. "We have a huge overhead with a hefty mortgage. Building maintenance. Landscaping service. The parsonage. Neville's salary which is at the top of his range with full benefits plus a retirement package. Carol on the payroll full time…"

"Well, if Neville's program gets us back on track, I'm all for it," Bill said.

"But this business of teaching and doing workshops is overkill," Marva continued. "After all, we're the ones who brought him here. We pay his salary."

"And a good salary it is," Paul nodded, looking at Bill.

"So he was hired on my watch," Bill said, his voice louder than it had to be. "But if you want the best, you have to pay for it."

"Don't be so sure," Paul declared.

Bill's face was turning red. "I know you and Billy Oliver were friends, but he wasn't what Amity needed. The world has changed and so has Worthington. People are alienated, separated, disenfranchised. We're all crying out for something more. Neville can bring this church around to where people reach their greatest potential and find that spark of divinity within. Call it being closer to God. Everyone knows I'm a skeptic. But his message resonates. There are others who feel the same.

"But people are talking," Gary insisted, making sure that Bill could see that he was no pushover.

"My point exactly," Bill replied. "The natives are getting restless. Amity's had had a time of quiet. No, let me correct that. We've had a time of drift. Now people are looking for something to happen and what better way to do that than by generating a fight. No thinking necessary. Just crank up the emotions and yell."

"This was supposed to be a party," I pleaded, afraid Gary had gone too far.

"What the hell. No one's listening anyway." Bill stood up, pausing for a moment to catch his balance. "I'll see if our table is ready. I could use a walk." And he moved purposefully into the dining room.

"Is he mad?" I asked, hoping that Gary would see what I meant.

"He'll be fine after he's had something to eat," Paul replied.

In a few minutes, Bill was back, saying they could seat us right away, so we picked up drinks and followed him into the dining room. We ordered steaks and the server he called Katie brought two bottles of Merlot without having to be asked. She fell all over Bill, calling him Mr. Presser and saying she was glad to see him and could she bring anything else. No doubt he's a big tipper.

"One more thing," Paul said, spearing a tomato from his salad. "I'm going to re-activate the Ministerial Advisory Committee." He looked at Bill. "What do you think?"

Marva studied her wineglass. Obviously she and Paul had already talked about it.

"Bad decision. But you're the president now. Do what you will and devil take the hindmost. I'm only a board member with a pretty lame portfolio at that. After all, who listens to Denominational Affairs?"

"I know it's my call, but I'm asking for your feedback," Paul insisted.

"Well, you might as well hang out a sign that says Ministers for Breakfast," Bill declared. "The vultures will eat him up. And this, my friend, will be on *your* watch."

Most of this was over my head. So I went to the lady's room to catch my breath and when I came back the steaks had arrived and everyone was smiling again.

"A toast to a bright future." Bill raised his glass and I joined in, glad the argument was over at least for now.

The next day, Marva explained about the Ministerial Advisory Committee which is a kind of go-between for when the congregation and minister are getting mad at one another and no longer talking. Three members along with the minister go over what each side wants or doesn't want. Marva said it was a big deal. I lost interest about five minutes into the explanation. Once anyone starts talking about firing someone, his days are numbered, so why pretend? Still, I felt sorry for him. And I felt sorry for Jason having to say goodbye to Hannah. I even felt sorry for Sheila, because they'd be moving again. But then, maybe not. Where's there's life, there's hope. As long as my own skirts didn't get dipped in the mud.

CHAPTER 22: LIZ

THE CALL FROM Paul Larson surprised me. Not that we'd had a falling out. But people do drift apart.

"I have a favor to ask of you, Liz. Do you have a minute?"

"Sure. John's down for his nap and Kelsey won't be home until three. What's up?"

"Do you remember about the Ministerial Advisory Committee?"

Did I remember the killer triumvirate with binding arbitration designed to solve problems when all else failed? "Oh, please Paul."

"It's not what you think, Liz. Last time around the MAC's power was abused. Today we're looking for something preemptive, a place to air grievances before they become serious."

"And you're asking me?"

"We need help, Liz. It's not just us. There have been rumblings."

"Like what?"

"That's for you to find out."

A series of faces paraded across my mind - Sheila, Joy, even Gerda - anyone of whom could stir up God only knows what. "It sounds ominous."

"Honestly Liz, this is only precautionary." He paused. "You have a level head and know how to keep things calm."

I took a deep breath. "Let me think about it."

"Thanks, Liz. I know you'll do the right thing." He cleared his throat. "So how are you and the kids doing?"

"We're fine. Kelsey is learning new skills little by little. New theories say that some Down's Syndrome persons actually learn to read. And John is growing like a weed. Tell Marva to bring Ashley and Taylor over for a play date. The kids always have so much fun together."

"I know. I'll tell her." Another pause. "How soon can I expect an answer?"

"I'd like to sleep on it."

"Tomorrow, then."

"Yes. Call me at this same time. I'll be home."

I went into the living room, shoved a bunch of golden books off the couch and sat down. The previous MAC had included members who'd been coming to Amity for years, all the way back before Dr. Walsh. They were decent people, but after all the gossip, innuendo and slander, two of them resigned. The third died the day after Billy left. Damn Paul anyway.

I told Dave about it after dinner and he said he's back me no matter what I decided. We continued talking sporadically all evening, finding reasons pro and con but when we went to bed, it was still up in the air.

At noon Paul called and told me that that Steve Rothberg, and Nancy Oberman, Carol's mother, had agreed to serve and would be the two others on the MAC. My God! Steve, who lets Mirabelle lead him around by the nose and Nancy who thinks a batch of chocolate chip cookies will cure anything. I'm not St. Teresa, but I know when I'm needed. So I said yes.

Steve called that same evening and we agreed to meet at noon on Saturday. I guess he was designated chair, or maybe he designated himself. It would be held at Nancy Oberman's.

Saturdays were always crazy at our house, but I managed to roll out of bed and pull myself together, hoping some of the chores got done by the time I came back home.

They were in the den at Nancy's sipping ice tea and admiring the cookies laid out on the table when I walked in. Neville got up to give me a peck on the cheek, asking about the family before sitting down again. "I was just telling Nancy how important Carol is to our work at Amity. Isn't it interesting how someone's light can remain hidden for such a long time and then suddenly, burst forth. On the other hand, those who knew her best were always aware of her ability."

The conversation went on as we assumed our respective roles - Steve as CEO, Nancy as Pollyanna, me as mediator, with Neville's role so far undefined.

Finally Steve cleared his throat. "We want to thank you for making your home available, Nancy. Now let's get to work."

"Saturday afternoons are precious, aren't they?" Nancy murmured.

"We've been given a mandate," Steve continued. "I brought my copy of Robert's Rules of Order in case we get bogged down."

I burst out laughing. "Isn't that a bit silly?"

Steve's face turned a mottled red. "We may also find it useful to have a scribe to take minutes. So if you would be so kind, Liz."

I glanced at Neville whose eyes were twinkling. "But I wasn't expecting to write."

Steve reached into his briefcase and pulled out a yellow legal pad. "You'll want to set up your own system later, but this should do for now."

I put the pad on my lap and sat with pen poised. "All right. Go ahead. I'm ready." Only Neville seemed to think it was funny.

"We might begin by asking Neville for his ideas of the ministry and how it relates to Amity. For my part, as chairman of the finance committee I would be especially interested in his perception in that regard," Steve said, leaning back in his seat.

"Although you haven't addressed me directly, I would be happy to answer," Neville smiled. "What do you want to know?"

"Bill Presser's study has come up with some stunning figures." Steve's voice had taken on an icy edge. Accountants don't like to be bested.

Neville nodded. "As finance chair, it's come to your attention, and rightly so. But a small decline in pledges is to be expected whenever there's a pulpit turnover. Different ministers will appeal to different members. One cannot be all things to all men."

"I'd hoped you'd bring back the Bible study," Nancy said. "Dr. Walsh held Bible study every Wednesday night, rain or shine and we got so much out of it. I could study the Bible forever and still find more to learn."

"You're absolutely right, Nancy." Neville's face was serious and sincere like a father talking to a child. "Unfortunately, when I tried to set it up, we couldn't find a date to satisfy everyone. Dr. Walsh might have cornered Wednesday nights, but nowadays Amity's schedule includes Little Theater, Cub Scouts, Bridge Club, Social Action, Circle Suppers, New Member Orientation as well as periodic Sunday school faculty, committee and board meetings. And that doesn't include the holidays or special events like the Sunday school festival that takes weeks to plan. If you could find enough people to commit themselves to Bible study and settle on a date, I would be happy to add it to my schedule."

Steve almost leaped out of his chair. "I hear you're teaching a class at the university. Are you being paid?"

Neville looked startled. "Of course. But the amount is nominal." He looked at Nancy. "Teachers are notoriously underpaid."

"The amount is not the issue. The issue is time. Teaching even one class takes time away from your work at Amity."

"It supplements my work at Amity, taking the form of outreach."

I looked up from my note pad. "I don't think Neville's schedule is within our mandate to facilitate communication."

"What's that supposed to mean?" Steve asked.

"If I wanted to participate in a gripe session, I could have stayed home to fight with my husband."

"Oh my dear, are you and David…"

"Nancy, I was being funny."

Neville shifted in his chair preparing to stand up. "I still have a lot to do and I also have plans for tonight. Let's settle on a meeting time and place. That should be sufficient for now."

"How about every Saturday at noon?"

"Once a week? Good Grief, Nancy, what on earth would we talk about?" I protested, thinking of all the chores waiting for me when I got home.

"We haven't really talked about anything yet," Steve said. "There's the church budget, the allocation of time Neville spends at the university, the Sunday morning service, the church program…"

"What do you mean, the Sunday morning service?" Neville asked, his face suddenly pale. "I came to Amity with top qualifications and have been told that my sermons are exemplary. As a matter of fact, some think they are worthy of publication. Furthermore, there's the matter of the free pulpit."

"You see, we do have things to talk about." Steve looked at his watch then back at Nancy. "So shall we meet here next Saturday at the same time?"

"I suppose. But every week?"

"Once things settle down, we can meet as the need arises. Let's see how it goes." Steve stood up and wrapped a gray scarf around his neck looking like a pasty-faced turtle. Then before Nancy could see him to the door, he scurried out, leaving the three of us staring at one another.

"Will someone please tell me what just happened?" I asked.

"The finance committee is getting ready for the annual fund drive so he's pretty stressed out. It's an occupational hazard," Neville smiled. "He'll be fine once the numbers are in. I'm sure they'll be positive."

"What study is he talking about? People keep tiptoeing around it."

"Bill Presser found a statistical device that's supposed to measure the financial health of an organization. It divides expenses by members in attendance on Sunday morning, dividing things like utilities, maintenance, minister's salary and so forth. Then it projects what it would take to grow. Taking into consideration the pledge difference between new and settled members, it sometimes shows that growth becomes a handicap rather than being beneficial. But like all short cuts, it doesn't tell the whole story." Neville looked at his watch. "But I do have to go. I promised Sheila I wouldn't be late." He stood up and taking a final cookie, headed out the door with a wink and a wave.

"Now don't you rush off too," Nancy said, turning to me. "We haven't had a nice talk since I can't remember when. How about a cup of coffee before you leave?"

I knew she'd gone to a lot of trouble preparing for this meeting. "Well, okay. Then I have to go."

She returned from the kitchen with a tray. "I added the cream and sugar for you. I hope you don't mind."

I took the cup and inhaled deeply before taking a sip. "Continental-freshly ground. You know what I like."

"We have the same taste."

"Yes we do. Born and bred in Worthington. It must be in the water."

"Nothing wrong with that. Carol thought Midwest University wasn't good enough. You see how much going away did for her."

"Carol is a loving daughter," I said softly. "She'll get her life back together. Just give her time."

"She'll be doing it by herself. I don't know why Tony even bothered with college, wasting all that money."

I winced. "Sales is a respected occupation. David has always taken good care of his family."

"My point exactly." She looked at me intently. "You sure everything is okay with you two? You and Dave are such a perfect couple and such good parents to your little ones, especially Kelsey. I guess what they say is true. What doesn't kill you makes you strong."

"When Paul asked me to serve on this committee, he wouldn't tell me what the problem was. Said it was our job to find out for ourselves."

"Well, Joy Volkman was upset about the young people's retreat but she wasn't specific. And Marva had a sour look after the workshop in January. I guess that's enough for starters."

"Do you remember the way people twisted words and took every little thing so personally when we were dealing with Billy Oliver? Do you see any of that happening?" I asked.

"I like Neville. I really do. Oh, I miss Bible study, but most of the time I bring it up because I can't think of anything else to say. As for Steve's comment about sermons, I have no idea where that came from."

"Do you think Amity is in trouble?"

"Oh God, Liz, don't say that. I almost had a stroke over the Billy Oliver thing. Once more and I'll be one of the people who leaves - or maybe they'll carry me out on a stretcher. On second thought, I can't leave. There have been too many years invested."

"Still, people have to adapt or die."

"So it will be our job to smooth troubled waters. Neville must be given every chance to make good. If we show solid support, we can silence the dissention."

"Nip it in the bud," I agreed. "So we're together?"

She laughed dryly. "It took greater effort to accept Tony than it would be to embrace Neville. After all, we only have to listen to a minister once a week."

I took a final swallow and got up to leave. "With all respect, Nancy, I'm glad you're not my mother-in-law."

"We reap what we sow. None of us are angels."

At the door, she gave me a big hug. "I didn't mean what I said about Kelsey. I hope you weren't offended."

"Of course not. Your support has been priceless and I can never express my gratitude. But Neville's support has also been meaningful." I shifted my purse and returned the hug. Then I went to my car and waved as I pulled into the street.

Dave had started dinner so there was only the laundry to deal with. I could finish that after the kids were in bed.

It was quiet in the cool basement except for the hum of the washer and drier. Moments like this were precious, times when I could reflect and reminisce. I had a loving husband, three great kids and best of all, roots. Central to that was Amity and the people whose love and support were unshakable. Surely that would never change. Yet I kept picturing Paul and Steve bending over a bloody Julius Caesar. Et tu Brutus. I breathed a prayer and went back upstairs.

Chapter 23: Joy

SWIMMING AND TRACK are sports I can relate to, so I watch the boys compete whenever I can. Sometimes I even run into someone I know so instead of sitting in the bleachers, leafing through old magazine with everything out of style, I have someone to talk to.

Of course this makes our lives busy, so we eat out a lot. On this particular day, the boys had just completed a track meet with Matt winning the mile and Jason's relay coming in third. Like always, we'd go to the club afterward where the boys could shower and change before we sat down to eat.

Sue Mason had come to watch, so I invited her to have dinner with us, which is no problem because I do like having her around, what with her being into cheerleading and all, something we have in common. Because it's spring, we also talked about summer fashions and how she'd get a job in one of the cool clothing shops once she turned sixteen. I would have enjoyed having her as a daughter.

Fridays at the club were busy, it being the end of the workweek. So it was no surprise to walk into the club and see Jan and Max Pollack waving us over. We started to introduce them to Sue, but Jan said she'd known the Masons for a long time, both families having lived in Worthington for years. "Tried to sell Dave a franchise but couldn't get him to buy," boomed Max. "Maybe you could do better," he continued, looking at Gary. "I know Dave's a crackerjack salesman. There are still plenty of opportunities downstate."

As we sat down, I asked what brought them to the club so early. It turned out that Jan had come into town for her annual physical and there's nothing she likes more than talking about herself. Sue acted like she was interested, asking questions which kept Jan on a roll. In the meantime, Max ordered another round of drinks.

When the boys came in from the locker room, Jan wasn't anywhere close to finishing her story, so we asked for a table in the dining room large enough to accommodate all seven of us and got one that seated ten giving us lots of elbowroom. I settled back, knowing this was going to be a long evening, there being no stopping Jan.

The Friday special happened to be a seafood platter. I know that eating fish on Friday is Catholic so I usually make it a practice not to order it. But I love seafood and the price was right so I gave in.

The salads came immediately, something to pay attention to beside Jan who kept going on and on about a hearing test and growing cataracts. I'll admit that my eyes began to wander although I am a very disciplined person and try not to be obvious.

By now the dining room was pretty full, and I knew the servers would want a quick turnover. Then off toward the entrance, I saw Neville, Sheila and Hannah, scanning the crowded room.

Jason saw them at the same time. Suddenly he came alive and stood up, waving. I could see it was either lose Jason or share our table with the Leightons so I interrupted as diplomatically as I could. "I see some friends without a table. Would you mind?"

Jan looked up. "Why, of course not. The more, the merrier." She nudged Max to move over while Gary got up to invite the Leightons to join us, making quick work of the introductions.

"Amity Community Church," Max murmured. "Bill Presser talks about it a lot. Heard all about your problems. Sorry picture. All fixed now, I suppose."

"We're Episcopalian," Jan declared. "Our priests wear turned around collars and read sermons delivered by Federal Express that no one listens to."

Neville laughed. "Don't they wish! As for people not listening, that's an occupational hazard in any denomination."

"Jan's pulling your leg, Neville," Max said cheerfully. "She likes to see how far she can go."

"I'm always delighted to meet someone with a sense of humor. There's not enough of that, I'm afraid." His benevolent smile was enough to make anyone melt.

"And do you like Worthington, Doctor Leighton?"

"I like it just fine and the people are all I could ask for -- the salt of the earth."

"You bet they are!" Jan nudged Max. "Just like Bill says. He tells it like it is."

Max leaned toward Neville. "We've got one of the best sales forces in mid-America. Headed by a guy named Gary Volkman. Aughta meet him. Holds his liquor like a man." He winked at Gary.

"Got a nice wife and kids too." Neville's smile went around the table, embracing everyone. "Family -- that's what counts."

"And how about yours?"

"Grown and flown. So now we're raising horses." The people at the next table turned and stared. "How about yours?"

"No horses allowed in the parsonage. So we'll keep Hannah and Adam a while longer." He smiled at Hannah as though they were sharing a private joke.

"Gary's like my own son." Max's tongue slurred over the 's' sounds. "He can drink anyone under the table. Almost out-did me. But I showed him up. Drinking takes practice, you know."

I almost cheered when the food arrived. "Oh yum. Shrimp, scallops, lobster…"

"You bet!" Max boomed. "And I'll have another. Anyone else?"

A blue vein pulsated in the middle of Gary's forehead. He put his hand over his glass. "I'm fine."

"So what does a minister do to fill his day besides writing his own sermons?" Jan continued, peering at Neville over her dinner plate.

He raised his shoulders non-committal. "No two days are alike. Today I was at the university with Carol, teaching a class in Sensitivity. In the afternoon we went to see about new teacher orientation."

Jan focused her attention like a bulldog. As Max slobbered over his dinner, she asked one question after another. What did the class include? How about Carol's input and most particularly, about ministerial counseling. Did he make home visitations? How about hospitals? Nursing homes? At first Neville was simply polite. Then his answers became more calculating. Max and Jan were town richies, and even Episcopalians were fair game, a prize to bring home to Steve and Paul.

Meanwhile Sheila sat mute, her bright red lipstick a bloody slash above her soft rounded chin. Poor thing. Desperate for a makeover.

The server came back asking about dessert and coffee. But Max was ready to go, or more accurately, there was no keeping him. So Gary walked him toward the door while Jan got their coats. Then they were outside, guiding Max to the car. Meanwhile the server had brought the check, which sat in the middle of the table while we all waited for Gary to return.

"Interesting people," Neville murmured. "So they've been in Worthington for a while?"

"Just Jan," Sue replied. "They're from Texas where her father made his money in oil. Max was a Midwest kid and went to military school upstate and then to college out east. After graduation he took a job at *Marty's*. By the time he met Jan, his life was pretty much locked in because Jan's father died and Max took over the business. Dad says Max doesn't even visit his family any more. No one around here knows them."

Jason and Matt were taking it all in, one more lesson in climbing the business ladder. There's more than one way to succeed. "I like Max," I said. "He's always been very nice to me. Gary's learned a lot since coming here."

"I'm sure," Sheila murmured.

"Life's filled with tradeoffs." And that was about the only wisdom I could offer.

Gary came back and as always, brought a breath of fresh air. "Let me work by the sweat of my brow and be paid for what I've earned. I'll match anyone at any time in any battle for any price and come out the winner." He leaned over the table and picked up the check. "Are we done?" He looked around the table. "More coffee? Dessert?"

"Did they find their car?" Neville asked. "It's getting dark."

"Oh, they're fine," Gary said in his hearty salesman's voice. "It's been a long week with lots going on. Max just needs to unwind. I'm glad we ran into them." Loyalty is important.

"Mrs. Pollack is probably used to it," Hannah offered.

"There are some things you never get used to."

Jason reached for Hannah's hand. "It's Friday. What's happening?"

Sheila shook her head in an amused way. "Kids and weekends."

I laughed. "Life gets serious soon enough."

We got up with not so much as a murmur from Neville and Sheila as Gary signed the check. I guess that's another fringe benefit.

Walking to the cars, Sheila talked about Adam's coming home during spring break, getting his room ready, cooking his favorite meals and buying new video games, like she knew exactly what he'd want. Meanwhile, Easter was around the corner. Soon it would be time to organize closets and switch wardrobes. And the kids chattered among themselves, echoing the voices of spring.

Chapter 24: Jayne

ADAM WAS COMING home. He'd take the red eye, arriving before dawn. Of course he'd sleep all day. But maybe he'd call. So I didn't mind, that is, *really* mind, baby-sitting right after school so Mom could go shopping even though I'd thought of going to *Sloppy Joe's* after school where the cool kids hang out, something that I'd always been afraid to do.

Mom's car was already in the driveway when I got home. "Ashley and Taylor are watching TV." She grabbed her purse on the hall table. "I wouldn't have asked except the stores are always such a mess before the holidays."

"That's okay Mom. Not much is happening at school."

She gave me a peck on the cheek. "Adam called. He'll be over at about four." And she was out the door.

My heart took a jump landing dead center, three inches above the collarbone.

After checking the kids, I went upstairs, tossed my books on the bed, and went into the bathroom to comb my hair and add a touch of lipstick. But after looking in the mirror, I could see I needed the works - face scrub, foundation, rouge, mascara and a touch of Mom's cologne. Short of a shower, it would have to do.

By three-thirty I was back downstairs watching *Sesame Street*, trying not to be nervous. After all, Adam and I were just friends. Would Sue be nervous? No way. She was a nervous giver, not a nervous getter. A guy would shake for a week before even saying Hi, hoping he wouldn't pee in his pants if she smiled back. I looked down at Ashley. She looked exactly like Mom, another nervous giver. Damn her anyway. Damn them both. And while I'm at it, damn the DNA that cheated me of anything resembling sex appeal. And damn the brains that are supposed to compensate. Apples and oranges - they're never an even trade.

The doorbell buzzed and I jumped. "That's okay. I'll get it," I called out, which didn't matter to little eyes glued to Big Bird and Cookie Monster.

He stood at the door, looking down at me. I'd forgotten how tall he was. Or maybe he'd grown. "Hi. Long time no see."

"Hey Jayne, how's it going? I called."

"I know. The kids are watching TV. Mom's at the store." I stood with my hand on the doorknob. "Coming in?"

"That's why I'm here." He leaned down and gave me a peck on the cheek. "I'm glad to see you."

"I'm glad to see you too," I said softly. And suddenly, everything was okay.

We sat in the living room, Adam on the recliner and me curled up on the couch. He leaned back so the footrest popped out with hands under his head casual-like. "So what's happening around here? Matt wasn't home when I called. Anything going on?"

I shrugged apologetically.

"Well, we'll have to get something going tomorrow. Any ideas?"

So I gave him a rundown on happenings in Worthington, things like the Mall, the movies or watching the amusement park being built. Maybe just hang out at the club.

"Sounds good."

I gulped. He didn't think I was a stupid kid after all.

Just then the garage door opened and Mom came in with a load of groceries and we got up to help. As we were putting things away, Paul walked in. So Adam said he'd call later. Then he left.

Saturdays are always busy but Mom had promised me a free day to spend with friends which meant being with Adam, of course. I'd decided to go semi-grub, it being a Saturday and all. Then I sent Adam an e-mail saying I was ready. Mom said guys are always late, it being a power thing, and I shouldn't take it personally. So I settled down to wait.

At about noon, I looked out the window and saw a van pulling up the driveway with Adam, all preppy with tan Dockers, an open-collared shirt and a sports jacket. Oh God! I was dressed all wrong.

Jerking the grungy sweatshirt over my head, I tossed it on the floor and threw on an oversized pink turtleneck. Next the blue jeans were replaced with stretch pants. I had a bulky sweater that went down to my knees, and I grabbed that just in case. Hearing Mom's footsteps in the hall, I flung open the door. "I'm not ready for this," I whispered, pulling her into my room.

"Don't be silly. You're going to the Volkman's to pick up the others. Then all of you will be going somewhere."

"It's Saturday, Mom. Kids don't dress like that!"

"He's fresh from a job interview and didn't have time to change." She looked me up and down. "You'll be fine."

"Oh sure - for church."

"You're going to have a good time. Just be sure to call if you're out past dinnertime." She smoothed my rumpled hair and gave me a pat on the butt, then pushed me out into the hall.

He was at the bottom of the stairs, looking up like someone waiting for the bride to descend. Stairs can be such a challenge. "Hey Adam. Sorry to keep you waiting."

"Lookin' good," he replied, his voice as smooth as butter. "I told your mom we'd hang out at the Volkman's for a while. After that, who knows?" He looked at Mom. "Right?"

"I trust you." It was the sort of thing you say to the babysitter. I could have died.

But he just nodded and put his hand on my shoulder, steering me out the door.

It took only a few minutes to get to the Volkman's. "Next year I'll be driving," I said as I got out of the car, then bit my tongue, knowing he could do the arithmetic.

"Sue drives."

"She's not supposed to." Another mistake. Change the subject. "Where was your interview?"

"At the Polo store. Just for the summer."

"You'll get it for sure."

We were at the front door and Matt opened it before the bell. "He'll get what?"

"He'll be getting down…" Adam sang, swinging his hips from side to side like someone in a rock band. "So why weren't you answering my calls?" he asked, giving Matt a playful jab.

"High times, my friend. I'll tell you later." Matt motioned us inside. "Everyone's downstairs. C'mon."

There were platters of sandwiches and chips and cans of pop on the bar. Jason was at the play station in one corner with Hannah leaning over his shoulder. A modified jukebox stood next to it. In the middle was a pool table and off to one side, a foosball game. "So how'd the interview go?" Sue chirped from her perch next to the bar.

"They said they'd call." Adam took off his jacket and threw it on the stool next to her. "Who's for a game of pool?"

So Matt and Adam had a match and I watched. Then Sue and Matt played a game and I watched. Jason peeled himself from the play station and came over with Hannah. We munched at the food and watched some more. No one invited me to play which was okay since I just plain don't know how.

Finally Adam put down his Coke and moved away from the bar, giving Matt a broad wink. "It's too nice a day to stay inside. Let's go for a drive."

No one objected, so we gathered up the food like polite teenagers and carried everything to the kitchen, finishing the cleanup just as Matt came down from his room carrying a backpack. "Where we heading?"

Adam shrugged. "Around."

"How about Summit South where we had the retreat?" I offered.

"Why not?"

And once more I was surprised. Maybe I would give *Sloppy Joe's* a try after all.

It was a beautiful drive into the country, with the sun warming the van enough to crack open the windows, taking our time and arriving at about three o'clock. The parking lot was empty. "Think they've booked?" Adam wondered.

"We might look around," Sue offered.

"Sure. Consider the possibilities," Matt said, and everyone laughed.

Our shoes crunched on the gravel as we walked up to the main building. The door was locked and we saw no one inside.

Continuing up the path we came to the row of cottages, stopping at the one where I'd stayed. "One of my cabin mates had a panic attack in the middle of the night. She just about broke down the door. Everyone was scared that we'd be stuck with paying for it so when it was time to go, we just jammed it shut." I pointed at the heavy door. "Looks like they still haven't fixed it."

It took less than a minute for Adam and Matt to pull the door out, motioning us to crawl inside.

The cottage was furnished with a set of bunk beds and a table surrounded by four chairs and two pull up chairs on either side of the fireplace. Off to the left was another room with two more bunk beds and a chest of drawers. To the right was the bathroom where Matt moved to check things out, turning on faucets, flushing the toilet and flipping on the lamps one by one. Everything worked. "Couldn't have planned it better myself." He ducked back out, returning with the backpack from which he pulled out two nickel bags. "How lucky can you get?"

The guys dragged the table and chairs toward the fireplace, making room for all of us. Then Matt rolled a joint, lighting it and passing it to on. I took tiny puffs, praying that I wouldn't choke and sent it on its way. Soon the room was blue with smoke with wisps curling up the open flu. "Like *The Night before Christmas,*" I giggled.

"You're out of it. Next Sunday is Easter," Sue snorted.

"No, no, no. Remember how Santa Claus comes down the chimney? Then it goes, it goes…" I couldn't remember the words.

"And the smoke curled around his head like a wreath," Adam said helpfully.

"Right. See how the smoke. .." They weren't interested.

"We should do more than sit and get stoned," Hannah said.

"Let's play twenty questions. The ones who don't guess have to take off their clothes." All the guys leered at Sue.

"What's twenty questions?"

"That's a question twenty times over." Everyone laughed.

"What's twenty questions? What's twenty questions? What's twenty questions…" The laughing got louder.

"Okay. I'll start. I'm thinking of an animal. You have to guess it in twenty questions," Adam said.

"What's an animal?" Jason asked, his tongue stumbling over the words.

"You are," Hannah replied.

More laughing.

"Your turn," Adam said, looking at me.

"Is it bigger than a bread box?"

"What's a breadbox?"

"Baker's Square," Adam replied, and that set everyone off again.

Questions went around four times. Is it in a zoo? Does it come stuffed? No one guessed that it was a rhinoceros. So everyone except Adam took off one shoe, tossing it in the middle of the table.

The next round was Sue's. It took only one question to guess that she was thinking of a red, white and blue pompon. Her other shoe hit the table.

Rings and watches didn't count. Five more questions and Sue was down to panties and bra. Everyone else wore a little more - pants, sweaters, tops - with me wearing the most. I might hate games but I'm good at puzzles.

Now it was Matt's turn. He reached for the bag and rolled another joint, taking a drag before handing it to Sue. "I'm thinking of something mineral."

"Is it bigger than a breadbox?"

"Would ten fit into a breadbox?"

"Would twenty?"

"Would I put it in a jewelry box?"

"Does it come in different colors?"

All the answers were no.

Three more rounds, and no one guessed. "Well?"

"It's an empty can of Campbell's Chicken Noodle Soup!" Matt crowed.

Now we were supposed to peel down one more. After all, rules are rules.

"No fair," I argued. "Guys can strip down a lot further than we can."

"And I'm not going to sit here butt naked," Sue said. "So I quit." She leaned over to get her clothes, but Matt grabbed them and held them over her head, out of reach.

"We can do it another way," Adam said helpfully. "Let's tattoo our clothes on."

"No way," Hannah said.

"Not real tattooing. We'll just paint them on. What can we use? Pens, pencils…"

Matt got up and dug into his backpack, coming up with a box of magic markers. Suddenly it was a new game. "Everyone has to peel down to the bare essentials. Then we'll begin. It's an exercise in trust." And everyone laughed.

I looked down at my pretty pink turtleneck. Oh, what the hell. I'd come this far. I pulled the shirt over my head, revealing nothing more than panties and bra. "I'm ready."

Matt began with a pink butterfly on each of Sue's shoulders. Hannah wanted a red bird winging its way across her bellybutton but Jason wasn't a very good artist so it looked more like a rust colored bat. I asked for a boa around my neck. It took Adam a long time, each feather a thin line, and I kept giggling because it tickled. Then I turned around and he added two pink dimples at the top of my butt because he though it was cute. We helped the guys draw snakes and hearts in the crooks of their arms with words printed across saying things like *Mother* and *Peace Now.* Then they drew peace symbols around their bare nipples and we laughed and laughed because it was so 60's.

By now it was getting late and we knew better than to turn on the lights even though we were pretty far off the road. So after putting the rest of the good stuff in Matt's backpack and flushing the ashes down the toilet, we got dressed and crawled back through the door wedge, propping it back so no one could tell we'd been there.

We were all hungry but Saturday night at the club was busy, mostly with grownups having dinner before going out on the town. *Topper's* was more to our liking. On the way there we all called home giving us freedom for the evening.

Toppers was crowded and we six had to squeeze around a table for four way in the back. Our food was a long time coming but we ate quickly, and when we finished, it was still early considering it was a Saturday night. Matt and Sue suggested we take in a movie, so once more I called home and Mom thought it would be okay. "Are you having a good time?" It's all she wanted to know.

After the movie we stopped back at *Topper's* for hot apple pie so it was past one when Adam pulled up in our driveway after dropping the others off. Hannah was in the back seat pretending to be asleep. The radio was humming softly as he turned off the engine. "I guess they're in bed," he said softly. "I'll walk you to the door."

This was it. He was going to kiss me goodnight. He wasn't gay after all.

Wordlessly I got out and he put his hand lightly on my shoulder as we went up the walk. "Mom always leaves the door open for me," I whispered. "It's her way of being motherly." I pulled the sweater tight around me. Opening the door, I stood with my face turned up to his. "I'm glad you came home so we could really get to know each other. I'd like to know you even better."

He put one hand under my chin, leaned down and kissed me ever so gently, sending an electric charge from my stomach down to my knees. "So am I. Everyone needs friends. And you're special, even though…" He straightened up and stroked my cheek. "You understand, don't you? We talked about it."

"Of course. That's what friends are for."

He ran his hand down my arm and squeezed my fingers. "See you in church?"

I nodded, glad it was too dark to see my face.

He turned and walked back to the van, waiting until I was inside to pull away.

As I mounted the stairs, there was a rustling sound in the hall. "Did you have a good time?" Mom had been asleep, her hair tousled, her fresh-scrubbed face wrinkled from the sheets.

"Oh yes. It was cool."

"Where did you go? What movie…"

"I'm really tired, Mom. I'm not used to…"

"I'll help you get ready for bed. We can talk." She began pulling at the pink turtleneck. "You haven't even washed your face. Can't do that to a teenage complexion."

Before I could move away, she had the turtleneck half off and stood staring at the boa painted around my neck.

"We were just fooling around, Mom. It was all innocent fun. It'll come off with soap or maybe nail polish remover," I whispered. "Please don't tell Paul."

What else did you take off?"

"What do you mean?"

"She looked me up and down. "Take off the tights."

"You don't think..."

She tugged at the pants and there they were, the two pink dimples. "What on earth happened? Was this some kind of orgy? I mean, we've had our talk, but..." She stared at me. "We'd better get you to a doctor."

Now I was crying. "Nothing happened, Mom. Honest. We just hung out for a while and then went to *Topper's* and then to a movie. Ask Adam. He can show you the movie stubs."

Her face was like stone. "Go to bed, Jayne. We'll talk about this in the morning."

"Tomorrow's Palm Sunday."

"Well then, later." She gave me her clinical look. "I have no idea what will get that stuff off."

I put my hands over my eyes.

"Okay. We'll talk about it tomorrow."

Then she was gone, leaving me to cry myself to sleep.

Chapter 25: Joy

MY SIXTH SENSE was telling me that things weren't quite right. It began simply enough. The schools were on spring break and the Leighton kids along with Sue and Jayne came to hang out. Elsie had made a tray of sandwiches and put out drinks and chips. With everything taken care of, I went shopping. Because the stores were crowded, I didn't get back until dinnertime. By then the kids had gone out and Elsie had left. Later Matt called saying they were going to a flick which was okay. Actually, it was more than okay because it allowed Gary and me to enjoy a quiet dinner by ourselves.

The next day was Palm Sunday and we went to the late service while the boys slept in, them having been out very late. The sanctuary was packed, it being entertainment time with two choirs, hand bells, and a harp along with the usual organ and grand piano. Lining the front were banks of Easter lilies, their sweet fragrance coming in waves to fill the room. And of course, Neville was superb in his robes of pure white with silver and gold brocade.

His sermon was short, celebrating traditions and holidays binding us together, looking at every man and woman like he was addressing them personally the way he always does. Afterward people drifted down to coffee hour and there were lots of smiles and hugs because Neville always made people feel so good about themselves that they wanted to prove how good they really were. I looked everywhere for Marva and Paul but I guess they'd stayed home. We did have a nice talk with Liz and Dave, that is, until Kelsey and John came bouncing up from Sunday school. But it was long enough for Liz, acting for Marva and the Women's Club, to get me committed to help set up the Easter coffee hour even though Gary and I would be something like guests of honor, being two of the new members in the induction ceremony.

I knew we'd decided on a spring theme for Easter, with hyacinths on the serving tables instead of the traditional baby orchids. Kim and Nancy, Carol's mother, would pour coffee and tea from the silver servers at opposite ends of the table with decorated petit fours and bite-sized creampuffs arranged on platters instead of the usual breads and rolls. Little girls in brand new Easter outfits would replenish the food from the kitchen. Others would circulate with Easter baskets containing chocolates and gourmet jellybeans. The youth group would do housekeeping, picking up stray napkins or collecting empty plates to take to the kitchen. Everything was planned to the smallest detail.

So the following day I arrived a little after ten to help with the set up, knowing it wouldn't take long. Carol and Liz were already there. "Hi!" My voice echoed in the empty room.

"Hi yourself. Marva's dropping some stuff off for Carrie. She'll be right back."

Carrie Cook was a college student hired to put together the monthly newsletter and be an office gopher. They call it an internship, which means they don't have to pay her, or at least not much. In between she helped Erma Willins, the vice president administration, plus Mary, the secretary, all of it adding up to a part-time job. Carrie talks with long words and looks down her nose when she speaks. She's studying journalism but fancies herself writing the Great American Novel. How small town can you get.

"Is everyone ready for Easter?" I asked, pulling out a chair next to Carol.

"I'm just buying some pre-filled baskets and be done with it. If Mother wants more, she's on her own."

I could have mentioned to Carol how I spent hours coloring Easter eggs, staying up until midnight to hide the jellybeans, about investing in

Easter outfits so they'd have a sense of religion even though we weren't going to church back then. But instead, I gave her strokes, saying, "You're so conscientious. Here I am on a perpetual diet, in and out of the gym, going to the Mall to try on this and that."

"It all evens out in the end."

I'd heard rumors as to why Carol and Tony got married, but I decided to change the subject since overweight people never take the hint anyway. I turned to Liz. "How about you?"

"I just drop Sue off at the Mall and she takes care of the rest. A few more months and she'll be driving. That'll help even more."

Down the hall, a door closed followed by the click of footsteps on the tile floor. Marva rounded the corner just in time to hear Liz's comment. "Jayne has six months to go before she can drive, and even then she might wait. As a matter of fact, we might insist."

"Where did that come from?" I asked, amazed at her turn around. "You said you couldn't wait for her to grow up."

"You're going overboard, Marva," Liz added. "It was just Magic Marker. No big deal."

"What Magic Marker?"

"Last Saturday the kids drove out to Summit, broke into a cottage and decided to give each other fake tattoos using Magic Marker," Liz explained. "It was just kids being kids."

"What kids? Ours? Neville's too? You're kidding!" Suddenly, it all made sense. Matt and Jason sleeping most of the day, wearing turtle neck shirts and long pants and ducking out as soon as they could. I started to laugh. "Well, at least Magic Marker comes off -- eventually."

"Jayne's were on her butt and down around her neck -- way down. Too far down." Marva's voice was accusing. "So when was the last time you checked on your own kids?" She turned toward Liz. "And maybe you should have a little talk with Sue. There might be things you aught to know about."

"Oh come now. They were just goofing around. I'll bet you did as much, or more, when you were young."

"They were trespassing," Marva insisted.

"If someone had seen them, they would have been sent home with a sharp reprimand -- nothing more. Dave and I talked about it. He agrees."

"Look at the big cities. Drugs, sex, gangs. We're nowhere near…"

Carol put her hands over her ears. "I don't want to hear it."

"City or country, it happened. Something more for the Advisory Committee to consider," Marva declared.

"Okay. Enough." It was Liz playing mediator. "What about Easter?"

So we returned to the schedule. Liz would pass out carnations to the women. Kids got candy. Men got boutonnieres. That would be my job. "Church will be packed. Maybe we should rent some tables and chairs and pray for good weather. Or maybe put up a tent."

"Prayer will have to do," Marva said. "There's no money for extras."

"More money *would* go a long way. At least it would make Steve a lot happier."

Marva and I exchanged glances. "So how often does your Advisory Committee meet?" I asked.

"Once a week - for now. But we're not supposed to talk about it."

"But you just said…"

"I didn't say what actually happened in the meeting."

"Well, Steve may be worried about the budget," I continued. "But for your information, there are some who worry about this sensitivity and self-actualizing business as well. You were at the retreat, Liz. Didn't you think some of it was out of place?"

"I'm just sorry there wasn't something like this when I was a teen," she replied. "Tears can be healing."

"Baloney," Marva snorted. "There's no such thing as a good cry."

"What else does the Advisory Committee talk about?" Carol asked.

"Well, right now we're focusing on the budget. That's the bottom line." Liz looked down at the papers in front of her. "But I really shouldn't be talking about it."

"Isn't the committee supposed to listen to what people say?" I persisted, trying to keep my voice innocent but friendly.

"I can listen," Liz replied, letting me know I was on the right track. "But I can't answer questions. That has to wait until the report comes out."

"Neville's playing with fire," Marva declared. "Psychologists spend years in training. Neville's doctorate is in education, not counseling. Mind games can be dangerous."

Carol thrust her chin. "Neville has the full confidence of Dr. Jones who happens to be a bona fide psychologist. He's won the hearts and minds of many others. I hope he will teach my kids to be the best they can be. As for Amity, I think Neville's the finest minister we've ever had, and that's saying a lot."

"This conversation is much too personal," Liz pleaded. "We shouldn't be talking this way."

"Actually, I like Neville," I said. "He keeps regular office hours, preaches a good sermon and is someone we can be proud of. That should be enough."

"The budget problem is not going away. A new direction will bring in new members," Carol declared. "And that's what Neville is trying to make happen."

"Maybe. But when it's being done in the name of Amity, we're also responsible." Marva insisted. "What if something goes wrong? Could we handle a lawsuit?"

"Look, I came here to plan for Sunday. If we're done, I'm leaving." Liz's voice was soft but her message was clear.

The silence could have been cut with a knife.

Then Marva spoke up, visibly pulling herself together. "You're right. There will be time enough later."

We finished by late morning and peeled off, one by one. Carol wanted to get a little more work done in her office before lunch. Liz had to pick up John from pre-school. That left Marva and me alone. So here was my chance. I followed her into the lady's room and after some prodding, got her to explain what had really happened with Jayne and why she'd missed church on Palm Sunday.

It all had to do with what had happened the day before. The way Marva told it, you'd think there'd been an orgy. Not that I approved. But Marva was in a real snit over the whole thing, a real turn around from the Mom who wanted her daughter to know everything about you know what. The upshot was that Jayne was grounded for the rest of spring break, killing any party plans, assuming of course that she'd been invited in the first place which was never a sure thing. When Marva gets mad, look out.

There was no talking to her. So finally I gave her a hug and told her she was still my best friend and hoped she wasn't mad at me, to which she replied that of course she wasn't. She was just upset that none of the kids had better sense and hoped I understood. So I left her there, putting on another touch of powder and lipstick, letting her cool off before going home. A friend can do just so much.

Back in the car, I just sat back and closed my eyes, letting the bright sun warm my face as I tried to return to my normal self, being relaxed and satisfied with my life as it was at the moment. I mean, why get all upset about something that's already happened or things you can't change?

Just then, a car squealed across the next aisle and onto the road, roaring around the corner toward the Interstate, narrowly missing two other cars. It was Jan Pollack in her Jaguar. I'd know it anywhere, that gorgeous piece of machinery outfitted with doggie kennels to chauffeur her animals to and from the vet. What in the hell was she doing at *my* church?

Chapter 26: Carol

Being a board membership makes people feel special. So there's never a shortage of candidates. People kiss up and strut or reminisce, dropping names as though there's no tomorrow. Although not a voting member, the Director or Religious Education holds a similar position of influence.

But there is always the accompanying grunt work, namely preparation for the meeting. Today I arrived early, and entered the deserted building, going to the Community room closet where the extra chairs were stored, placing twelve around the long table. I brought out glasses, napkins and ice water from the kitchen, along with note paper and ballpoint pens. Paul would bring the agenda and other handouts for distribution. Then I stood back, surveying the results. It had been a wonderfully warm day. Outside, the sun, a bright orange ball, was about to sink below the trees. Forty-five minutes to go. I turned and walked toward my office. Might as well use the time productively.

As I approached Neville's office, I heard him call out to turn on the lights. "Can't let you stumble and fall."

Obediently, I flipped the switch. "And you shouldn't be working in the dark," I added.

He looked up and squinted. "What time is it?"

"After seven. What are you working on?"

"It's that workshop in D.C. I was telling you about. The Board wanted the request in writing. Triplicate. With individual copies for each."

"I remember. But you didn't expect it to be ready by tonight."

He looked at me ruefully. "It's not. But space is limited so I have to get it in."

He'd told me about it a few weeks back after a particularly successful class session at the university when both of us were too excited to go home so we'd stopped for coffee. Conducted by psychologists, sociologists and theologians, it led to a certificate in group dynamics and counseling. It might serve to quiet the negative whispers coming from the Ministerial Advisory Committee. "Even if Amity isn't interested, I know Ken Jones will be pleased." I moved closer. "Anything I can do to help?"

He shook his head. "I'm almost done. Thanks anyway."

"Then I'll leave you." I closed the door behind me, returning to the main room.

Steve had arrived with financial statements to distribute. He now sat with Paul at the head of the table, the ledgers spread out in front of them.

Paul glanced up, his voice soft but tense. "Take a look at this, Carol. Attendance is down six percent and pledges are off by eight. Neville was supposed to raise those numbers."

I shrugged. "Another study by someone with an ax to grind."

"Figures don't lie," Steve shot back.

"Monthly bills. Sounds like home." As board secretary, Dave Mason's lack of secretarial skill made his job more inspirational than administrative. His big smile could disarm the toughest critic, convince the hardened skeptic. He could even sell the proverbial ice box to an Eskimo. Tony might have taken lessons from him. *What do you mean you don't need any more XYZ? Why, only last week I sold three times as much your neighbor. But I have something even better. Be the first one on your block…*

The other board members were now drifting in with Bill Presser dominating, as usual. "Long agenda, Paul. Need to get right down to business."

I got up to call Neville.

The board consisted of nine voting members, with Neville, Carrie Cook and I being ex-officio. They included Jared Cole, treasurer, Erma

Willins, vice president-administration and Debbie Conroy, vice president-program. These were the wimpy three who were no match for the established power base of Bill, Paul and Steve with Dave being the swing vote on many issues. Still, their votes had to be reckoned with.

When Neville and I returned, all had arrived, going over the spreadsheets in front of them.

"The meeting is called to order. The chair will entertain a motion to dispense with reading the minutes," Paul began.

"So moved," Debbie Conroy chirped.

"A second?"

"Second," Dave nodded.

"All in favor?"

The ayes were unanimous.

Then came Jared's report, monies spent on landscaping, window washing, copy machine maintenance… Bills were piling up. He suggested a special collection. Erma thought we should have a bake sale or maybe a carnival to raise funds. The Annual Pledge drive was around the corner. Not a good time to face a deficit. The board took the problem under advisement. Membership committee needed to be alerted. Hospitality too. Smiles faded. I looked at Neville, trying to read his expression, watching his eyes move from one face to another.

Next came Bill Presser's report from denominational headquarters. We were in arrears in our annual contribution. It was followed by Erma Willins' report on the decrepit copy machine. Payments on a new one would be added outlay. Carrie Cook offered to cut the newsletter pages in half to lessen the load but was told not to, given its importance as public relations. Sarcasm? Maybe.

I got up to refill the water pitchers while others stood and stretched. Next item on the agenda was the Minister's Advisory Committee.

Paul cleared his throat and everyone sat back down. "The Ministerial Advisory Committee has met and will continue as long as necessary. Of course, their deliberations are absolutely confidential."

Confidential? The MAC was a cauldron of gossip, innuendo and half-truths, each member trying to out-do the other, taking the discussions back home which, with luck, might remain secret until morning. "It's a good way to monitor a smooth transition," I offered. My voice sounded hollow.

Everyone looked at Neville.

"Comment?" Paul asked.

Neville shook his head.

Carrie leaned forward. "Maybe I should report it in the newsletter."

"It's confidential, Carrie," Paul said dryly. "So you need only announce that MAC exists, and indicate which members can be contacted."

"As old news," I muttered.

Paul now turned toward Neville.

"My turn?" Neville smiled.

"I'm sorry you had to wait," Paul said easily. "Unfortunately, tonight's agenda was long."

"No problem. It's just as well." Neville reached into his folder and pulled out copies of his proposal, distributing them around the table. "I'm applying for admission into the International Progressive Training Conference for Applied Behavioral Science Program for Community Change Specialists. It's a month-long certification program in Washington D.C. that will enhance my inter-personal skills and make me a better pastor and counselor. Only 36 persons in the entire United States will be accepted, and the registration deadline is at the end of this month." He took a deep breath. "The cost is about ten thousand dollars. Now, I know that's a lot of money, but I would be happy to drive, which would eliminate the plane fare. Of course, you would have to fill the pulpit in my absence. But I have two weeks vacation coming so I'm asking for only two weeks additional time."

The room was silent except for the rustling of papers. Paul looked up. "That's a pretty big chunk of money, Neville, given the financial rut we're in. Could we tweak it into something more manageable?"

Steve leaned forward. "Especially with all the other financial goings on. I hear you're on the payroll at the university. Couldn't that finance your trip? And by the way, how come we weren't told about it at the beginning?"

Neville seemed bemused. "It's not exactly a secret. If you'll notice, it's been on my schedule for weeks. Anyone interested could see it logged on in the office. These classes constitute my contribution to the community. It puts Amity on the forefront."

"With pay."

"Yes, of course. I'm a professional. You should understand that."

"In other words, it's a side job. And now you want even more time to pursue these interests," he persisted.

"The money wouldn't come close to covering the amount. Look at the numbers."

"You're also getting a stipend from the Housing Center?" Steve continued.

"It's a Federal grant that runs for a year. Again, it's a pittance."

"That may well be. But meanwhile, the attendance at Amity is falling and pledges are in arrears." Steve's voice was taking on the edge of a prosecutor.

Neville's gaze was unflinching. "The total time spent is what would normally amount to my days off. The rest is devoted to Amity. Would you rather I be lounging in a hammock or getting drunk with the boys?"

"You also have occasional income from weddings and funerals. And there are speaking engagements or writings available for added income," Steve continued. "Wouldn't that apply?"

"Hold on now," Bill interjected. "Neville has made a simple request to address one of our concerns. We should applaud that. I'd take a month off myself if I thought it'd help."

"I'll second that," Dave cried cheerfully.

"But what about the Sunday services?" Debbie Conroy wailed. "The program committee's budget is mighty slim."

"I know several seminarians who would be happy to speak without fee on any given Sunday. Most would jump at the chance," Neville replied.

"No doubt," Debbie nodded. "But we've just gotten off that merry-go-round."

There was a murmur of agreement.

"What's so important about this conference anyway?" Paul asked.

Neville settled back in his chair the way he does when preparing a speech. "This church can be a catalyst for community change. Our future can be glowing, and exceed our shining past. To do so requires members to become more aware, more enlightened, more cognizant of self. Now I understand that some people might find this threatening. They don't want to look inside. They don't want to examine how their very beings affect the others with whom they come in contact. Yet if we are to lead, that should come first." He looked directly at Paul. "Oh yes, I know there were feelings relating to the first Leadership Training class. And I have apologized. I wasn't being sufficiently sensitive. I have promised to do better."

I could feel Paul tense up. "This is not the time..."

Neville turned to Dave. "There were things being said about the Youth Group's retreat. But young people need to connect and trust one another, even if the process is painful. Many felt it was worthwhile. Some actually sought me out afterward to thank me. Not only after the retreat, but weeks later. So the program did have an impact."

"I never criticized the retreat," Dave murmured. "That must have been someone else."

"This conference will make me a better leader and organizer," Neville continued. "It will help me pace these programs so the participants will feel more comfortable with the process. It will make me a better minister and counselor and eventually contribute to the entire community. People talk about what Amity used to be. Well, those glory days are far from over."

"Is this workshop or conference or whatever it is going to provide you with additional certification?" Paul asked.

"Yes of course."

"By whose authority? The state? The American Psychological Association? The American Council of Churches? Who is to certify you? And how will this add to your qualifications? For example, as an architect, I must take certain classes to maintain my license. At the end I pass a test and am qualified to do certain things I wasn't qualified to do before. Is that what…"

"…this course does? Well, not exactly. It's more specialized than that. Ministers, psychologists, social workers will be applying from across the country, men and women with advanced degrees and diverse experience. I'm sure community outreach will provide press coverage across the country and Amity will be so honored."

"Sound more like public relations," Debbie said. "That may enhance our image, but we need something more solid."

"We don't want to preempt the MAC," Paul worried. "They're the ones who should determine the wishes of the congregation in matters such as this. Maybe a questionnaire…"

Bill shifted in his chair. "Let me suggest a compromise. Neville can take his vacation time and we'll fill the pulpit as needed. We do have five thousand budgeted for professional development. The rest will have to be carried by Neville himself." He looked around the table. "…if he still wants to go."

But Steve wasn't finished. "And what about the other matter -- teaching and working outside jobs? Shouldn't the board have been consulted?"

"One thing at a time," Bill replied. "Are we agreed that Neville should go to the conference?"

"That needs to be put in the form of a motion," Paul declared.

I pretended to study the handouts. There'd been some murmurings after the retreat and I'd become uneasy, knowing that Joy made some inferences about Neville and me – all untrue. I'd decided that trying to explain would only make matters worse. Now I wondered whether that had been a mistake. Certainly, trusting her was.

Finally at ten o'clock the motion passed with Paul and Steve voting the negative. Neville would be given the time off. Amity would subsidize half the cost. The rest would come out of Neville's pocket. Meeting adjourned.

The guys began to stack the chairs back in the storage closet and I returned to my office, hoping to find Neville and give him a few quiet words of encouragement.

The lights from the parking lot reflected eerie shadows as I entered the room, and flipped on the desk lamp. Steve and Paul, a conspiracy for power, turning a hiccup into an earthquake. What one didn't think of, the other did.

"Are you okay?" I hadn't heard Neville come in. Now he stood in the doorway, his smile warm and cheerful.

"Oh Neville, I'm so sorry."

He came to my desk and bent over, looking earnestly in my face. "It was more than I had the right to expect. I wouldn't have been able to go otherwise."

"A whole month?"

He nodded.

"I'll keep you posted on what's going on at Amity. You need to keep your fingers on the pulse."

"Good. Between your report and Sheila's, it'll be like I'm still here." He touched my shoulder.

"Are you almost finished?" Carrie had come down the hall and stood framed in the doorway. "Everyone else has left."

Neville took two steps back. "Yes. We were just closing shop." He looked at his watch, then back at Carrie. "It's still early. Could I interest you lovely ladies in a nightcap or a little wine before packing it in? I think the club stays open until midnight."

Carrie raised her eyebrows. "You're a man of boundless energy." But her smile said she was tempted.

He turned toward me. "Carol?"

I shook my head. With Carrie there, real conversation would be impossible. "Morning comes early at my house. But you two go ahead. I'll stay and lock up."

He turned to Carrie, his manner almost lighthearted. "My car is right outside."

I watched as they disappeared down the hall. Then shaking my head, turned to clear my desk. Obviously, I still had a lot to learn.

CHAPTER 27: JOY

A PLEDGE DRIVE is not a party. But this one came close, a catered affair with a string quartet playing soft elevator music as servers in black tuxedoes moved around with trays of canapés, asking whether anyone wanted something more to drink. Worthington Country Club had several private dining rooms and Amity had rented the one with wood paneling and thick carpets, the biggest and best. The lights were dim and candles on the tables gave a soft glow, all intended to loosen everyone up, or at least loosen up their checkbooks, the goal being to raise everyone's pledge by ten percent or more.

We sat with Paul and Marva, them having no special responsibility tonight since this was the Finance Committee's bash. As usual, Marva was gorgeous and dressed to kill in a black sheath that looked like Bloomingdale's but more likely came from Penney's after-Easter sale. Kim and Bill Presser joined us a few minutes later. We hadn't see Gerda and Werner Stahl for some time so it was a surprise when they asked if the other seats were taken. So that made up our table of eight.

Dinner was prime rib, au gratin potatoes, fresh asparagus with hollandaise plus Caesar salad and two different wines. Dessert was cherries jubilee flambé, served the way they do in British movies with the waiters marching in with trays all on fire held high over their heads. Everything was free, including the bar. It began at seven and by the time dinner was over and people had mellowed out, it was close to nine. Time to get serious.

The head table looked like a Senate hearing with committee members having a gold lettered name tag in front. The center of the table held an arrangement of spring flowers with ivy cascading gracefully over the pleated skirt. Off to one side was a computer to be used in Steve's presentation, its lights blinking red, amber and green.

I could see Steve smoothing his lapel and straightening his tie as he prepared to speak. Poor guy. Out-dressed by the kitchen help. Finally he stood and held up his hand for silence which took a while, the audience being prepped with hard liquor and good will. "Welcome, members and friends of Amity. Our pledge drive is one of the highlights of the year. We hope you are enjoying the evening."

The applause was loud and enthusiastic.

"I'd like to ask that you recognize members of the committee who have made this possible." He held up his hands like an orchestra conductor, motioning the members to stand amid scraping of chairs.

More applause.

"As we all know," he continued, "this year has been a busy one for Amity. After years of uncertainty, we have hired a minister and now have the stability we've yearned for." There was a further smattering of applause and Neville stood to take a bow.

"We've also hit numerous byways and turns," Steve went on, "burdened with financial commitments and budget shortfalls. In addition, there were the usual changes in the congregation as people moved away or changed their life styles, replaced by younger blood that might have hardier constitutions but thinner pocketbooks."

A chuckle rippled across the room.

Steve walked to the computer table and upon a hidden signal, a large screen behind the table dropped down. The program began with displays of the current budget, proposed budget and current balance sheet.

Paul and Bill sat with eyes glued to the screen while Gary flirted politely with Gerda, and Marva and I began to whisper about Sheila's outfit that was circa 1980s. Kim and Werner stroked their wine glasses and others fiddled with their drinks or shifted in their seats, waiting for a chance to escape now that the fun was over.

Then came Debbie Conroy, the Program Committee person who bounced up and down, acting all excited and up-beat about art fairs, concerts, monthly forums, theater groups and a well-stocked library, all which the Rotary Club did better and cheaper. I'd attended lots of these programs with Gary at places like Hawaii or Palm Springs, showing salesmen how to make a pitch. Speakers would show how to warm up the audience, got them to feel personally involved, then hit them with the pitch. *1) This is our product. 2) This is how it relates to you.* 3) *This is how much it will cost.* Bingo. The sale was made and they signed on the dotted line. Steve's program was a good start with a dinner that showed a picture of Amity. That was Number One. But Debbie's number two had nothing new to offer. Steve's number three had even less. So it added up to a net loss.

Then Neville stood up. "I'd like to add a little something to Debbie's list." He smiled as he walked toward the head table. "And that's our new program of leadership training." He turned toward his audience.

"Last August, I was introduced to a new world. Amity Congregational Church asked me to be its minister and I accepted. Although I don't like analogies, I must say it has been a happy courtship, at least as far as I'm concerned." Neville's baritone voice projected to the far reaches of the hall. "I am getting to know you and you are getting to know me. I hope you like what you see." There was a ripple of applause. "Together, we can make Amity a power in the community, a voice to be heard, a commanding influence not only within its walls, but stretching out to Worthington and beyond. Equally important is that I know myself and you know yourself. Philosophers have said it, psychologists picked up on it and theologians embraced it. Know yourself and recognize who you are and what you can still become. After that, all things are possible. That was Jesus' message. It is in essence, the message of all great religions. Learn to love yourself. Then you can love your neighbor."

Gary and I exchanged glances. Neville had taken over.

"In January we embarked on an adventure together," Neville continued. "We called it Leadership Training. Through it we are learning to listen to one another and work as one, empowering us to understand, not just on the surface but within the deepest reaches of our innermost being. This is unique. It is something that contributes not only to one another but to the community as a whole."

Now I happen to know that half of Amity's members have ongoing relationships with their shrink. Not that I mind psychiatrists making a living. And people have to spend their money somewhere. It might as well be on making themselves feel good. On the other hand, the church could be cheaper and less painful. As for me, keeping a Positive Mental Attitude does the trick.

"Because your comments have indicated a responsive chord," Neville's voice now rang out like a TV evangelist, "we will be embarking on a second round of Leadership Participation. There will be several groups. I can even foresee a need for Leadership III in the near future."

A smatter of applause. Close, but no cigar.

Suddenly Bill Presser stood up. "Although at first skeptical, I like the direction this is taking. As a matter of fact, I enthusiastically endorse Neville's program because, to be frank, I have reaped its rewards in a very personal way. I know it works." He moved toward the center where Neville stood. "Amity needs someone like Neville to take the lead and give us a new direction. Worthington is changing. We must also change."

I looked at Kim whose eyes were fastened on her wine glass, her face without expression. Carol and Tony were at the next table their backs to us and I couldn't see their response. Mirabelle, in a seat across from them, sat impassively, her face inscrutably Indian. But at most of the other tables, people were responding with smiles.

Bill continued, his voice rising to a bellow, his great bulk towering over Neville. "So I want to be the first submitting my pledge for the next fiscal year. As an expression of our support, Kim and I will increase our pledge by 50%. And I challenge the rest of you to increase yours as well -- as much as you are able."

After a moment of stunned silence, members of the finance committee leaped up and started circulating from one table to the next, armed with pledge cards to be signed right then and there.

Before I could gulp down my surprise, Gary stepped forward to say how much Amity had meant to us as a family. Then he pledged a generous increase as well. Bill came over and slapped him on the shoulder like a good buddy. Suddenly I saw the new bedroom furniture I'd been promoting going out the window. But I pasted a smile on my face and applauded with the rest of them. Bill's contacts had made many things possible. This was not the time to argue.

Werner and Gerda were whispering to one another. I wasn't sure whether they'd signed the membership book, and a pledge wasn't required anyway, but when they were handed the form, it was signed with a big smile and placed in the collection basket.

Now Neville, Bill and Gary moved from table to table, glad-handing like Hollywood promoters. Marva and Sheila sat open mouthed and Steve's face was sour as usual. No one likes being up-staged. Of course pledges are only IOUs, but they're a start. Who was in and who was out? The pledges would tell.

Steve stood up, anxious to take the meeting back. "Let's say it again. Amity has a mission. Amity is important to Worthington. Amity will survive!"

Survive? Was it that bad? There was a moment of silence, or maybe it was surprise. Then everyone continued talking and the room became cheerful again.

In the middle of the hubbub, servers began moving back and forth, clearing the tables. It was time to go. Neville stepped forward, then called for silence to pronounce a blessing on our journey back home.

I leaned over to Marva. "Staying for a nightcap?"

She looked startled. "Oh I don't know. It's pretty late."

"Oh c'mon. It's not even eleven."

"He's planning another series of Leadership Training," she hissed.

"Well, no one *has* to participate. It's strictly voluntary," I replied, trying to calm her down.

"Since when did you change sides?"

"Well, some of his ideas do make sense. I mean, saying we need to understand ourselves before we can understand someone else is pretty positive." I glanced at Bill and Gary standing elbow to elbow. I know what side my bread is buttered on.

"Joy, he's using the name of Amity. That means if something happens, we're all responsible."

I was getting annoyed, or maybe it was because I'd had a few drinks and it was late. "Quit beating a dead horse."

She looked like I'd slapped her.

I almost apologized but then Gary came over carrying my coat. "How about a nightcap? Some are staying." That meant Bill was staying. Never pass up an opportunity.

She shook her head. "Paul has an important meeting in the morning."

There was a dark tone in her voice, like a warning. So I let it go and told her I'd call her.

At the bar there was a lot of self-congratulation, exactly the way it should be after a successful fund drive even though it probably wasn't. Sheila and Kim managed to smile and tell a few lame jokes. The Finance Committee came a few minutes later, joining in as much as they could even though they're a pretty serious bunch, especially when headed by someone like Steve whom Gary calls anal retentive.

Last call from the bartender was at midnight and we were out of there soon after, parading to the parking lot like good buddies. The evening had seemed kind of strange without Marva, but if she didn't want to participate, so be it. Gary and I have always been able to make our own fun. Not many people can say that. Not even Marva.

Chapter 28: Kim

I HATE ENTERTAINING. But when Bill wants something, there's no stopping him. So I agreed to invite some friends for an early summer event before things got too busy. It would be the last time I gave in before deciding about school.

Poets sing of June and I heard myself humming in spite of myself as I watched our summer furniture being pulled out of storage and placed onto the deck. Maybe the evening would be warm so people could spill outdoors to the scent of flowers and newly mown lawn. The caterers were to arrive at five-thirty and the guests about seven when Bill was scheduled to come home. There was a time when he arrived early, but I cured him of that.

Back inside, I went into the library and raised the windows. Taking a deep breath, I allowed my mind to wander. Kimberley Crawford. Class valedictorian with a size seven hat and a thirty-six inch bust. Vassar wasn't know for its psychologist program. Maybe I could go to the University of Chicago, UCLA or Berkeley. California might be a good choice.

I sat back on the recliner, picturing myself on the beach, hair bleached like straw down to my waist. Or walking into *City Lights Bookstore* on the North Beach. Maybe students still practiced pagan rites under a full moon, whirling in and out of the trees while a crackling bonfire sent sparks into the sky.

"We're finished with the deck, Mrs. Presser. Is there anything else?"

I looked up. "Did you hang the lanterns? I'm hoping that people can stay outside for a while."

"Yes Ma'am. All cleaned and filled with fresh kerosene."

Sam and Will had been doing odd jobs for Bill's family long before I entered the picture. They lived down the hill and had been there forever. Roots. They'd never wanted anything more, working beside their father after school, then doing the handyman chores when Leroy could no longer lift the tool box. "Thank you. You did a nice job."

When the caterers arrived, I went upstairs to get ready, taking my time in the shower. Just as I turned off the water, there was a tap on the bedroom door. "Kim baby, I'm home."

I reached for my satin robe, a gift from Bill that was absolutely useless but one he insisted I wear. "Good. You can check to see that the bar's set up. I'll be down in half an hour."

His voice grew louder. "Open up. I've got something to tell you."

"Later. I'm still getting dressed."

"That's okay. Let me in. This is important."

Reluctantly, I opened the door.

"Not to worry. They've got the downstairs under control," he declared, locking the door behind him.

"I have my own routine and you're a distraction," I insisted, pulling my sash tighter. "Makeup takes ten minutes and I haven't even decided on what to wear. I'll never be ready on time."

Our bedroom is divided between the sleeping area and another section furnished with settee, chairs, lamps, and so on. When we first married, Bill had a canopy with draperies constructed over our bed, saying it made him feel like Louis XV overlooking Versailles. But after almost suffocating, he agreed to tie back the curtains and finally gave it up entirely, won over by the waterbed. Now I crossed to the dressing table, pressing my body protectively against the back of the chair.

He sat across from me and watched as I applied clarifier, then smoothed on liquid makeup to cover the fine lines beginning to appear. "Neville and Sheila are coming tonight."

"You already told me that," I said, eyeing him through the mirror.

"Neville told me about a nifty retreat in California. I think I might go."

"Why so tentative?" I turned and faced him. "Do you need my approval?"

"You've been talking about going back to school. I just wanted you to know that I might have my own plans."

"Are you jealous? Or is it the money?" I reached for the lipstick brush. "Because I fully intend to finance it myself - if I do go."

"Now who's tentative?"

"You're always telling me to keep my options open." I ran a comb through my hair. "I'm just following your advice."

"Your flattery warms the cockles of my heart."

"I knew it would." Hitching up my robe a few inches, I moved toward the dressing room door, closing it behind me.

"Sanctuary! No gentleman would dare invade a woman's boudoir, right? Room's too damned small to accommodate both of us anyway." His voice reverberated through the door.I opened the door a crack. "We're not alone, you know. Do you want all of Worthington to hear?"

He got up. "Believe it or not, I just came up to talk. Thought you'd like that. Christ! There's no pleasing you." He turned toward the door. "You're right. Someone needs to check the bar."

I heard the bedroom door close and I reached for the black dress and pearls. Guests were expected any minute and I still had to check on the caterers.

The first to arrive were Gerda and Werner who quickly established their spot next to the bar for the rest of the evening. Next came Carol and Tony along with Nancy, Carol's mother, which meant they'd hired a babysitter, a real compliment although given Carol's job, something they could probably now afford. Joy and Gary Volkman were next, arriving with great fanfare, as usual. Bill had chosen to take them under his wing - another area of disagreement. Good looking, but too pushy for my taste. Then more people came in groups of two or more - Dave and Liz, and Scottie Smythe with her new boyfriend, Herb. There were others, all sustaining members of the church. By the time Neville and Sheila came, everyone was mingling comfortably throughout the house and onto the deck as I'd hoped.

After seeing that everyone was taken care of, I got some wine and a few canapés for myself and went out on the deck. The moon was high in the sky, a sliver of light against the pinkish glow of the setting sun. Lanterns gently swayed back and forth on hooks extended from the rail overlooking the lawn. In one corner of the deck, an electric waterfall splashed against gnomes and frogs along its watery path.

"Hey Kim, come and join us. Plenty of room." Dave stood up and pulled out a chair. "We were talking about the pledge drive. I think it's going to be okay."

I sat down, my glass on the table in front of me. "Are the pledges coming in?"

"I didn't say that. I said it's going to be okay. Leadership II is fully subscribed and there are two more leadership classes in the works, with a number of non-members enrolled, namely business leaders with plenty of clout. So growth is on the horizon. We're going to weather the storm and prove that there's more than one way to skin a cat."

"Too bad Steve and Mirabelle had to be out of town," I said.

"His mother hasn't been well," Nancy murmured.

"Then that's where he belongs," Liz agreed.

"So where do we go from here?"

Everyone turned toward Neville who was leaning against a post with his arm draped casually around Sheila's shoulder. "You have to decide how much you want to take on," he smiled. "As we become more loving, more engaged, more forthcoming in our daily lives - and I say we, because I benefit as much if not more than anyone - people will want to know why and how. Once that happens, we'll not only increase in membership but will be making a real impact on the community."

"I'm for that, at least the loving part," Tony declared, raising his glass.

"And maybe we could begin a Bible class," Nancy murmured. "I can't tell you how much I've missed those weekly gatherings."

"Tell us about California," Liz interjected.

"Yes. How long before it falls into the ocean?" Bill asked.

"I can swim," I replied easily.

"So you've decided?" Liz asked.

"I didn't know it was common knowledge. But yes, I'm going back to school."

"In seminary?"

"No, of course not. But then again, it's something to think about." I held up my glass, struggling to maintain a sense of confidence. "Anyone need a refresher? I'll have some more canapés brought out while I get a refill."

"Thatta girl," Bill declared. "Live it up."

I gritted my teeth. "I intend to."

The living room was bright and noisy and I worked my way toward the bar, trying to be a good host, determined to be more engaged, more forthcoming. Gerda was draped languorously on the couch, her fingers caressing her glass, her foot swinging provocatively. Despite everything, she seemed quite alone. "Looks like you found your niche," I smiled. "Everything okay?"

"Couldn't be better."

"Still house hunting?"

"I'm beginning to like hotel living. Werner doesn't mind and it makes life so much easier."

"I'm sure it does." I patted her on the shoulder and moved on, my pity muted by scorn. A woman living in her husband's shadow. She had only herself to blame.

I swallowed the last of my wine and arrived at the bar for a refill then asked a server to bring a tray of canapés out to the deck.

Back outside, the sun had set and the lanterns' flickering light bounced across the tables, throwing enough warmth to feel comfortable. The patio was deserted. Then a voice came out of the shadows. "Bill's showing everyone where he's going to put the swimming pool. I said I'd stay behind in case you needed anything." Gary stood up swaying before he pulled out a chair next to me. "But I don't think you're a lady who does."

"Need something?" I steadied myself against his shoulder. "Oh my dear friend, if only you knew. And another drink won't help, I'm afraid." It was more than I'd intended to say.

"You don't say? Actually, that's what I was thinking. Like I felt it all along. Like a sixth sense."

The server had followed with the canapés and set the tray on the table in front of us. "I didn't know it was obvious."

"Kim, *obvious* is the last word I'd use to describe you. I mean, some people are obvious, like Jan and Max. Not that I don't like them, mind you. As a matter of fact, Max is the best boss I ever had. Totally up front. *What You See Is What You Get.*" A lock of hair had fallen across his forehead and he appeared almost boyish. "Know what I mean?"

I nodded. "I feel like I've known them for years."

"It's kind of sad."

"I've tried to help him. I really have."

"A lot of people have. That's why it's so sad." He moved the plate of canapés closer. "I noticed you at their Christmas party. You were so kind and gentle."

"Really? I wasn't aware of you at all. I suppose that's what happens at large parties. Everything is so confusing."

"I noticed you right away and told myself that you were someone I should know better. So I'm finally getting my chance."

I took a canapé, then sat back against the cushions. "I'm going back to school, you know. I'll be studying psychology."

"Is that so? Well good for you! I'll tell you, psychologists are really needed. You wouldn't believe all that's going on in the world."

"I'm more worldly than you think. Years ago I was marching, carrying a sign saying *Make Love, Not War,* participating in campus sit ins…"

"Well I do admire you for that. And now you want to help people again. Bill's a lucky man."

"Bill thinks I should mind my own business."

"Maybe he's just trying to protect you. Like I say, there are some strange ones out there."

"Max isn't strange. He's just sick. He needs to get help." I lowered my voice to a whisper.

"You mean rehab?"

"That's what I was trying to tell Jan."

He was quiet for a long moment. "Well, maybe I shouldn't be saying this." He held up his right hand. "But if you promise not to tell..."

"I promise."

"We think Jan's coming to Neville for counseling. Joy saw her a couple of times leaving the parking lot."

"You're suggesting...?"

"Not for herself. For Max. It has to be hush-hush because of business. Imagine how this could impact our creditors. The bankers would flip."

"Maybe..."

"Sh - they're coming back. Now remember, you promised."

Bill's voice echoed from below. "Skinny dipping in the moonlight. Sure can't do that in the club." He trudged up the steps, breathing hard. "Invitation only, and no peeking."

"Better than a hot tub," Carol laughed.

"So what do you think?" Bill asked, sliding on the chair across from me. "Have I your approval Madam Counselor?"

"You'll do as you choose. But my decision has suddenly gotten easier," I replied.

"I thought it was a done deal." Bill leaned back and addressed Neville who'd just come up from the lawn. "Isn't that what all the telephoning and e-mailing and networking was all about?"

"Kim is a strong woman. What she does is for you two to decide," Neville smiled. "I just work here."

"Men!" I snorted. "You think you know everything. But you don't know me - not any of you." I took a long swallow of wine.

There was a long silence as everyone looked at me. Suddenly my heart began to pound. My stomach felt like lead and I could feel a cold sweat creeping up my arms and forehead.

"Oh Christ, get her to the bathroom."

Suddenly I was on the couch staring up at dozens of heads, all jockeying to get a better look. Slowly everything gray began to turn back to its natural color. Phil, a member of Amity's council and a hospital internist was holding my hand. "We'll keep the blanket on you for a while. Don't want you to go into shock."

"At least we know she's not pregnant," Bill said, and everyone chuckled.

"I fainted?"

"Gary carried you inside." Joy smiled. "He works out every morning at the club. Might as well put it to use."

"Did I say anything? I mean, afterward."

"This was not a death bed scene, Kim. You just passed out."

I looked at Gary. "Thank you."

"It was nothing."

"You're a good listener."

His eyes softened. "Any time."

I looked around anxiously. "This wasn't much of a party."

"Oh yes it was!" Carol cried, and everyone laughed.

"But it is time to go. Enough excitement for one evening," Phil said as he reached to check my pulse.

So between Neville and Sheila and Liz and a few others, the party wound down while I was unceremoniously put to bed.

The next morning, I felt much better and concluded I must have picked up a virus. But Bill gave me no quarter. From his standpoint I was drunk which was less of a sin than not being able to hold my liquor. So much for love and understanding.

Chapter 29: Joy

THIS SUMMER THERE'S so much to worry about. Jason hopes for a job at the Club, but his chances are slim being only fifteen. Matt has a year to go in school. I don't know if I could handle graduation on top of everything else like holding Gary's hand when he comes home what with everyone's waiting for Max to be put out to pasture and no one knowing who will take his place. Then there's Marva in a snit, sitting at home, sulking about God only knows what. On top of all that, Kim is treating Gary like her new best friend never having seen through Gary's song and dance learned at his high school drama class. No wonder her boys are such dorks. Bill's world isn't exactly on the cutting edge but at least he keeps up his end of the conversation. Kim just sits and looks at you with those droopy eyes. If only she'd say something, even something weird or goofy so we could have a chance to laugh.

And another thing. Neville will be leaving for D.C. in about a week and he's so busy with that and his sermons are getting boring. So everyone's playing the rating game, keeping score. Was it a hit or a home run? I have to admit I'm not much at knowing the difference. I'm still working on getting up early on Sundays. Gary says *The Bloom Is off the Rose*, which sounds like he heard it from Kim.

Actually, all this is under the surface and not much is really happening which makes me restless. Spring shopping is done and there's not much money left for extras, what with Gary's increase at the pledge drive which of course we have to honor since he committed it there in front of everybody. Imagine us bailing out the church. What happened to *God helps those who help themselves?*

Still, I didn't hold it against him even though he knew I'd had my heart set on re-decorating our bedroom. I'd even had the colors picked out. But being a good wife, I started looking around for things that would occupy my time while I waited for him to make it up to me. The Club was pretty well run and I'm not into sports except for sitting at the pool sipping a cold something. Maybe I could become more active with Amity. With Marva losing interest, there was definitely a space to fill.

So today being Sunday, it would be a good time to look around. The church was dressed for summer with tulips and azaleas in the atrium and the front of the church. Even the choir was lightweight, singing songs where you could actually understand the words. I nodded toward Bill and Kim as we passed toward our seats, glad they'd found their spot so we wouldn't have to be sitting with them. Liz and Dave had said good morning when we came in, then gone downstairs to take their turn with the little ones. Sheila must have been to the early service since she was nowhere around. And if anyone manages to stay visible, it's the minister's wife.

A few stragglers came in after us and it took the usual few minutes for everyone to settle in. Out of the corner of my eye I saw Paul come in alone and take a seat toward the back. Then the organ swelled into Neville's theme song and our attention was front and center.

Neville began with a couple of readings from the Bible like *To everything there is a season, and a time to every purpose under the heaven…a time to love, a time to hate…* and something else about potters having power over the clay. He read a couple of poems. We sang a couple of hymns. The choir stood in their white summer robes and did their thing while the ushers passed the collection baskets, all in preparation for the main attraction -- Neville's sermon.

As usual, his voice was casual, his eyes friendly. "I've been a closet bird watcher from way back," he began. A smile tugged at the corners of his mouth. "Now I don't know how many of you browse the Net, but for me, it's like eating popcorn. You can't do just one. So I indulged myself, stopping for a moment at the site describing the American eagle. Suddenly, the topic of this Sunday's sermon, the one before going on my sabbatical jumped out at me. It has to do with the coming of spring and the beginning of summer, of birth and re-birth, metaphorically speaking."

I looked at the ceiling. Bird watching on the Internet. Ho hum.

Neville continued talking about how eagles mated for life. How they selected another mate only when one of them died. How they could live up to thirty years. After mating, how the female laid two to three eggs and how duties of both parents are shared. "So why is this a Sunday morning sermon? My purpose is not to teach you to be bird watchers." He paused. "It's something more internal, more central to whom we are. It's about how eagles relate and how you and I also relate.

"The eagle's nest is made up of twigs, moss, grass, feathers and conifer branches. Both parents take turns sitting on the eggs. But taking turns is not all sweetness and light. She may have to coax him to take over. Or she may not want to move and *let* him take over. There's pushing, shoving, and occasionally one gets hurt. *My turn* is not necessarily the same as *your turn*."

He leaned forward. "Now I've read lots of articles about men and women being on different wave lengths. She's caring for the children while he's pursuing his career. Then when the kids are grown and flown, she's ready to pursue her career, while he is finally ready to relate to his family. Some cast blame on society, on personality or even on finances. Granted, this can be painful and even threatening. On the other hand, it can also prove exhilarating and fulfilling."

My mind began to drift, wondering when the outside pool at the club would open, wondering if Jason might qualify as a lifeguard. I ran through SAT reviews I'd heard of, thinking that Matt might want to take it a second time to boost his score.

"Newly hatched eaglets are helpless," Neville continued. "But once the fledglings are ten to thirteen weeks old, the down is replaced with strong feathers. They're now ready to fly. At that point, the parents are ready for tough love. No more feeding. No more comfortable brooding, sheltered from the cold winds at night. The eaglet must learn to stand alone."

Matt and Jason ready to fly? I looked up at Gary but his eyes said he was daydreaming, his thoughts a million miles away.

"The eaglet's parents fly by with fresh kill, darting ever so close but never quite offering the food. Finally, the day comes when the parents swing by once more, tantalizingly close. At the same time, there is a gust of wind and the young bird, hungry almost to the point of starvation, is lifted and soars over the treetop, landing far below in the valley. He pounces on the piece of flesh the parent has dropped for him, eating for the first time in days. Nothing has ever tasted so good. The rest is practice."

Neville took a step back, his hands resting lightly on the edge of the podium. "Becoming is not easy. Learning is not easy. Each of us must face the first flight, surmount the barricade on the edge of the nest and with the help of those around us and a fortuitous gust of wind, soar over the valley and become what we were meant to be."

He was winding down. What I was meant to be. What you were meant to be. What Amity was meant to be. And then the clincher. "We get from here to there by following the path I've just laid out. Listening and learning to love. Amen."

My empty stomach rumbled, anticipating brunch.

In the foyer, we did the usual greetings, handshaking and kissie-kissing then made a beeline for the club. Paul had disappeared, so I didn't get to ask him about Marva and why she hadn't called. In the parking lot we were joined by Bill and Kim and since we were going to the same place, decided to all go in their car.

"Well, what did you think?" Bill asked, his voice rumbling over the sound of the air conditioner.

"One of his best," Gary replied, knowing that's what Bill wanted him to say.

"Right. None of that Bible crap about miracles or magic. Hells bells, there's already too damned much of that on TV. Refreshing to hear something original."

"It stands on its own merit," Kim declared. "You don't have to take it any further." She turned to Gary. "Don't you agree?"

"Neville always does a good job."

"It's like he's talking directly to me," she continued.

"He has a way of doing that," I agreed. Let her let her live in her own fantasyland.

"He knows how to connect with his audience. No script. No notes. Just human interaction straight from the heart. He's willing to put away the books and live a little."

Kim stiffened. "I happen to find comfort in the world of ideas."

"That's you. But Neville's grounded in reality," Bill replied, "not pie in the sky. God formed our bodies to be more than a stick supporting the brain." He pulled into a parking space and turned off the engine.

She eyed him up and down as she got out of the car. "Except, it's been a while."

If it had been Carol, we might have laughed.

Bill remained unruffled. "We go around this life only once. So I intend to make the best of it. I'll feast my eyes on beauty, utilize all of my senses and savor my surroundings." With that, he put out his arm and steered me inside, leaving Kim and Gary to follow.

We found Steve and Mirabelle, back from visiting Steve's mother at the last empty large table and cheerfully joined them, knowing the spaces would be filled shortly. The server was right there with the champagne, although Steve and Mirabelle declined which wasn't a surprise since I'd spotted Steve as a recovering alcoholic from the get go. As for Mirabelle, she was a person who spent all of her energy making life hard. The more it hurt, the better.

"Beautiful day," I murmured. "Almost warm enough to go swimming."

"What did you think of the sermon?" Mirabelle asked. Nothing like the direct approach.

"Pretty interesting," I replied, trying not to be too specific.

"Some say it's the turkey that should be our national bird," Bill nodded, winking at me. "I'd vote for that."

"We go to church to be inspired and uplifted. I want to hear what God had to say. I want something spiritual. Birds can be studied at home."

Bill's expression darkened. "So can the Bible." He turned toward the buffet table. "The line looks like it's thinning out. How about it?"

We got up, leaving Mirabelle and Steve to their complaints. When we returned, Gerda and Werner had squeezed in next to them along with Liz and Dave.

"Sue's working at Bergner's in the Mall," Liz said as I took the chair next to her. "She didn't tell them her age. We'll have to chauffer her, but that's okay. It'll keep her busy."

I watched as she got up and walked toward the buffet. Solid Liz. Everyone's big sister and Marva's best friend. At least she was until I came along. Just goes to show how flighty Marva could be.

"So what does everyone think of the Eagle's Nest? Anyone taking bets?" Werner preferred guy talk.

"It was a homerun," Gary replied. "A worthy speech for closure."

The chit-chat continued which allowed me to concentrate on brunch. From time to time a few sentences would carry over from the other side of the table. Neville, pledge units, program, budget, and mostly about money. Not that everyone had suddenly gotten poor. Far from it. Worthington was booming along with the Chamber of Commerce, the Elks, Lions, Country Club and even the churches. All except Amity.

Meanwhile, I focused on Liz, talking about new clothing, makeup style and summer plans. If Kim and Mirabelle felt left out, too bad. As for Gerda, she just smiled and nodded dreamily, a woman permanently out of it.

Later, people began moving around the room, which is what the Club membership is all about. Then, lucky for us - meaning just the opposite - Gary spotted Max and Jan coming in and they sat at the table with Neville and Sheila. Since we'd brought the Leightons and Pollachs together in the first place, Gary saw it his duty to go over and say hello. Pretty soon Steve and Mirabelle got up and left along with Gerda and Werner, the coming and going natural at a Sunday buffet. Bill and Kim left next after I told them we could get a ride back with someone else, moving close to Liz and Dave, giving them my animated best. And pretty soon Liz was laughing and showing she had a lighter side and could actually be funny. By the time Gary came back from his tour of the dining room, we were having such a good time I'd almost forgotten about Amity's problems. I'd even put Max and Jan out of my mind. Of course Liz and Dave offered to drop us off seeing we were the only ones left.

Walking back to the car, it was like we'd known each other forever. And why not? We had a lot in common. Gary and Dave were in sales and Liz and I stay at home moms. Like I say, every woman needs a best friend.

CHAPTER 30: LIZ

DIPLOMACY IS HARD work. And when faced with a crisis, you need all the help you can get. We were counting, aware that attendance was shrinking faster than the usual summer decline. It wasn't time for panic, but getting close.

Neville had returned from his D.C. training lab filled with enthusiasm, ready to expand his sensitivity workshops. He presented his ideas to a handful of followers and even though he'd been selective, the notion spread that this had become some kind of mystery cult. Steve scheduled a Minster's Advisory Committee meeting two days later.

I tried to make the best of it.

Nancy once more provided cookies and ice tea and if Steve hadn't looked so grim, it would have been a pleasant afternoon. But this was all business. No small talk or chit-chat allowed.

Armed with an array of papers, Steve began by handing out the financial report. Pledges were being paid too slowly, already behind projections by ten percent. Sunday collections were soft. "Granted, people are on vacation. But this goes beyond the norm. We've got to stop the bleeding." He stared at Neville. "Any ideas?"

"Are you suggesting this is my fault?"

"I'm suggesting that you be part of the solution."

Nancy turned to Neville. "We need to come up with some ideas to stimulate attendance. Being without a minister for a whole month was hard. Guest speakers were interesting, but it's never the same."

"I've scheduled two more sensitivity workshops. I had a meeting just last week and got volunteers to be trained as leaders. By fall we should have several more in place. That should stem the tide and add to the numbers." Neville leaned forward. "Let me tell you all the good things that happened in D.C."

"We need results today, not three months down the road. How about if we went back to some Bible study and a little more of the traditional like Daily Vacation Bible School. That could be in place by the end of the month."

"Fine, but we need something that's not available in every Protestant church within fifty miles." Neville's expression was intense. "I tell you, when people are on the same wave, they emit a glow that is downright saintly. I saw it in D.C. I know we can have it here. Just plant the seeds, then stand back to watch it develop into something wonderful that will change Amity, change Worthington, change the world."

"Your ambition is commendable. But first we have to pay our bills. And that's becoming a problem," Steve declared. "I'd like us to consider this." He reached over to his stack of papers for another handout. It included a questionnaire rating each sermon and detailing all of Neville's activities, a form to be filled out every other week and submitted to the board.

Neville glanced at it and turned pale. "You're very efficient."

"We need information. Can you think of a better way?"

I poured more ice tea into my glass. "Anyone want more cookies? Neville? Steve?" I held out the plate.

Their gesture was a dismissal. When two men play King of the Mountain, little can be done until they settle the score.

"I see nothing wrong with a questionnaire," Nancy offered as the two men glared at one another. "I always get something out of Neville's sermons and I wouldn't mind saying so."

"Like the Eagle's Nest?" Steve's voice dripped with sarcasm.

"I thought it was one of his best," she replied.

"People are usually willing to go along provided it's temporary," I added.

Neville had been painted into a corner. "All right. We'll give it a try. But understand that there's a fine line between critiquing sermons and censoring them."

"Oh, of course!" we cried in unison.

"And I want to have input on the questions asked. Agreed?"

Steve nodded his assent.

"Then I accept, but only temporarily."

Steve looked at his watch. "So your homework will be to come up with appropriate questions. When that's done, we'll submit them to the board for approval."

The room felt stuffy and I was as eager as anyone to go home. Steve had declared the meeting adjourned and left, but I felt the need to reassure Neville who sat slumped in his chair. "We'll work this through, Neville. Just hang in there."

"I have distributed my energies into specific activities and projects, following the wishes identified at the neighborhood meetings," he began. "Democratic procedures, adult education, social responsibility, variety of worship, and long range building needs." He looked up. "I thought we'd made good progress."

"And so we have," Nancy soothed. "But some feel you've isolated yourself. Emphasis on personal growth has made the quality of Sunday service deteriorate."

"You might consider broadening your focus," I added gently. "Even though you plan to train more leaders, it might be well to curtail the expansion, make it less aggressive, leaving room for other activities."

He winced. "Ministerial time need not be at the expense of counseling or education. Twenty-eight percent of my time is already spent in administration. Much of this could be handled by committee heads or volunteers from the congregation. I'm preacher, teacher, administrator and pastor, representing the church in the community and in the church. That's a large undertaking. Now this."

"Don't be so hard on yourself, Neville. I know you minister to those in need. My own family is an example. I don't know what I'd have done without you and Sheila when Sue had her accident. I will always be grateful."

"Well, maybe progress has been at the price of unity and understanding. I have not effectively conveyed my intentions nor shared my plans. For this I offer my deepest apologies."

"Oh my dear man, there is no reason!" Nancy seemed close to tears. "It's just that this congregation has been through so much."

"I know. But what starts as an honest disagreement can turn brother against sister, friend against friend. It grows without anyone wanting it to. Pretty soon the congregation is divided, the minister's reputation in shreds, the church in shambles." He reached out and patted her hand. "But here I'm among friends."

"That's it. That's it exactly. And we're not the only ones. I know that to be true."

"Intrinsic to any group is the possibility of dissent with a handful of people taking pleasure in fomenting differences. If not dealt with, it's fatal. That's why I'm so anxious to continue the programs of sensitivity training. We need to listen to one another, really listen so dissent is first understood and dealt with, then replaced by true Christian love and understanding."

"Yes. So we won't pay attention to Steve," Nancy sniffed. "He's one of *those*."

"No, my dear. We can't afford to lose anyone. Not even those who disagree."

"That's very generous of you," she said, dabbing at her eyes.

"Meanwhile, we do have to garner new members as well."

"I really liked *The Eagle's Nest*. Carol even had a copy run off and brought it to me one afternoon. I read it three times. You should submit it somewhere for publication."

He laughed, visibly relaxed. "Actually, the basic idea has been used before. But thank you anyway."

It was like the sun had come back out and I could smile again. "I'm glad I stayed for a while," I said, tucking the handouts into my purse. "But Saturdays are always so busy…"

His embrace was familiar and warm, like from a big brother or a favorite uncle.

"You belong here, Neville. And we're going to see that you stay," Nancy declared.

"I hope so." He moved toward the door. "By the way, how is Marva? I haven't seen her for a while. Has she been sick?"

"I really don't know." I hesitated. "We've been out of touch."

"I'd call except the last time I saw her, she seemed distant. We'd had a little disagreement that I thought was settled, but if she's still, well, you know, I don't want to stir things up."

"Of course. I'll probably see her at the club. That is, unless I see her in church tomorrow."

Before I could follow Neville out the door, I felt Nancy's hand on my arm. "He's got a point, you know. Marva and Paul are two people we can't afford to lose."

"Lose? We'd better not! Paul's president."

"Unless there's pillow talk."

My jaw tightened. "I have no idea what's eating Marva," I said, feeling a surge of anger. "If he wants to reach her, he should try going through Joy."

"Just give her a call. I know it's hard. But do it for Neville. Or do it for Amity." She squeezed my hand. "Do it for me."

"I'll think about it."

"Let me know. Okay?"

"I won't have to. You'll hear it through the grapevine."

"People around her don't gossip," she said reproachfully.

"Right. And if you believe that, then let me show you a thriving ski resort a few miles down the road."

On the way home, I stopped at the cleaners and bought a few groceries. Then I swung around to pick up Sue from Bergner's and it was early evening before we got home. John and Kelsey had been playing in the dirt and were grimy from head to toe so by the time I cleaned them up it was time to sit down to dinner.

"A bunch of us are going to an early flick," Sue declared as we began to pass the food. "They'll be picking me up in an hour."

"Decent of you to let us know," Dave replied. "How many bananas in your bunch?"

"The usual. Kids from school, church…"

"Like who?"

"Oh, you know. The Leightons, Volkmans…" She made a face. "Jayne's coming too."

"All in one car?"

"Adam's getting the van."

I reached over and moved the plate away from Kelsey who was making a mess with her spoon. "Be home by midnight. Tomorrow's Sunday."

"What happened at your meeting?" she asked.

"Don't change the subject."

"No, I'm really interested."

"I'm not supposed to talk about it. Even with your father."

"I know. So what happened?"

"Nothing. Neville just wanted me to call Marva so ask why she hasn't been coming to church."

"You don't want to call her?"

"Really Sue."

"Well, if you don't want to call, ask Jayne. That might be easier."

"Some choice."

"If we don't get this kid away from the table, we'll have wasted a perfectly good bath," Dave said, lifting Kelsey from her chair. "Who's on dishes tonight?"

"You are, Dad, remember?"

"Baby sitting *and* dishes? What happened to my weekend?" He looked at Sue. "Wanna trade?"

"No way!" She got up from her chair, give John a peck on the cheek and headed for the stairs. "If Matt comes, tell him to wait."

"I thought Adam was..." Dave looked at me. "What do you suppose would happen if I told him she'd gone out with someone else?"

"I think you'd lose your happy home."

"Gonna talk to Jayne?"

"Maybe. See how it goes."

"Steve's got it in for Neville, doesn't he?"

I nodded. "I don't know why."

"Looks like Marva does too."

"Two babies, a demanding husband... Some people buckle easily. Neville's convenient." I wiped off John's hands and face with a washcloth, then lifted him down to the floor watching him scurry to the family room where Kelsey was watching cartoons. "I just hope the poison doesn't spread."

"It's that bad?"

A commotion outside was followed by the slam of car doors as five teenagers spilled onto the lawn. "Traffic was terrible. Stoplights on Main Street were out. Sue'd better be ready. The flick's already started." Matt sprinted toward the door dressed in blue jeans and t-shirt, a sweater tied casually around his shoulders.

"Sue's life is one big interruption. Come on in. I'll call her." Dave looked over my shoulder, gazing meaningfully toward Jayne.

"Yes, come in. She'll be down in a minute. Everyone had dinner? There's some leftover chicken."

"We're saving room for popcorn." Matt shifted impatiently from one foot to another. "We wanted to be early, avoid the crowd."

"Well, sometimes it just doesn't work out." I turned toward Jayne. "How's your mother? I haven't seen her for a while."

"She's fine." She paused. "How've you been?"

"Fine." I laughed nervously. "It's been a while, hasn't it?"

She nodded. "We've been pretty busy."

"Wouldn't you like to come in and sit down? I'll see what's keeping Sue."

Just then Sue made her appearance, coming down two steps at a time. "What are you waiting for? We're late."

Within minutes they were gone.

"So much for talking to Jayne," Dave declared, closing the door.

"She didn't have a clue as to what I was getting at."

"That could be good."

"I suppose you're right," I sighed. "How did I get pushed into this?"

We walked back into the kitchen to finish our coffee. "You don't have to be pushed unless you want to be," he said, reaching across the table to pop a piece of chicken into his mouth. "In the grand scheme of things, Amity isn't all that important."

"You sound like Bill."

"If you questioned Neville closely, you'd find him saying the same thing. Life is too short to dwell on pettiness. If something is making you unhappy, get rid of it. It's as simple as that."

"If only it were," I murmured.

"Look. Marva was a good friend. Something's eating her and she's hibernating. So be it. Find another friend. How about Joy? At least your kids are compatible. That's more than there was between you and Marva."

I shook my head. "Never mind. I'll work it out."

So we went on to talk about other things and after we put the kids to bed, one thing led to another, and then we fell asleep, so we didn't even hear whether or not Sue made it home by midnight. And I forgot to ask. Not that I didn't trust her. But with all that was going on, I needed to keep reminding myself that my first responsibility was to my family.

CHAPTER 31: JOY

A WIFE AND mother should always willing to listen or offer advice. For example, when Gary tells me that sales are up big time, partly because of his sales contests, the newest one with a weekend in Las Vegas, I nod and marvel at how valuable he is to the company. And when he wonders if he is becoming Max's fair-haired boy, getting a hearty handshake every time they meet, I assure him that of course he is, along with the six martini lunches where everyone else is jockeying to be his fair-haired boy.

Then there are the boys and their summer schedule. Gary wangled a summer for Matt in *Marty's* mail room. And Jason got a job working at the club golf shop. All this keeps them busy which is good, especially with Sue and Hannah hanging around. So we talk about being on time and giving a hundred and ten percent because that's what it takes to climb the ladder of success.

But after a while, being there for others gets tiresome and I need a change of pace to charge my own batteries. What better way than to go shopping?

The Club happened to be having a charity luncheon and style show coming up which is right up my alley, but I hate going to these things alone. I mean, what's the point of looking at new styles if you can't compare notes? So after ruling out Marva since she'd been so cold to me and getting no answer in my call to Liz, I decided to ask Sheila to come as my guest. She might even learn something about style. God only knows, she needs it.

The call took only five minutes. But it took an hour and three other call-backs for her to make up her mind. Then she had to go to Nancy Oberman's and deliver a letter Neville had forgotten to mail, which I would think he could have done for himself. I told her as much but she still insisted we stop. So by the time we got to the Club, the show was half over, with most of the fashions hanging in a room just off of the lobby available for sale but not half as much fun as seeing them being modeled. But once I start something, I give it my all.

So we hunkered down to lunch which was over in nothing flat since Sheila isn't the greatest conversationalist. Then we went out to the lobby to look through the clothes, the only reason I came. And I was ready. "The colors for summer are in the green palette," I said, taking Sheila's arm and steering her toward one of the racks. "Look at all the luscious tones." I reached for a blouse in soft cotton, holding it up to her. "It has just a hint of blue, perfect for your coloring. I took her hand and led her to a full length mirror. "See how this brightens your cheeks and brings out the blue in your eyes?"

She was skeptical. "My closet's full of summer clothes. I really don't need any more."

"Bright colors can overwhelm you. Stay clear of anything heavy -- colors, fabrics…" I ran my hand lightly over her arm. "Everything about you is soft. Your clothes should reflect that."

She smiled uncertainly. *Show what is possible. Establish the need…*

"You don't have to wear everything out before buying new," I teased. "Clothes do more than cover the body." I leaned closer. "They allow a woman to be all she can be."

"Joy, you're shameless." She was laughing.

"Let me buy this for you. Call it my contribution to charity." Her stunned expression told me I'd said it wrong. "I mean the Club's…"

"No, that's okay." She turned this way and that, studying her reflection in the mirror. "It really does something for me, doesn't it?"

"Trust me."

"Well then…"

It was much more expensive that it would have been at the Mall. But she didn't blink twice when the clerk returned her credit card for signature, raising my opinion of her several notches. A woman can learn a lot from her husband and Neville was no slouch when it came to expensive clothes.

While she was doing that, I wandered around looking at scarves and jewelry, choosing a match for the top she'd just bought. Again she refused to let me pay, simply adding it to her purchase.

By now the room was pretty empty, with even the models getting ready to leave. Gathering our packages, we crossed the lobby, taking a short cut past the pool, squeezing past umbrella tables and lounge chairs, holding our packages carefully in front of us. I was so busy protecting our purchases, I didn't look up until we got to the shallow end and spotted Marva and Liz oiling their skins and having a great old time while they watched over the little ones. Seeing Sheila, they waved in a casual kind of way. I don't think they saw me until I waved back.

"Doesn't look like you're going swimming," Liz smiled, eyeing us up and down.

"We came for lunch and the style show. Then we did a little shopping."

"Right. Knowing you…"

I turned to Sheila. "Show them what you bought."

Opening her bag, she pulled out the blouse, draping the silk scarf around the neckline. "And a pin for the finishing touch," she added proudly.

"Expensive," Marva murmured.

"But exquisite," Liz declared. "You do have good taste."

"So what's happening?" I asked, pulling out a chair, starved for some real conversation.

Marva and Liz exchanged glances. "Not much. What's with you?"

"The same. Haven't seen you around. I've been meaning to call."

Marva shrugged. "We've been busy."

Just then Ashley and Taylor came bounding out of the water, demanding attention. And of course, they got it.

In between, I kept looking at Marva and Liz, trying to read what was going on, watching as they talked to each other about kids, family, the weather, the Club. It was as though the past weeks, the past year, had never happened. But there was also a certain reserve. Was it me or Sheila? I couldn't tell, and I had a hunch that a phone call wouldn't produce much.

I motioned toward the chair next to me. "Sit down, Sheila. We don't have to go right away, do we?"

Her worried look had reappeared. "I told Neville it wouldn't take long. He's expecting me."

"You make it sound like a dental appointment," Liz laughed.

"Women go shopping to nourish their souls," I said. "We're entitled."

Marva reached for her towel, calling to Ashley and Taylor who had gone back into the water. "Start gathering up your toys. We'll be going soon."

"We really should get together," I said friendly-like. "It's been a while."

She looked around distractedly. "I'm sorry. I can't talk now. You know how it is."

"Oh, do I ever! When the boys were little, it was all I could do to keep an eye on them, especially in the summer when all they wanted to do was play. You're lucky to have Jayne to give you a hand."

Her expression hardened. "Jayne is fine. No need to worry."

"Of course. If Jayne were the biggest worry in the world, we'd be in pretty good shape," I said, eyeing Sheila and Liz for affirmation.

Marva turned toward the pool to retrieve toys and kids along with the usual odds and ends. The conversation was over.

"I think we'd better go," said Sheila. "Neville is probably home by now."

I nodded, standing up and gathering our packages. "We really should get together," I said turning to Liz. "Maybe we can do lunch."

She smiled politely. "The summer is usually so busy."

I thought of her family, of Sue, of poor retarded Kelsey and baby John, of how people said she never complained. Poor Dave. It must be hell to live with a saint. "All the more reason…"

She didn't hear me. So I gave all my attention to Sheila who should appreciate it more. After all, didn't I just achieve a break-through, discussing clothes and hair styles and got her to actually listen? In the car we continued talking about things like fabrics and color tones. We even got into the benefits of a weekly massage although maybe that was a little over her head. Meanwhile, I mentally went over a list of possible playmates, knowing that all work and no play makes for a dull summer.

After dropping Sheila off, I returned to my empty house, going into the den. Surely there were dozens of prospects, even in podunk Worthington. Why, even Jan might qualify. At least she was conscious.

As I approached the desk, I saw the message light blinking. It was Gary. His big Las Vegas trip was going to include the wives. And by the way, Max and Jan would be there too. Did I want to go? Well bless his heart, of course I did.

Good thing I'm adaptable. I had three days to get ready.

But what to do with the boys? Too old for a baby sitter, too young to be home alone. Then there were their jobs. Could they stay with friends? Neville and Sheila welcomed them with open arms. I guess the Club lunch paid off after all. The boys would stay there Friday and Saturday. We'd be home by Sunday. Trust in God. I was tempted to take the house keys away from them, but that would have been too much.

Matt drove us to the airport. It would be a short trip, enough time for a little chit-chat as I warmed up to Jan, and a nap before the captain's instruction to fasten seat belts and prepare for landing.

Gary's expense account had taken me to some very nice hotels and this was one of the best. Our party of forty occupied two floors. Each room included two vibrating beds and a whirlpool bath. We were welcomed with a carafe of wine and a plate of nuts on a table near the windows that overlooked the mountains. Coming back to the hotel at night, we'd find our beds turned down with two mints on each pillow. We could even have our shoes shined if we placed them outside the door at night. In addition to the hotel package, everyone, husbands and wives, got three hundred dollars in gambling chips. When it came to having a good time, no one could accuse Max of being cheap.

Gary's main job would be to bring everyone together for an hour or so on Saturday and give his inspirational talk. We'd attend the Friday night dinner at the hotel and the more formal banquet and show on Saturday. The rest of the time we'd be on our own.

After unpacking, we went down to the Casino. By noon, I'd lost a hundred dollars on the slots. Gary had won sixty dollars at roulette and offered to split it with me. We ate lunch in the hotel dining room where they had a spectacular buffet complete with ice sculptures and miniature fountains that emptied into pools with real water lilies. Afterward, Gary wanted to take a walk on the Strip, but it was too hot so we waited until evening, first going into the bar to get something cool to drink. And of course, there were Jan and Max.

"I'll have a Tom Collins," I told the smiling bartender, sliding onto the stool next to Jan.

She looked up from the gambling screen embedded in the bar. "Well, Joy! All settled in? What do you think?" As slways, her voice was a notch louder than necessary.

"The mountains are beautiful. Quite a change from Worthington." I moved closer, looking over her shoulder. "Are you winning?"

"I don't know." She looked at Max. "Am I?" Click, click, click…

"Two hundred thirty to the good along with three Martinis for me and two beers on the side." He put his arm around Gary. "Sales up. Morale high. Gary should be Man of the Year. How about it, Jan?"

She put in another chip. Bling bling. "You bet!" Her eyes were like Max's, friendly, yet preoccupied. "Business is booming." Five chips burped out of the machine. Click, click, click… Another chip. Then another. "How're things at Amity?"

"Okay, I suppose." I remembered her car leaving the parking lot. "Neville got you interested?"

"Neville's a good man. Got his head screwed on straight. Deserves more than he's getting," she declared.

"Well, he'll probably get a raise if the pledges come in."

"That's not what I meant." She moved a fresh martini out of Max's reach so he ordered another one. "It takes a while for someone to settle into a new job. Gotta give him some slack." Her eyes were on Gary. "Like with you. What if Max didn't let you run this contest? After all, it wasn't cheap. Not that I'm saying it was a mistake. But Max cut you a lot of slack. So sales jumped through the roof. Who would've thought?"

I looked away. *Marty's* was a two-bit franchise company located in a cow town, run by a drunk and owned by a loud-mouth who looked ready to gamble away next year's profit. Before Gary arrived, they were muddling along with no growth, no policy and no strategic plan. Whatever changes happened were because of him.

Gary was unruffled. "In sales, it all boils down to a Positive Mental Attitude. If you believe, you can achieve. Success isn't a goal. It's a journey. I hope my sons follow the same path."

"Couldn't have said it better myself!" Max cried, slapping him on the back. He turned to Jan. "Listen up, Mamma. Gary's preaching the Gospel truth."

"You bet!" Another dollar went into the machine. This time she hit, sending off a series of whistles and flashing lights. Them that has, gits.

"Hey, the lady's hot! Time for another round," Max bellowed, gesturing to the gathering crowd. "It's on the house," he added, and everyone laughed because in Vegas all the drinks are on the house.

I think they stayed there all afternoon. We saw them again at dinner but spent less time with them because Gary and I needed to circulate, this being one reason we were there.

The dinner was outstanding, with Caesar salad, poached salmon, filet mignon and baked Alaska for dessert. I never eat more than half of what is on my plate. An ounce of prevention is worth a pound of dieting. Because I finish before everyone else, I kill time by going to the restroom for about ten or fifteen minutes. That let me see the inside of a lot of bathrooms which is an education in itself, meeting women like Gerda ready to pass out, or silly little girls sneaking a smoke or trying to pull themselves together after being rumpled up on their first date.

This bathroom scenario was even more dicey because I would never in a million years have expected to find Jan boohooing in a stall, her voice unmistakable with a half a dozen women at the vanity acting like they didn't hear a thing. Luckily, they weren't from our party so I spun around, beating a fast retreat. Watching Mrs. Boss fall apart was not at the top of my agenda, thank you. Pretty soon Jan returned, back to her old self. Sometimes a woman just needs a good cry, and I respect that.

Saturday was Gary's big day with a morning meeting and an after lunch gathering to inspire. I joined the wives at poolside for conversation, then a massage and sauna. I called Sheila and there being no answer, left a message. In the afternoon we rented a car and drove to Hoover Dam, returning in time for the reception, dinner and show. A very full day. On Sunday we returned home.

Matt came alone to pick us up at the airport. Jason was at work, Sundays being especially busy at the Club.

"Are your things back at the house or do we have to stop at the Leightons?" I asked as Gary took the wheel, pulling out of the parking lot.

"We took them home this morning while everyone was at church. And I'm still pretty tired and need to take a nap. So maybe you can pick up Jason. He's off at five."

I didn't check the mail until morning. By then everyone was talking about the bombshell Neville had fired off to Nancy Oberman and published in the newsletter causing all hell to break loose.

CHAPTER 32: JAYNE

THE GODS ARE raging on Mount Olympus. Bad enough that Mom had it in for me and Adam for no reason. Now she's turned on all the others, blaming them for God only knows what. Then came Dr. Leighton's editorial in the church newsletter. Mom's even mad at Carrie Cook who was just doing her job putting out the newsletter. Worse, Paul is right there agreeing with whatever Mom says. Christian love. Except it's closer to hate.

I've read Dr. Leighton's editorial so many times it's practically worn through and I still can't see what the flap is all about. It's just telling about the Minister's Advisory Committee and how people were supposed to suggest what they liked in his sermons. Mom calls that divisive. Then it said he was going to spend more time with sensitivity training which was enough to make Mom go postal. She probably thinks they're some pagan rites just like she did with us.

Pretty soon she and Paul were burning up the wires between Worthington and the East Coast like it was a Constitutional crisis. So now the phone's tied up all day long and I can't turn on the computer without facing a blizzard of e-mails. All I hear is Neville did this and Billy did that. Mom's even got someone in Boston checking on Dr. Leighton's credentials and she actually asked me what I've heard although I don't know anything, having pretty much lost whatever friends I had. I can't even open my mouth without getting all these extra chores dumped on me. Before all this happened, I begged her to let me get a summer job, but she said I was needed at home. I'm needed all right. But not a way that's normal. After all, this is her house and her kids and she's the one who is supposed to take care of things. Or maybe she thinks teenagers are supposed to be rebellious and so she might as well go with it.

Mom and I used to be close, at least, I thought we were, having long talks, cuddling together after she'd read me a bedtime story. She'd tell me about life and being grown up and I'd talk about school and teachers and some of the kids. Back then she was hip and understood me even though I wasn't cool like Sue or some of the other kids. But Dr. Leighton has really turned her off. She won't tell me why or explain what happen, no matter how much I ask. Last night we had a big argument, mostly about Adam, and I cried myself to sleep - again.

This morning I offered to take Ashley and Taylor to the pool. It was my way of getting out of the house. No one's there in the afternoon except babies and old ladies and I couldn't possibly run into anyone. And it's a lot better than sitting here, listening to Mom pace up and down, feeling her vibes jangling all over the house.

She must have wanted her own peace and quiet because she pulled herself together in a hurry and had everything ready by the time Ashley and Taylor woke from their naps. She even gave me permission to go to the snack bar and get treats as long as it wasn't too close to suppertime. Then she arranged for Paul to pick us up after work.

So after getting into our suits, we got drinks and chips and carried them outside, putting them on a table at the shallow end of the pool. Ashley was fearless as usual, jumping in and dog paddling to the side. Taylor was happy with her water wings, pretending she could swim. Of course I was right there in the water with them, making sure nothing happened. Later, I'd take them to the shallow baby pool where they could play while I buried my misery inside a book. Surprisingly, the activity felt good.

After about an hour, we got out and went to our table for a snack. Suddenly I heard someone call my name. It was Jason, waving from the parking lot. It took a minute to register. Then I remembered he had a summer job working in the golf shop. Some people have all the luck.

I waved back, wondering what he wanted.

He sprinted over the low shrubs outlining the walkway and leaned against the chain-link fence. "Hey, Jayne, what's happening?"

"I'm giving my mom a breather. What's with you?"

"Not much. Just dealing with a hysterical girlfriend. Got a minute?"

Jason coming to talk with me? I tried not to look flustered. "Sure. Why not?"

"Be right there." He ducked around through the clubhouse, crossing the deck to where we were. "Sun's hot. Mind if I take off my shoes?"

"Join the crowd." I watched as he kicked his loafers and peeled off his socks. "Finished with work?"

He nodded. "Matt's supposed to pick me up. But he's late -- as usual."

We stared at one another and I groped for something to say. "We'll both be taking American Lit next year."

"Is that the next level?"

"I think so. You'll be in AP won't you?" I'd gotten accepted for Advanced Placement a week before.

"I'm not sure." He studied his fingernails.

"Didn't you sign up? You have to put in a request, you know. Maybe it's not too late."

"It's about your mom and all the ruckus she's started at the church."

I took a deep breath, feeling my stomach flutter. "Let's go by the kiddy pool. It's quieter there."

We loaded the stuff to where the Ashley and Taylor could splash and play on their own while I braced myself for God only knows what.

"Neville's been here less than a year," he began. "And already people are beginning to snipe at him. He should be given a better chance. I mean, what's a year? My dad started selling shoes fresh out of high school. Every new job after that was a promotion and now he's an executive. All this takes time."

"What's that got to do with my mom?"

"It's not fair what she's saying."

Suddenly I wished I'd paid more attention. "Like what?"

"You know. Like asking for Neville's transcripts and evaluations from other churches. I mean, all that is past history."

Jason is one of the nicer cool kids but that doesn't make him perfect. Not that Mom is perfect either. But she *is* my mom and that goes back a lot further. I felt my back stiffen. "First Sue's mom comes at me with polite questions like how's your mom and long time no see as though it's some kind of code. Now you want me to do something. Honestly, why can't people just talk to each other without a third party in the middle?"

"Because she's making trouble, Jayne. I'm telling you, church headquarters is having a real cow. This guy Billy Oliver is sitting at denomination headquarters just waiting to get even. Meanwhile, she's feeding him stuff big time. I mean, this is serious."

I looked over at Ashley and Taylor to make sure they were all right. "Dr. Leighton wrote a letter to Mrs. Oberman. Mrs. Oberman showed it to Carol Stone. Carol showed it to Carrie Cook. Carrie put it in the newsletter which went out to all the churches. My mother had nothing to do with any of it."

Jason looked like he was ready to cry. "Do you know how many times Adam and Hannah have moved? Well, I'll tell you. Hannah's gone to seven grammar schools. Adam's gone to nine. Think about it. And now she's going to move again. How'd you like that to happen to you?"

I thought of Mom sitting at the phone, talking to Billy Oliver, to Dr. Jones, to Washington, hearing her voice, sensible but urgent. *I'm just calling for information.* "I read the newsletter. It seemed perfectly okay to me."

"That's what I'm saying. It's what your mom is doing that's causing all the trouble."

Just then Matt's voice came from across the parking lot, hollering our names.

"We're at the kiddy pool," Jason called. "C'mon over."

Matt rounded to the clubhouse and came from inside carrying an armload of snacks, ready to settle in. "Hey, man, what's happening?"

"You're late."

"All the more time to chill out," he grinned, opening a bag of chips. He turned to me. "You going to the cookout on the Fourth?"

He meant the annual event along the river with local bands, followed by a huge fireworks display after dark. Amity's youth group had even planned an evening cookout beforehand. It was the sort of thing you were invited to and Adam hadn't called. "I'm not sure," I replied.

"It'll be a blast," Matt declared.

"Jason doesn't think so."

They exchanged looks. "You've been talking?"

Jason nodded.

"Look, I don't care about the church except for my friends. But people are taking sides and that shouldn't happen," Matt said.

"Well then, talk to Sue's mom or the MAC and let them know how you feel."

Matt laughed dryly. "No one listens to us. Look at how your mom is giving you a hard time about going out to Summit South. Does she listen?"

"We were just goofing around."

"*We* know that, but try getting any grownups to believe it. Even my mom gave us a real talking to."

"So what do you want from me?" I cried.

"Get your mom to back off before it's too late."

I tried to remember what happened when Dr. Walsh died and Reverend Oliver came to Amity. It was about the time that Dad moved out and Mom filed for divorce. Then with Paul coming around and everything else different, Amity was just a fly speck on the wall. "I wouldn't know what to say. And she wouldn't listen anyway." It was true. Maybe we were close -- but not that close.

"Someone is handing out a petition to recall." Matt's voice was barely a whisper. "They already have the twenty percent needed."

Ashley and Taylor had come out of the pool. They were now at my side, wet and clingy. I put my arms around them both. "Then it's too late."

"No it's not," Jason insisted. "Hannah says we can stop it if we act now."

"How does she know that?"

"Christ! She's a minister's daughter. She knows."

I'd lived in Worthington all my life. For me, moving would be an adventure. "Maybe they'll vote to keep him."

"Yeah? Try living with that."

I put my hands over my eyes and Taylor began to whimper. "You're saying it's my mom's petition."

They nodded. "All she has to do is forget about submitting it to the board and it'll die," Jason declared.

I was skeptical. "What about all the people who signed it? They'd still be around and, like you say, making trouble."

"All he's asking for is a little time to prove himself. If it doesn't work..."

"By then, Hannah will have had a chance to graduate," Jason added. "It's not too much to ask, to graduate with your friends."

I didn't reply.

"Adam wanted me to tell you Hello." Matt continued. "He said he would have called.

I felt a rush of anger. "So now you're offering me a carrot?"

Jason knelt down on all fours and pretended to be a horse, whinnying and tossing his head toward Ashley and Taylor. Within minutes they were on his back, screaming with glee. Moving carefully, he carried them back toward the playground next to the pool, and pretty soon they were on the swings being pushed by an accommodating Jason.

"A distraction. That's all we need, Jayne. A couple of successes, then see what happens." Matt's voice was warm and coaxing. "We'd all be so grateful."

There was no place to turn. Mom barely talked to me any more. As for friends, there was only Adam, and he'd become one of *them.* "I don't know. This has gotten so complicated."

"Just try. That's all we're asking."

The sun was going down and I was blinded by the light. I nodded, unable to speak.

"Good girl! I knew we could count on you." Matt grabbed my shoulders and gave them a squeeze.

"What about Mrs. Mason?" I asked, still not sure. "She and Mom were close."

"Sue's working on her. And my folks have an in with the Pressers. Maybe we can make a difference after all." He called toward the playground. "Hey Jason, she'll do it."

Jason came galloping over. "Cool! I'll tell Hannah." He gave me a hug and then cupped my face in both hands, his expression sober. "You're a good friend. I'll never forget this."

Just then a car drove up into the parking lot, the bright sun reflecting on its surface. It was Paul, home early on a Friday. He greeted the boys politely then loaded the kids into the car. Mom must have whispered in his ear. Married folks are like that. And suddenly, I saw this to be a lot harder than I imagined.

CHAPTER 33: JOY

"MARVA, ANSWER THE phone."
Silence.

"Talk to me. I know you're there."

The phone felt hollow in my hand, my voice a metallic echo. Then there was a click followed by a hum. I looked at Jason huddled in the armchair next to me. "She hung up."

His face was ashen. "It's not fair. Jayne promised."

"I'm sure she did her best."

"What am I supposed to tell Hannah?" he wailed.

"She's probably more prepared than you think. And nothing's final. They might decide not to vote after all or vote to keep him."

"Can I go?"

"Honey, it will be crowded. Anyway, you're too young to vote."

"All the kids are going. We want our voices heard. We'll just sit in the back and watch."

"I'd be interested to see how you'd do both at the same time."

"I have the right." His voice had an aggressive edge.

"Well yes, I suppose you do." I pictured thirty or forty grubby teens huddled in the back. I always saw to it that Jason and Matt looked their best. But with all of Neville's outside contacts, anything could happen.

"So it's okay?"

"Just don't embarrass me."

"Is Dad going?"

I nodded. "This is important."

"Which way will you vote?"

"Jason, I don't know that it will even come to a vote. We'll have to see."

"They have more than enough signatures."

I sighed. At fifteen, everything is urgent. "Twenty percent of the members are needed to call a meeting. Then they have to convince two thirds to vote for recall. To make it even harder, should it not pass, they have to wait another six months to begin all over again. So stop worrying. Hannah will be here for a good long while."

"I was just asking."

"Why so curious?"

He stood up. "Because it's hell to move every few years, especially when you're in school."

So it wasn't just Hannah. Not that I didn't like the girl. But a minister's daughter? He could do better. "It'll be okay, Jason. You'll see." I reached up to give him a hug but he ducked and was halfway up the stairs to his room before I could say anything more.

I don't know how Neville could have been preaching Sunday after Sunday with all this going on, but he carried it off pretty well even though attendance was shrinking before our very eyes.

Meanwhile, our house remained the gathering place for Matt and Jason's friends. They'd come around after their summer jobs or whenever they got tired of the club, relaxing on the deck or cooling off in the game room downstairs. On the Fourth of July, we had a big cookout before the fireworks. Sue was her normal self and I spent a big chunk of time talking with her because we get along so well. But she didn't come up with anything I didn't already know. Poor Jayne didn't even show up, probably too ashamed after her big promise to help. As for Adam and Hannah, if they were stressed, it didn't show.

The big congregational meeting was scheduled for mid-July on a Saturday night. It was announced in the newsletter with few details. Who would be in charge? Would there be coffee hour afterward? A little wine?

Would we drag out the silver or just use paper cups? What is the proper etiquette to fire a minister?

It turned out to be the responsibility of the board, with the meeting to be held in the sanctuary because they expected a big crowd, with both sides calling past members, hoping they'd put a check in the collection plate at Christmas or sent in a few dollars to stay on the mailing list making them entitled to vote. The district representative would also be there. And at the last minute, Billy Oliver decided to come, spending the weekend with Marva and Paul. They probably would have invited Dr. Jefferson Walsh, except that he was dead.

Finally Saturday came. We decided to take two cars, the boys having their own agenda. It was scheduled to start at seven and we wanted to get there early.

The parking lot was half full when we arrived with people streaming into the building like at a PTA Open House. "Doesn't look good," Gary muttered.

"Where did all these people come from?"

"Probably clackers, hired to stir up the crowd. Sometimes that's enough to tip the undecided."

Inside, the people hurried to their seats, brushing past ushers who stood armed with extra copies of the agenda. The air conditioning was going full blast. We found two empty seats toward the center.

Up front, the potted plants had been pushed to the side and a long table set up, converting the sanctuary into a meeting hall. Five empty chairs faced the audience with microphones, pads of paper and bottled water at each place. Board members were milling around, talking to one another in hushed voices. Marva sat in the second row, giving her full attention to a short pudgy man in a rumpled suit probably in his late forties, his hair combed the way balding men do. I assumed that was Billy Oliver. Next to him was a younger man, his dark suit and tie looking like he was from the east coast. Liz and Nancy sat in the row behind them with Carol and Tony at the opposite end. The Leightons were nowhere in sight. It was a quarter to seven.

"Marva didn't call me back. Have you had a chance to talk with Paul?" I whispered.

Gary shook his head. "I only talked with Bill Presser and that was mostly about *Marty's.*"

"I suppose that's best. Never mix business and pleasure."

He nodded. "We need to back off a little, at least until this blows over. The way things are building at work, we can't afford to get on the wrong side of anyone."

There was a stir at the back and a large group of teenagers took seats, Matt and Jason among them, filling three tightly packed rows. "They promised to be quiet," I whispered, hoping it was true. Our own row was filling with people I'd never seen before so I simply smiled, then turned and faced forward.

As it crept closer to seven, the hum of conversation became more hushed. Those standing in front moved to sit down and Paul, Carol and the gentleman in the dark suit took their places at the long table. They were joined by Steve. Then there was a rustle from stage right, and Neville emerged the way he did every Sunday. Moving easily, he brushed past the potted palms and came down the steps from the stage, taking the last seat at the table next to Carol. The room became silent.

Paul stood up and took a gavel from his briefcase, placing it in front of him. "The meeting of Amity Congregational Church will come to order." His voice bounced off the walls toward the back, his face serous. "We meet in response to a petition signed by twenty-three percent of our membership requesting a vote of ministerial recall. As stated in the agenda, we will allow time for each side to present their position and for members to express their comments before the vote is taken."

He paused. "But first, I would like to introduce the individuals at this table. To my far left, Dr. Neville Leighton, our minister, next to him, Carol Stone, Director of Religious Education, both of them staff members. At my far right is Steve Rothberg, chair of the Ministerial Advisory Committee, and next to him, Dr. Cliff Hamilton, chairman of the

Department of Ministry. I have asked Dr. Hamilton to give the invocation."

The dark suit stood up, and the congregation got to its feet. Bowing his head, he began. "We are gathered here, people of good will, to address our differences and make peace with those who are angry, puzzled or distraught. We seek to have our hearts filled with compassion, to open up and truly listen to one another. We recognize that each in his or her own way wishes only good for our church community, knowing that the Lord's work travels on many different paths. So we ask God's blessing tonight. May it end with love, not rancor. May friendships be deepened and faith sustained. May our differences serve as an ultimate bond through God. Amen."

I could feel the electricity in the air. There was no question which side he was on.

"We will now proceed with the business at hand," Paul continued. "First on the agenda is a report from the Minister's Advisory Committee Chair."

I studied Paul's face, remembering the good times we'd had, going out to dinner or attending jazz festivals, sometimes with all the kids in tow, having a blast. I'd never seen Paul like this, so serious, almost grim.

Steve stood up, shuffled some papers, and began. "In the last few months, there has been much concern with what the minister is and is not doing. A key issue has been the growth of the church. Although there was a mandate from the congregation to expand our program and encourage growth, that expansion has not been successful, at least so far as our financial stability is concerned. Pledges and collections are down as are attendance and new member growth.

"In order to address these problems, the board appointed me, along with Nancy Oberman and Liz Mason to explore the problems and propose ways to solve them. We have met almost weekly and discussed the following points. First, that the policy regarding minister-congregational relations should be spelled out with greater clarity. Second, that academic and denominational counsel should be sought regarding the use of the minister's time. Third, that an effective measurement of program needs and interests of the congregation be implemented. And finally, that the congregational welfare have priority over the personal interests of the minister.

"Unfortunately, before we were able to make our findings known in the proper and expected order, Dr. Leighton chose to appeal directly to the congregation via an editorial in our newsletter, knowing full well that such mailings went to all our churches across the country as well as the regional and denomination headquarters out east, in effect, washing our dirty linen in public." He paused to take a sip of water.

I saw Liz and Nancy whispering to one another, their faces worried.

"In addition, there have been some real concerns as to the welfare of our young people," Steve went on. "Granted the group is growing, but at what price? Topics such as outings that encourage inappropriate intimacy is not the domain of church retreats, especially for teenagers. Quite the contrary. It is our responsibility to provide nurturance and care so they become worthy citizens of society and faithful members of the church.

"And finally, there has been a great deal of concern regarding the amount of time Dr. Leighton spends not only in community outreach but in private counseling, the question being that of his qualifications and the church's subsequent liability. Is Dr. Leighton a licensed psychotherapist? A qualified counselor? Ministers certainly do pastoral counseling, but what happens when he takes on outsiders? If done on church property, are we then liable? We need to explore those matters not only for Dr. Leighton's edification, but for our own protection as well."

Steve sat down and a number of hands went up.

Paul tapped the gavel. "I'd like all the speakers to have their say before there is a motion on the floor. After that, there'll be general discussion. You will have your chance, I promise."

Next was Dr. Hamilton. "I've been coming here a bit more than I'd like, first to participate at Dr. Walsh's funeral, a very sad day for us all. Jefferson was a good friend. I will miss him. I'm sure you feel the same.

Then there were the years when I thought you'd come to love your guest ministers, and would never get around to filling the pulpit permanently."

Soft laughter rippled through the audience.

"So when you called Dr. Neville Leighton to candidate, I saw light at the end of the tunnel." He turned toward Neville. "Dr. Leighton has much to commend him, and your search committee concurred, finding him the best choice for Amity and recommending his call. Yet after barely a year, there is dissent. Tonight, without expressing any opinion in either direction, I hope this can be resolved because we all know how quickly molehills can become mountains." He stopped and cleared his throat. "But I wouldn't be an administrator if I didn't have a few recommendations of my own."

More laughter.

"I would like to offer the following. First, that you give this matter more time to get to know one another. If you want to assign a reasonable target date to give the Ministerial Advisory Committee more time to work, that would make sense. Meanwhile, this congregation should actively work with that committee to settle differences and disagreements. During that time, Dr. Leighton should seek out denominational headquarters and ministerial peers for professional advice. Second, that you review the budget carefully, continuing to work toward increased membership while at the same time examining where it could be adapted for this period which I'm sure is temporary. And finally, that the board and the ministerial advisory committee work together, examining Amity's purpose and direction, not the way it was but the way it should be." He held out his hands like in a statue of Jesus. "Whatever your decision, it should be thoughtful, serious and loving, worthy of this congregation, its members and all those involved." He sat down to light applause.

Now it was Neville's turn. He stood up and took a deep breath. "I would like to begin by saying that I like being here as Amity's minister and think that, for the most part, this is a good fit. So I'd like to lay out where I'm coming from and where I see some problems.

"A church is a community of persons whose loyalty is to transcending values and traditions which guide and judge their lives and by the standards which emerge from their individual and communal encounters with those standards, from which they derive their understanding of their task in the world and their policy and program." I looked at Gary and could see his eyes glaze.

"When the community or a portion thereof becomes an end in itself, we have a perversion of the church," Neville continued. "Amity doesn't seem to understand this. It has fellowship and cohesion, but as with all cohesive groups, has lost its ability to be self critical. It has become sterile and ingrown seeing any efforts to restore vitality and direction as critical and negative attacks. Several indications of the validity are as follows. The growing willingness of some members to openly disavow the need to consider Amity's goals, indicating that we, this warm little group, are happy as we are. Second, the open disparagement of personal growth as a basic concern of our church. And third, the tendency of many to flaut democratic principle in the name of democracy and the upholding of this practice by the group exemplified by persons who are dissatisfied, tending to withdraw and withhold financial support rather than expressing their dissent and open it to discussion. Some members even lauded rather than criticized them for this questionable practice, leaving the group vulnerable to the tyranny of the minority. An expert on strategy once said, 'Above all, never hesitate. Never qualify what you say. Never concede an inch to the other side. Paint all contrasts in black and white.'"

I could feel Gary's body tighten and he shook his head ever so slightly. "Hitler," he mumbled.

"During these past weeks, I have been told of numerous mistakes, many of which I have openly acknowledged not once but on several occasions," Neville continued. "Has my apology been accepted? I hope so, for I regret the times I have been tactless and negligent of my duty. I regret my attitude and conduct toward our board. But I too have experienced wrongs. I have been attacked professionally as incompetent in the pulpit and unqualified as a counselor. I have been described as unfit to hold this or any other office. I found myself wondering how I could continue as your minister under such circumstances. Since this is a large congregation, I thought the best way to reach out was through the newsletter. Now I have another matter calling for an apology. And I do apologize for causing distress. But in this church, we still believe in freedom of speech, freedom of the pulpit and freedom of expression. You may not agree with what I said, but surely, you must affirm my right to say it.

"You may wonder how I can re-establish a relationship with the congregation. Another questions might be to ask how this congregation can become a church that receives and supports a minister. This meeting can indicate our direction and hopefully, clear the air."

There was a whoop from the back and the three rows of kids stood up, applauding wildly, followed by a number of adults cheering them on.

"Order, order…" Paul cried, pounding the gavel. "If you don't come to order, I will have you removed!"

The room quieted, and Paul stood collecting himself, his face pale. "The chair is ready to entertain a motion from the floor. After that, we have general discussion, followed by a vote."

Marva stood up, reading from a small card in her hand. "I move that the members of Amity Congregational Church, terminate the employment of Neville Leighton for cause, beginning August 31, after which he and his family will vacate the parsonage and he will receive 90 days base salary as is indicated in the constitution."

There was a gasp. Six weeks? Churches with vacancies needed to learn he was available. Then there was candidating and church visits. Meanwhile, where would he go?

"Is there a second?"

A second came from somewhere in back of the room.

"Discussion?"

Dozens of hands flew up, and the stillness turned to bedlam. Finally, Bill Presser got the floor. He turned to the audience, his voice booming toward the back, one of the few people on this earth who never needed a microphone. "Over the years, I've sat on the board and on various committees, chairing many of them. I was on the candidating committee that called Neville Leighton to this pulpit. I'm also a member of this community and know how business works. In a job of this magnitude where the entire community is affected, it's important to understand group dynamics." He tilted his head, looking through the tops of his glasses. "Amity has shown itself to have a miserable track record. But it's never too late to learn. Neville can teach us. He has impressive academic credentials. He has served several churches with distinction. Several of his sermons have been published. We will look long and hard to find another minister with such a laudable record. As such, I urge everyone to consider carefully and vote against this motion."

More applause as Paul banged the gavel.

Marva stood up, facing the congregation. Her face was flushed, her hair rumpled, looking like someone headed for a nervous breakdown. "I too have been a member for a long time. I have served on committees and chaired numerous important events. I remember Dr. Walsh and the ministers who followed. I assure you, Dr. Leighton is no Dr. Walsh. Instead, he is a promoter of the first water, ingratiating himself to every segment of the church whether he agrees with their thinking or not, choosing to use his charm to manipulate others. He used the vulnerability of our young people to play mind games until they were agitated and distraught, then sent them home with no advice about how to handle it. This, from a man with no credentials in sociology, psychology or even pastoral counseling other than what is covered in an ordinary seminary curriculum. He will tell you he went to Washington D.C. to take a course in counseling. But his certificate of completion is nothing more than a piece of paper from a diploma mill, validated by no one with any professional authority. It was a case of the blind leading the blind. So not only is Neville unqualified, he is also dishonest."

The next speaker was Carol who gave a testimonial about how Neville had changed her life, comparing him to Dr. Walsh whom everyone seemed to see as the new messiah even though he'd been close to being fired himself. She was followed by a string of people from the housing project, swearing that Neville had enabled them to face obstacles, learn new things, find new hope. Paul shouldn't have allowed them to speak, them being non-members, but by then people were bouncing up and down like yo-yos, taking the floor at will. For every positive remark, there was a matching negative with voices getting louder and more insistent. Even the kids chimed in from the back of the room, swearing that Neville was a cool dude and threatening a boycott Amity if he was forced to leave. I watched Marva, seeing her shoulders begin to sag. Half were speaking for Neville, half against.

Then Billy Oliver moved toward the front, leaning toward Paul and whispering in his ear. Ministers sure know how to take command because the room became silent.

After a few minutes, Paul stood up. "Like any democratic institution, Amity's meetings are open, and rightly so. But voting on important matters is restricted to bona fide members. Again, rightly so. Now, there is a motion on the floor. Before we can proceed to vote on that motion, membership must be verified and a quorum established. All this is time consuming and it's getting late. So with the consent of the lady whose motion is on the floor and her subsequent second, it has been suggested that we take a straw vote before going further."

Each side sat glued to their seats, assuming to have won.

He took a deep breath. "Hearing no objection, I ask the ushers to please come forward."

"What's going on?" I whispered to Gary.

"If they can't fire him today, they'll have to wait six months before bringing it up again," he muttered. "So they want to be sure the motion won't be voted down."

Someone in the back stood up. "I move the vote be by secret ballot."

Another voice. "I second."

Slips of paper were handed to the ushers who carefully distributed them. Of course, with so many people, there was no telling who would be voting legitimately. But no one was going to be fussy. "A Yes vote means to terminate, the No means not to." Paul's voice was shaking.

The collection plates were filled to overflowing. Then the counting started and people got up and stretched, making small talk. Although I never missed a chance to meet and greet, we were sitting among strangers and their expressions scared me. So I took a walk to the lady's room.

When I came back, one of the ushers was back at the table whispering to Paul who tapped the gavel as everyone scurried to their places. "The results of the straw poll are as follows. Yes, two hundred seventy two. No, two hundred seven. A majority but not two-thirds."

The cheer could have been heard all the way to China, with the kids in the back jumping up and down, stamping their feet. Then before anyone could comment, a voice came from off side making another motion, this time to Postpone Indefinitely followed by a second and someone else yelling "Question!" which meant no further discussion.

The Ayes shook the rafters. And that was the end of it. Marva's motion was taken off the table to live another day.

I sat back, feeling perspiration beading on my forehead as Paul called for a motion to adjourn. Within ten minutes the sanctuary was close to empty with two clusters of people at the front, one of supporters surrounding Neville, another smaller group talking to Marva, Paul, Billy and Dr. Hamilton. "We ought to congratulate Neville," I whispered.

Gary nodded. "Except that he didn't win." He pulled me to my feet. "But we should go through the motions."

And so we did.

Back home, Gary and I stayed up for hours talking, killing a whole bottle of wine. I thought we'd pretty much run our church life dry now that all the important people were leaving. Sure, the man could be fired. So let him pull up his socks, straighten his spine and get on with his life. But Gary insisted that Bill Presser was still an important key. When the boys came home, the argument took a different slant with them saying how Neville was so misunderstood, which seemed odd since they never went to church. What a thing to tell my mother. Except she'd never understand.

CHAPTER 34: CAROL

THAT SATURDAY WAS the worst day of my life. Well, maybe not the worst, but it came close. During the speeches and the vote, there were people muttering awful things like how Neville had been divorced and was in therapy. Then Marva tried to bring up Neville's ministry to other churches, implying he'd been fired, which was neither here nor there. After all, which of us has never been fired? *Remove the moat from your own eye.* Some even suggested plagiarism, because he'd gotten sermon ideas from the Internet. I'd wanted to talk to Neville afterward, but he'd gone home for which I can't blame him. So I locked myself in the bathroom, crying for Dr. Walsh. Then I cried for Neville, for Amity and finally for myself.

The next day we had Ken Jones who'd actually been scheduled ahead of time as guest speaker. Most people knew he was highly respected in his field, but the church was still half empty.

Afterward, Ken and I went to my office to talk. Marva had opened a can of worms and the end was inevitable. Even if we persuaded her to cease and desist, there would be someone else to take her place. People are like that.

In the following weeks, there were countless meetings and conferences, or more accurately, strategic caucuses. I think the MAC also met twice. I was getting concerned about Mother's blood pressure although she refused to talk about it. Then the August board meeting turned into a shouting match with Steve grilling Neville like a prosecutor about the falling pledges and Neville accusing Paul of maneuvering at denominational headquarters. All this in the space of a few weeks.

Meanwhile, I had work to do. The new school year was coming up and I needed to find volunteer teachers, a number almost impossible to calculate given the absenteeism and falling enrollment. There was curriculum to modify and distribute to say nothing of completing the summer program. I needed some peace and quiet.

But I couldn't concentrate for all the raucous noise down the hall. You'd think people would show some respect. After all, this *is* a church. I got up to close the door and then recognized the voices of Carrie Cook and Erma Willins coming from the business office. They sounded so agitated that I walked down the hall to investigate, fearful that something had happened.

The room was crowded with two copiers, a stamp machine, three beat-up desks, and a scattering of unmatched chairs and bookcases filled with dusty folders. Both copying machines were grinding away and the room smelled like a print shop. Erma and Carrie sat across from one another, one folding sheets, the other stuffing them into waiting envelopes, maintaining an animated conversation above the noise. I banged on the open door. "Hi. What's happening?"

Carrie looked up. "Paul brought in a special mailing that needs to get out by the end of the day. Can you imagine?"

"What special mailing?" I picked up a sheet, glancing at the Amity heading.

"He brought it in about an hour ago. As if we didn't have enough to do."

I began to read. "In order to avoid special congregational meetings to question the continued employment of the minister, and in order to relieve the pressing dissatisfactions of the petitioners…"

I pulled up a chair and sat down. "Where did this come from?"

"I told you. Paul dropped it off."

"No -- when did the board arrive at this?"

"Paul called a special meeting day before yesterday. They'd gone into executive session and come out with this resolution. Staff people weren't invited."

The letter continued. '...be it resolved, whereas Dr. Neville Leighton has, through verbal statements, represented his participation and the participation of the society in the Technical Assistance Corp as being an act of social responsibility, and... whereas Dr. Leighton has had the additional motive of personal financial gain, and... whereas Dr. Leighton has misrepresented his qualifications to counsel and advise, and... whereas through this and other conduct unbecoming to the ministry, Dr. Leighton has destroyed or damaged the desired condition of faith and trust between his office and the membership of the society; therefore, the Executive Board of Amity Congregational Church hereby formally censures and condemns such conduct and misrepresentation by the minister and hereby agrees to advise the membership of the basis of this censure through a special mailing to the membership.'

"The full board agreed to this?" I could barely get the words out.

"Paul said it was pretty cut and dried." Erma ran her fingers along the edge of the stack, straightening out the bundle.

"Cut and dried!" I almost shouted. "You're talking about a man's life work. His career. His reputation. Weren't you paying attention?"

"We only work here, Carol. We do what we're told."

"Where was Bill? Why wasn't he there to sit on Paul?"

"Bill was out of town. Anyway, for your information, the vote was unanimous - minus Bill, of course."

The copiers had finished their cycle and the room was dead silent. "Erma, you can't send this out," I cried. "It's a travesty, it's slanderous."

"It's a report. And truth is an absolute defense."

"Does Neville know?" I demanded. "Did you at least have the courtesy..."

"Go ask him." They turned back to their work.

I grabbed a copy and stomped down the hall. Neville's door was closed. I tapped lightly.

Footsteps, then the door opened. "Oh, Carol. Come in. I thought it might be..."

"Were you expecting...?"

"Not at all. Come in."

I wanted to put my arms around him. But instead, I only could only murmur, "I've seen the letter. I'm so sorry."

"Well, they had good intentions." He motioned me inside and shut the door, blocking out most of the noise that had now resumed. "Sit down. I could use another perspective. Sheila and I sat up all night, talking. So if I don't make much sense, it's fatigue, not you."

I sank into a chair across from him, limp with sadness. "Are they right? Will this quiet the dissent?"

"If so it'll be news to me." He smiled ruefully. "It's a little like chemotherapy. If it doesn't kill you first."

"A general letter seems so extreme. Recording this in the minutes should be enough to satisfy them."

His face was drawn. "Therein lies the key. People continue to turn over every rock, and the rocks are legion."

Sounds from down the hall throbbed through the silence. Then there was a tap on the door followed by a loud Hello as a fleshy hand with bright-red nail polish flung it open. "Ah, you're here! I was afraid you'd forgotten about me."

Startled, Neville leaped to his feet. Then just as quickly, the magnetic charm returned. "Forget you? Perish the thought." He turned toward me. "I think you've met Jan Pollack."

"Of course. At the club. Nice to see you."

She grabbed my hand and pumped it up and down. "I've seen you with your two little ones at the pool. Mine are grown and flown so now I just sit and watch. I was never much of a swimmer anyhow."

"Oh, ha ha. Very funny."

"Jan and I have an appointment," Neville explained.

"You bet. This man is the best," Jan cried, and I half expected her to slap him on the back. "Neville can zero in like you wouldn't believe." She swung her shoulders appreciatively. "I'm getting myself self-actualized." Her laugh was loud and raucous.

We were standing, facing one another. Clearly they were waiting for me to go.

"I'll catch you later," Neville murmured.

Back in my office, I closed the door and stared at the clock. If only some magic could send it in reverse, taking us back to spring, to Christmas, or to that lovely moment when Neville first arrived, when we were so optimistic, almost giddy with the promise of a bright future. After all, who else had connected so well with the youth group? Who else embraced so many diverse personalities and still kept peace among them? Who else showed how he cared, for only a saint could put up with the likes of Gerda, Mirabelle and Joy, not as a duty but out of love.

I reached for the file of potential teachers, determined to get back to work. But the noise had re-erupted. Damn them anyway. I went to the door, ready for a confrontation.

This time it was Jan's voice, echoing from the opposite direction followed by Neville's more soothing baritone. "He makes me so mad! Sometimes I could just..."

I could feel my stomach flutter, for in a flash, I'd found the solution. One word from her, accompanied by a sizeable check to spell out her gratitude, and the dissenters would have to be silenced. I pressed my ear to the door, ready to bear witness to Neville's vindication.

Their voices continued with Jan crying out her rage and frustration, followed by Neville voice urging her on. "Tell it like it is, Jan. You're entitled."

Both voices were now raised in such intensity that it took no effort to understand their words. I prayed that Carrie and Erma had finished their work and gone home.

"He promised when we married..."

"How does that make you feel?

There was a long pause.

Neville's voice was urgent. "Keep going. What would you like to do?"

Silence. Then a sound like someone had picked up an object and slammed it on the desk.

"What would you like to really do?"

"I don't know." Her voice was like a wounded animal.

"Would you like to send him away? Get rid of him?"

"I can't. I love him."

"Don't be afraid. Get in touch with your feelings. You're entitled."

"I can't. I just can't."

"Yes you can. Yes you can…" And the desk thumping continued.

I felt like a Peeping Tom. Only this was far worse, for I'd witnessed the raw, naked emotions of someone in pain. And I hadn't been invited in.

Trembling, I went back to my desk and pulled out a note pad. My mission was clear. First, I'd call Jan on some pretext, maybe ask her to help with something or other. Then I'd shift the subject and talk to her about Neville. People like Jan were always hungry for friends.

Justifiable? It amounted to the least harm and the greater good. I took a deep breath and said a silent prayer. Oh God, please, make it worth while.

Chapter 35: Joy

One look at Jan Pollack and you know she's a fighter. But taking on all of Amity when you're not even a member is quite a challenge. So here we go again. Another congregational meeting, this time with serious charges. Neville was pounding the desk and his hand slipped. Simple as that. Yet Jan's black eye couldn't be ignored. In this, even Carol had to agree. So much for making Jan a brilliant example of Neville's success.

Jan wasn't satisfied with letting the world know what happened. She wanted revenge. I guess that's the way they do things in Texas. So first she went to the MAC which met in special session just for her. That turned into a screaming confrontation and the police had to be called. Then she approached the board. They went into executive session and came out with a decision to call a special meeting to change the constitution, so that it required only a majority to fire the minister instead of a two-thirds vote. If passed, it would be followed immediately by a vote to recall the minister. That would end the battle for sure, since they'd been pretty close to fifty percent before the last meeting and no one seemed to have changed their minds. It was a coup de grace which means something like Gotcha and perfectly legal. Worst of all, Jan had turned on Gary, blaming him for introducing her to Neville in the first place. That could mark the end of a promising future with *Marty's.* And to think of all the time I spent being nice to her.

The night of the meeting we'd called out for pizza, not feeling much like going to the club for dinner. Gary told the boys he'd started sending out his resume, saying he just wanted to know what was out there. They could tell he was trying to let it sink in slowly, having been there before. I tried to be more cheerful, suggesting that Max might go into rehab and come out cured, making all of this unnecessary. The boys mumbled their own plans, trying to find a last minute solution, but we all knew that there wasn't one.

At a little before seven we all got in the car, pretty sure this would be the final act, yet determined to see it through. Once more the parking lot was filled with people streaming toward the sanctuary. Inside, the place was hushed with a sense of doom as though everyone knew this was the end. The table had been set up in front like before, this time with seats for the entire board as well as the Ministerial Advisory Committee. Cliff Hamilton and Billy Oliver would not be there. It was as if everyone had given up, knowing we were at the end.

At seven, Paul called the meeting to order. Minutes were dispensed with and Paul said he would entertain a motion to change the by-laws. It was a motion requiring a two-thirds vote and Neville's final hope.

But before that could happen, Bill stood up, asking for something called personal privilege.

Clearly surprised, Paul mumbled something like "of course," and sat back down. Bill still wielded power at Amity.

Moving up in front, Bill began. "I was out of town during several board meeting. Had I known their importance, I would have arranged otherwise." He glared at Paul who looked the other way.

"For a period of some months, we have struggled in vain to reconcile the differences between our minister and some members of our congregation," he continued. "The reasons for this titanic struggle are somewhat clouded. Some put forward that our minister is destroying Amity Congregational Church. Some of the means are said to be exceeding limits of pastoral counseling, frequently changing his mind, acting in deceitful ways, and most recently, deliberately lying to this board and therefore to our congregation. Such actions and performances can not be condoned and must be dealt with promptly and firmly. There are various ways of dealing with such performances.

"The positive methods generally correct the problem in the best interests of both sides. The negative methods take many forms. The malcontents of our society have selected what historically has proven to be the most effective, short of outright assassination. This method is that of witch hunting. The master hunter, until recently has been Marva Larson, who has acknowledged her pursuit. Her tool, the most effective available for this sport, is rumor and innuendo, the very method in which she hotly accused others of using against previous ministers. Now maybe the causes really justify the means and I would like to examine this."

There was a loud murmur as everyone turned and looked toward Marva who sat unmoving, her shoulders set.

"First is our minister exceeding matters of pastoral counseling, a charge very grave indeed, and potentially dangerous for our society," he went on. "Yet not one board member, president included, made any effort to convene a panel of counselors to establish the minister's credentials and determine its scope to protect our society from the danger of such things as a malpractice suit. In fact, our president has labored untiringly to discredit and disqualify our minister in this area.

"Our second point concerns our minister changing his mind. Everyone does this, depending on the person or situation. Even Mr. Larson does this as he so recently demonstrated with his desire to change our constitution, something he heretofore has so forcefully defended.

"Point three: deceitful ways. This is a most serous charge. The board feels, and rightfully so, that the minister has deceived by not revealing his gainful employment at the university. In addition, he did not tell the board how he would drastically change the format of his counseling program and the policies of this society until it was discovered by us."

I could see the panel sitting up straighter. Gary saw it too.

"But how it pales when held side by side with the deceit that has been practiced by the president of our society, not only toward the board but most poignantly to the minister in regard to our denominational headquarters. Here the tactics of witch hunting parallels, a dreadful accusation brought against a defendant when he cannot offer rebuttal. The minds then close tightly to any future protestations from the accused." Bill's voice had softened to almost a whisper but resonating to the very back of the sanctuary.

"Now let us consider the final point of the brief list of disclosures of accusations against the minister, the deliberate lie in which Dr. Leighton diametrically contradicts prior statements. Indeed, our primary purpose here tonight is to confirm such charges, and when confirmed, they should present the most serous problem this board has yet faced. The fact is, confirmation of the charge will reduced the prior discourse to positions of relative unimportance. We would have only one course of action. And that would be to dismiss Dr. Leighton from the position of minister of Amity Congregational Church, subject to the approval of the congregation. For it will be impossible for honest and upright people to allow a person to so continue as their leader when he breaches the inherent trust of his position.

"Yet this produces a strange situation, for at the beginning of this conflict, Mr. Larson in his capacity as president of this board also lied directly to the minister and the board concerning the now controversial letter from the minister, for contrary to what was stated, Carrie Cook did indeed seek his advice before incorporating it within the newsletter. Yet when Mr. Larson admitted to this lie, there was no chastising nor outcries for censure. Once again, this board failed its responsibilities and did not act. Who is really trying to destroy this society? And what, therefore should be our conclusion? I can conclude only that Mr. Larson as first officer has miserably failed his responsibilities and abused his position. He has consistently acted to destroy the cohesiveness against the wishes of the majority. He has acted in a deceptive fashion and used his position to revile and degrade the minister, members of the board and members of this congregation."

Bill's voice was getting louder, matched by the rumbling in the congregation itself. *A plague on both your houses.* If one is guilty, all are guilty. But there was more.

"Other members of this board have also failed the society," he declared. "Mr. Rothberg has continually harassed the minister, increasing the internal tensions among members yet provided no positive suggestions for solving the problem. Other members, including myself, are also guilty of neglect in that we have not responded to the gross misuse of the Chair. Therefore, it is in the best interest of this society and its members that Mr. Larson resign from this board immediately. Next, that the treasurer, Jared Cole, assume the chair to represent this board and the congregation as a whole for disposition at their pleasure, for he is one of the few who has resisted dipping his oar into this unseemly mess."

Now people were standing like pit bulls preparing for battle or flapping fingers that threatened to gouge their neighbors' eyes. Amid the confusion there was the bang, bang, bang of Paul's gavel and his cry of "Order, order…" with no one paying attention. A few people began to leave. Neville fired and now Paul? What kind of solution would that be? It took about five minutes of shouting before they sat back down, exhausted. "This meeting was called for a specific purpose," Paul began, looking like he'd been horse whipped. "The chair granted this board member time to speak out of courtesy, but it cannot entertain such a motion because it was not included in the specific call. Therefore, let us move on with the next item on the agenda." He looked down at his papers. "The chair will entertain a motion to amend the constitution."

The constitution was changed by a fifty vote margin. The following vote to fire the minister was closer, but undisputed. Neville would be relieved of his duties immediately. Three months salary as severance was little consolation, but that's all that was written in his contract. After all, he'd been with Amity barely a year.

Bill was right. *A plague on all their houses.* It was time to move on, with or without Paul, with or without Neville, and for me, with or without Amity, Worthington or the two-faced jerks in this podunk town.

I want to sleep in on Sunday morning, care for my family and enjoy my home. I could feel my heart swell with love and appreciation. Gary had always taken good care of us. God help the rest.

CHAPTER 36: KIM

WORTHINGTON IS MY home. Still, it will be a relief to leave. My move was precipitated by disaster, but once that passed, the sun came out.

Berkeley isn't anywhere near Hollywood, thank God. On the Bay, I'll be able to access the library and meet stimulating colleagues that contribute to the expansion of my intellect. They will see that I have a brain.

Bill has encouraging me throughout and actually become a good friend. It was a simple divorce, a case of irreconcilable differences. No one was surprised, least of all the boys. I was probably the last to acknowledge it. Strange how we cling to the familiar.

Neville and Sheila have moved back to Santa Ana, acting like their year in Worthington was nothing more than an extended vacation. We said we'd keep in touch, but I don't expect that to materialize. Divorced people divide everything, even friends, and I was never close to them.

As for Bill, he will stay in Worthington. His practice is here and the swimming pool is almost complete. These days he's spending more and more time at the club. I hear that one of the servers is the attraction, someone he calls Katie or Sue. A May-December relationship. I visualize them skinny-dipping in the moonlight or making love in front of a roaring fire. What some won't do for money.

Because today is the last Sunday before I leave, I decided to go to church, just for old times' sake. I'd considered a farewell party, inviting our friends to join in. After all, Bill and I still live in the same house. But he vetoed the plan. So much for outreach.

Bill had already left for church, having some remaining business with the board. His term was coming to an end and he would not be seeking office again, mumbling something about using the time to travel. Why not? It could be a new beginning for him as well.

I got in my car and opened all the windows. The trees were beginning to hint at their autumn transformation. Let Bill take care of the falling leaves. Or maybe his tart from the Club would do it, something to see when I came back. *If* I came back. With the boys gone and the family immersed in their own lives, the decision is open. Another tantalizing possibility.

Taking a roundabout tour, I went past the university, past the tea house where I'd occasionally lunched with Neville, then down the hill toward the parsonage which now lay dank and empty, its windows covered with dust, the yard overgrown. In the overwhelming silence, I felt nothing, neither sadness, nor guilt. Neville had gotten himself into this. Although I believed Jan's black eye to have been an accident, a matter of her getting in the way of a demonstrative gesture, it smacked of assault and no jury would be convinced otherwise. After sitting in contemplation, I turned toward Amity for a final goodbye.

The parking lot was half empty. Bill said that Amity might return to one service on Sundays which would lighten the load for the guest speakers, hardly a cheerful thought, all things considered. Still, pennies count. I took a deep breath. Another problem to leave behind. *Shake the dust off your shoes...*

Inside, the foyer was unusually quiet. I was surprised to see the Volkman boys at the inner door, serving as ushers. Already they were scraping the bottom of the barrel for personnel. "How nice of you to volunteer," I said.

Jason, the younger one, smiled as he handed me a program. "Carol wanted us to participate. It turns out we won't be here much longer anyway."

"Well, it's still a good thing to do," I said. "And I'm sure it's appreciated."

The service was shorter than usual, conducted by a seminarian who spoke about forgiveness and healing of wounds. He must have though he was being original. The reading was done by Sue Mason, a nice enough kid but badly in need of a speaking coach.

Downstairs, the mingling was a bit more animated and generated more warmth, aided by the young people. Of course their presence had also diminished, but the breads and baked goods were still substantial.

At the refreshment table, I was handed a cup of coffee by Mirabelle assisting at that end. "Good morning," I smiled, wondering what her take would be on all of this. But she merely nodded, giving her attention to the next person in line. No matter. She'd die of anorexia soon enough.

I helped myself to a piece of nut bread and moved to an empty table, watching people stand in clusters, balancing their plates or trying to break through to one another with little success. Neville was right. Amity needed lessons in sensitivity.

Off to one side, Joy and Gary Volkman had descended upon the Masons and were regaling them with new opportunities, for Gary's new job in Los Angles had been confirmed. "*Botanic Whole* is going to be the next McDonald's," Gary asserted, and people turned to smile. "They have twenty-seven restaurant on the west coast and moving east at the rate of one store every month. Imagine, a hamburger that's all organic - from beef fattened without chemicals, the burgers covered with lettuce and tomatoes organically grown. Even the mustard and mayo are made in-house to guarantee they're organic. Health food. It's the coming thing."

I shook my head. Gary, the super-salesman. His sympathetic manner had been so seductive, convincing me that Neville might indeed be a help to Max and Jan. But Gary had his own agenda. Then it all backfired and Jan sued everyone in sight. That Gary himself came out unscathed while Joy strutted her Hollywood image added to the irony.

"Hey Kim, don't just sit there. Come and join us." Gary's voice rang out across the room. Some people have no shame.

"I wasn't planning on staying," I began.

"All the more reason," he cried, pulling out a chair next to him. "I hear you're moving out to the west coast. So are we. What a coincidence."

I moved slowly toward their table. "I'm leaving tomorrow. School starts in a week. I have a lot to do."

"I hear Adam Leighton was accepted at Berkeley. You might even run into him. Of course you'll be in grad school and him being a college freshman, but it would still be a familiar face. Generations don't really matter, do they? I mean, Sue and I are friends even though she's the same age as my own son." Joy's face glowed with enthusiasm.

"Has anyone heard from them?" Dave asked.

"Hannah and Jason want to keep in touch. After all, Los Angeles isn't very far. But maybe that's not such a good idea under the circumstances." Joy had just learned a new word.

"Moving to the coast is going to another world," Gary insisted. "Anything can happen."

"Sue said Matt could get into the movies and become a star. I told her if he did, she could marry him." Dave grinned at Joy. "They could do worse."

"Two dynasties joined in love. Eloise and Abelard. Anthony and Cleopatra. Susan and Matthew." Bill had come from behind and now stood at the back of my chair. "And to think it happened in little old Worthington. Who would have thought?"

I smiled up at him. "Such charming repartee. I will miss you, my dear."

"I just talked to Paul," Dave said, turning to Bill. "A number of things need to be done and we could use your help - informally, of course. Can we count on you?"

Bill seemed wary. "Maybe. Depends on who's involved."

"No one you know. I promise."

So we were back to square one. Off with the old, on with the new. But not quite. Marva and Liz were back to being best friends. And the other factions remained on their perches. I excused myself and wandered down the hall, peering in the offices until I came to Neville's, vacated almost a month ago. The furniture remained with only a few of the figurines removed, his own personal belongings. The room was still smart and neat, so unlike the drab vacant parsonage.

Down the hall I heard the murmur of voices. Carol's door was open and I peered in. "Oh Kim, do come and join us. Scottie and I were just talking." She drew up a chair. "All set for your trip?"

I hesitated. "I don't want to intrude."

"Not at all. Maybe you can contribute some words of wisdom. God only knows, we need them."

Sighing, I sat down. "Joy and Gary are out there pummeling everyone with PMA. Talk about landing on your feet."

"They're going to la-la land where they belong. Glitz, tinsel and tanning salons. No telling how long that'll last. At least they're out of here," Carol said fervently.

"What about the others?"

"Marva is still Marva. And Paul continues in office although he might be the next target. Depends on whose ox is gored. Gerda and Werner have pulled back and haven't been seen in months. Word is that Werner's fishing for a transfer. Why not? They're still living out of a suitcase. My mother's staying in the shadows which is just as well since she took this all very hard." Carol shrugged. "Better than having a heart attack. But enough doom and gloom. How about you?"

"I'm leaving tomorrow. Free at last."

"But as a psychologist, you'll be intimately involved…"

"Ironic, isn't it? But that's what I want to do."

Scottie leaned back and smiled. "There'll be plenty of work when you return. The procession is endless."

"He sure did open a can of worms, didn't he?"

"It was so unfair," Carol whispered. "I don't know if I can ever find forgiveness in my heart. Poor Neville."

We were talking at cross purposes. Poor Neville? What about Jan and all the others? "I guess it will be a while before Amity does any more candidating."

"Not really. I understand they're already forming a search committee."

"I'm just concerned about the kids," Scottie added. "They don't conveniently stop growing whenever there's a crisis. I'm especially worried about Jayne. She seems so lost."

"It's hell to be a teenager," I agreed. "I don't know anyone who looks back fondly at those years. Which means you'll have to reach out to her. That's what a church is all about."

"You sound like Neville. And look at what happened to him." Her face was turning a blotchy red.

"Carol, I didn't mean…"

"This church is populated by barracudas," she cried. "A man dedicates himself to God and to his fellow-man and is destroyed in the process. Not once, but twice. Amity Congregational Church. We violate every word in the name. As long as we keep our fellows at arm's length, all goes well. But let us step closer and it becomes too much. Mirabelle wants us to focus on the Bible. My Lord, what's more distant than a book thousands of years old? Yet when Neville wanted to make it relevant, he was subjected to critiques by amateurs. Christian love is scary. Neville only wanted to be your friend and mine. But the sharks wouldn't let him." She looked like she was ready to cry. "And once more we're left picking up the pieces. When will it end?" She buried her face in her hands. "When will it end?"

I went to her chair and, kneeling down, put my arms around her. "Man learns from his mistakes. There's no need to blame God."

"Mistakes? These weren't mistakes. They were contrived power plays using people's deepest needs as antes."

I looked up at Scottie who sat frozen in her chair. "So you'll start over. Next time it will be better. Each step you take…"

Scottie shook her head and got up, quietly leaving the room.

After a few minutes, I returned to my chair, studying her as she pulled herself together. "Do you want me to stay?"

"No, that's okay. I can work this out for myself. You go ahead. I'm sure you have a lot to do." Carol, everyone's little sister, never taken seriously. On the other hand, I had myself to think of.

Patting her on the shoulder, I turned and walked out, detouring through the back entrance and into the parking lot. No need to go to the club. It would only be more of the same.

I got into my car and steered it toward home, Bill's home. Tomorrow I would load it up with basic needs - books, computer and clothes. Once I'd found a place to stay, Bill would send the other things we'd agreed were mine. A new beginning. Maybe Bill was right. This is all there is. Make the best of it.

Tomorrow I would click the garage door closed for the last time. There would be no ghosts for I knew what I wanted. Meanwhile, the world stretched out before me. My time had come.

~ End ~

Made in the USA
Monee, IL
20 May 2023

33843150R00152